How Many Frogs Does It Take?

PAULINE VERHOEFF

How Many Frogs Does It Take?

Pauline Verhoeff

Cover designed by Pauline Verhoeff & The Little French eBooks

Edited by Mel Jones

Published by The Little French eBooks

All rights reserved. No part of this book may be used or reproduced in any manner whatsoever without written permission, except in the case of brief quotations embodied in critical articles or reviews.

Copyright Pauline Verhoeff 2023

Published 2023

Index

Introduction to Modern Grannies	7
The Holidays	23
Faith Healer (New Title Carrot -Man)	67
The Ikea Whisperers	83
Blue-Stocking Spinsters	93
The Beauty Parlor	99
Http://Www.Rent Me A Guy.Com	109
Will Married Men Leave Their Wives?	121
Robo Comes Home	145
Social and Sexual Interaction	173
The Pin Code	185
Leisure Time	201
Cerebral Cortex	207
Santa	213
The Revelation	245
Expectations	251

The Pewter Pot	259
A Convicted Criminal	269
Mark	275
Downward Facing Dog	289
Hospital Gate	301
Recovering	313
QT	317

A juicy tale with a twist

Introduction to Modern Grannies

Just suppose you are a man that likes to date older women. What exactly are you looking for. Of course, you have seen older women, your granny, for instance. What a sweet old lady, baking cookies and knitting an endless supply of colorful scarfs that you never wear. In her purse you find only peppermints and hankies.

At best, she wears a cotton frock that has seen better days and a droopy blouse and, of course, no bra. No! Granny wants to be comfortable.

Now let's head to the nearest shopping mall and in particular to the more expensive shops like Gucci and Dior. Ah, good, you are inside now! Proceed to the makeup counter that is usually on the ground floor and look around. Your eye will immediately spot several older women trying out eye shadow, powders, creams and lipsticks. Some men would call it a witches' brew a woman can't be without. But we call it our first aid kit. It's our arsenal of tricks that keeps us looking young and attractive.

Generally speaking, we golden-agers are the best customers as we have the most money to spare and the most blemishes to be fixed. Every morning, it takes us considerably longer and longer to be somewhat presentable when we look in the mirror. Yes! Look carefully now - you have just identified the modern granny. Gone are the days we sat behind geraniums spying on our neighbors.

The modern granny hikes, runs marathons, and plays tennis. Some might even do kickboxing. And if that wasn't enough, we are vibrant and sexually active partners. And we are not usually looking for any commitment. A win-win situation for any man.

And as we are past menopause, we don't have to worry about getting pregnant. It's a well-known fact that men's sexuality peaks in their early twenties while we take far longer. So, we can out-sex any man, if that's an expression anyway.

And yes, people might give us disapproving looks, especially if we are dating a much younger man, but get used to it. It's not the end of the world. The days when grannies stayed at home are long past.

Most grannies of our generation own a car, have a good job, some money in the bank, and a sherry addiction at four in the afternoon. And don't forget we worked twice as hard as men to enter their executive world.

Now let's talk for a moment about me. Let's face it I am officially an old tart of 54 years. Luckily, there are plenty of men younger who love dating me. Although last night was a mistake. The guy I dated turned out to be a cheapskate; he even went as far as to nick the sugar bags that came with the coffee. The evening started off by ordering the cheapest bottle of red on the menu which was basically undrinkable. Then he asked.

"Do you like hamburgers?" It was only later that I realized it was because it was the cheapest dish on the menu. While we ate, he kept stealing my French fries (as he hadn't ordered them), and even my tomato and cucumber slices were not safe from his thieving hands. But the worst thing was that when the bill came, he ordered a Cinnabon bun to take away and could I please pay as he had left his wallet behind, and yes, he would pay me back later. Fuming, I did. I grabbed my bag and headed towards the exit passing the reception counter, which held a bowl containing candy. His hand shot out and he literally pocketed the whole bowl of fresh mints. Mortified and disgusted with his behavior, I walked out, hailed a taxi and turned around.

"Don't bother getting to come with me, you cheapskate," I said and slammed the door in his face. I told the chauffeur to drive off, leaving my date standing on the curb with his mouth open. When I arrived home, I opened a bottle of red wine and, still fuming, switched on the TV.

The wine went down exceptionally well, and hours later, intoxicated, I rolled into bed. What a jerk! The trouble is that when you are older, alcohol doesn't always agree with you as well as it did when you were in your twenties. I woke up, stumbled to the bathroom and looked in the mirror.

Hell! I have trouble recognizing the bloated face that looks back at me from the mirror as my own. I cleared my throat. Christ, did I drink that much? I look at my bleary piss-holes-in-the-snow eyes, gray unhealthy skin and decide that a major repair job is called for. After spending a good two hours in the bathroom, I am hopelessly late for work, and I am sure that my boss will go for my throat. But as it turns out, I am fortunate this morning he isn't there! The moment I enter my office, I head straight for the coffee maker, and after several cups, I begin to feel human again.

I walk to my desk and flip my computer on. The datasheet that I want is, for some weird reason, scrambled. Dam, has that ever happened to you dear? I need that data. In despair, I hammer on the keyboard, and the screen turns black for a moment, then a new window pops up.

The program to which you are referring has limited access. I hit the keyboard again in puzzled silence at the cryptic message, and a billion microseconds passed in anxious silence. Then finally, the computer sluggishly responds in a language no human can understand.

"AZY DZY 0023E - ERROR 01 ST ABORT / RETRY / IGNORE."

Randomly I hit another key, and a memory dump follows. When the computer finally starts up again, another message pops up!

'Download the free trial version of! Hacker-Proof app! For a moment, I am tempted, but then I remember that even for a free trial, a credit card is needed, and I decline. What now? In vain, I scout around the office for somebody to help me, but I see nobody that is of any help. What now? Shall I call tech support again? I sigh, remembering the last time, which didn't work out too well. Tech-support lost his cool and hung up on me. I had a slight suspicion he was located in India or the Philippines. No wonder the whole country is without jobs, letting these bozo's do our work for virtually nothing. I mean, how much is Microsoft paying them? 300 a month is my guess if they are lucky.

Requirements; English, no patience, and partial understanding of computer problems. You must admit it's not very patriotic from

Microsoft but hey, do I have an alternative? I find the support page, dial, and apprehensively adjust my receiver grip.

Tech Support: "Hi, my name is Habib, (confirming my thoughts) how may I help you?"

Me: "Hi, my datasheet is scrambled. I don't know what to do."

Tech Support: What program did you use to archive your files?"

Me: "What do you mean?"

Tech Support: "OK, what program are you using?"

Me: "When I came in this morning, I just switched my computer on."

Tech Support: "Do you have a valid backup?"

Me: "Yes, of course."

Tech Support: "How old is your backup?"

Me: "How should I know?'

Support: "Just hit a key." And read to me what it says."

Me: "The program you are referring to has limited access.

Tech Support: "OK, what is the document called?"

Me: "I forgot I wrote it about a year or so ago; that's why I need it."

Tech support; "Don't worry, mam; I am sure it's on the server somewhere."

Me; "Are you making this up?"

Tech support; "No, mam. With network drive did you save it to?"

Me; "Network drive?" God, is he speaking Hindu now? "I am not sure."

Tech support: "Again, miss, what is the name of the document?"

Me; "I don't remember!"

Tech support: "Tell me what client you are referring to."

Me; "It's a data sheet."

Tech support: "Ummm, well, there are several hundred thousand documents on the server, so unless we have some more information it's going to be tough to find."

Me; "Can you restore it from the backup?" I really need this document!"

Tech support: "What do you see on your computer now?"

Me: "A sticker of a doggy."

Tech support; Puzzled, a "sticker?"

Me: "Yes."

Tech support: (Chuckles), "no mam, I mean on the screen!"

Me: A "ZY DZY 0023E - ERROR ABORT / RETRY/ IGNORE."

Tech support: "What operating system are you using, mam?"

Me: "What do you mean?"

Tech support: "Do you have windows 10?"

Me: "Yes."

Tech Support: "Right-click on 'My Computer,' and select properties on the menu."

Me: "Your computer? It's my computer!"

Tech support: "No, no mam, the little picture called 'My Computer' on your desktop."

Me: "Oh OK, nothing is happening."

Tech Support: "OK, so we have to use your backup copy!"

Me: "Copy? What copy?" WE DON'T HAVE A COPY!!!" I am yelling now.

Tech support: "When I asked you if you were backed up, you said YES!"

Me: "That's because we are backed up. We are, in fact, so backed up that we don't have time to make backup disks."

Tech support: "Hmm, let's try another solution; your outdated spyware might be the problem."

Before I can say anything else, the phone goes Peep-peep-peep.

"Ahhhhrhhhh!" I shriek; I can't believe this crap; Tech-support has hung up on me! AGAIN! Before I can re-dial the number, my boss comes in asking me if I can fetch some urgent mail from the mailroom. I get up, grab my empty cup from the desk, go for a refill, and head downstairs. When I enter, I'm having trouble remembering why I came, as I am still trying to work out what went wrong with my data file. I vaguely registered or somebody wandered in after me.

Hello! Where did he come from? Now that is what I call a man. Mentally I tick off his assets: tall, graying hair at the temples, well dressed, casual, yet elegant, and when he walks past me, and I smell a whiff of some expensive aftershave. He stops at a desk, where a young technician is working behind a computer. Mr. Gorgeous leans over and lectures the young boy about the misuse of the program, sounding confident and firm. I couldn't believe my luck. Can he possibly be my next wiz-computer-boyfriend? What a turn on, if I can find a man who can casually bring up terms like backup, formatting- deleting, then casually stroll over to me asking: "I hope you have installed a good virus program. If not, I can help you." While I am daydreaming, Mr. Computer looks in my direction, gives me a cursory nod, and turns his attention back to the staff that seems somewhat in awe as he strides through the mailroom with confidence and poise. Things definitely look promising, and I decide that my goal for today is to find out who he is, even if it is the last thing I do!

I swirl around and take a closer look at him; he is standing in the middle of the room talking to another employee, the one I so casually tossed away as my new boyfriend last week. Why had I never seen Mr. Computer before? I plaster a smile on my face, and just as I decide to walk towards him introducing myself and ask if he can help me with my computer, my cell phone rings - loudly- Quickly I try locating it in my handbag, but as usual, it's never easy to find anything among all the clutter After searching aimlessly for what seemed like an eternity, I finally grab it just when it stops its loud ringing.

Now, you should know that when you enter our building, there is a sign that forbids the use of all personal phones. In my haste to get to work this morning, I forgot to switch it off. Flustered, I look up; everyone is staring at me with a look of horror on their faces. Casually I put the phone back in my purse and stepped out of the room. No harm done; I think. I always find it a stupid rule not to be able to use one's phone. What good is it, to own a cell phone if you can't use it? I lean back against the door and thank my lucky stars that none of my bosses had noticed my little debacle, but silly me, soon I will learn how wrong I was!

As soon as I sit behind my desk again, I sort some papers thinking about Mr. Whizz. When I am done, I don't want to go back to the computer, and I look out of the window. A bird flies by, and I envy its freedom. It barely flips his wings up and down and seems without a worry in the world. Then I am shaken out of my reverence because the phone on my desk rings. I pick it up and learn that I am being summoned upstairs; oh bugger: One of the top managers wants to speak with me. I can only just contain the use of a four-letter word in public. That's all that I need to make this morning a complete nightmare!

Don't panic, I tell myself, and storm out of my room to the elevator that brings me to the forbidden floor. I have only been there once when one of my new bosses lectured me about strict rules. And yes, that included the no-phone-rule and the no-pants-to-the-office-rule, and headscarves only for the girls, but even so, how silly!

The other half a dozen stupid rules I can't even remember. I stepped out of the elevator. I am in unfamiliar territory and am slightly intimidated.

As any good secretary, lets me wait at least 20 minutes to show me she is ranking higher in the pecking order and wants me to know it. Her beady eyes look me carefully over through her thick-rimmed glasses.

"Sit down, Madam. You will be called in."

I grit my teeth aware of her power and throws her a murderous look, as if I have to go to the lady's room. Finally, she gracefully waves her hand, allowing me into the Kingdom, confirming my thought that she likes to abuse her power. I open the door, and my feet sink deep into the luxurious carpet, and I wonder what it must have cost! As I am still mentally calculating, I look up, and the guy from the postal room walks in my direction. Are my dreams already coming true?

"You must be the mobile phone woman?" He inquires sarcastically in an icy voice.

I can't believe this is happening; Christ, is he one of the bosses now? Since when? And why wasn't informed? I realize all those questions are purely theoretical. Since I belong to the lower ranks. Nobody is under no obligation to notify me of anything, let alone any chance of the guards, kings, or bosses. I am tempted to lie, but then I decide that a meek approach is not in my best defense or character and look him straight in the eye.

"Yes, I am," I informed him. "Are you having a problem with that?"

The surprised look on his face makes me realize that once again, I behave like a fool. Why can I never keep my big mouth shut? He is not smiling, but can I imagine a glint in his eyes? Could it be that this is the human boss who sees how silly the cell-phone rule is? He turns around, walks to his desk, sits down facing me. I've not imagined it: I can see a definite smile around his lips. While I am composing my next retort, he beckons me to come closer, and I walk up to his desk, trying to look as if I am in control. OK, let's be honest. I am probably not being summoned to get a raise, but what the heck. Pity I could have done with one, so I could have bought that beautiful- to-die-for pair of boots I saw in the shop yesterday without feeling guilty for spending all that money.

Then when I am happily dreaming away about my new boots, forgetting my predicament, my boss drops a bombshell on my unsuspecting head. He gives me a curt nod and scowls impassively.

"You are fired, madam Telephone!"

For a minute, I am silent! I can't believe he said 'fired' My controlled look falls off my face. Did he say 'fired'? Fired? For not turning off my stupid phone? My mind goes round and round, trying to grasp what he just said. I swallow and look at him sitting behind his imposing expensive oak desk, all overbearing and arrogant, and I'm at a loss for words - something that doesn't happen too often. Weakly I lean against the desk, and when I finally open my mouth, croak a reply that sounds something like:

"Fired, you are firing me?"

"Yes," you were told of the company rules. In fact, we have provided you with a list; you can pick up your paycheck on the way out." With that, he swivels his chair around, picks up the telephone and dials a number, leaving me standing with my mouth open like a dead fish.

Desperately I swallow and turn around. Flushed with embarrassment, I walk slowly towards the door, feeling like I am about to have a panic attack.

Then when I go over what just happened, sanity takes over; I mean what would you have done? I change my mind about leaving, turn around once more, walk towards the desk, grab the phone from his hand, slam it down on its cradle and yell," un-fucking-believable!"

His jaw tightens, his eyes widen, fast as lightning. He grabs my arm and snarls, "what do you think you are doing?"

A rush of adrenaline surges through my body at the contact as he is so close, I can smell a delicious waft of expensive aftershave.

"Hell!" How can you fire somebody for forgetting something? Do you never forget anything, Mr. Perfect? What's next? Fire somebody for breathing?"

I am beyond anger, and I hurl an insult at him. He looks stumped, and his grip tightens; I wince, take a deep breath and, for good measure, yell in an outraged manner; "stop manhandling me, or I will file a sexual harassment suit take your hands off me."

His grip slackens marginally, and his grim face travels over me, taking in my flushed face, fierce eyes, and disheveled hair.

"You wouldn't dare!" He blurts out and slides forward on his seat.

"Try me:" I hissed.

It's clearly a stalemate, but unexpectedly the door opens, and his secretary comes in, practically drooling as she takes in the scene. Mr. Not-so-forceful-now releases my arm to face her.

"What do you want," he snarls, wired up. "Can't you see I am busy?"

"Sorry, Mr. Brent, your 11-o'clock appointment is here."

My gaze darts to the look of embarrassment on her face, and just for the fun of it, I confuse her even more, asking.

"Gloria, he is so wired up that he is he's manhandling me. What do you think? Can I take him to court and file for sexual harassment?" My face is a picture of innocence.

Gloria looks confused at dear Brent, who gets up from his chair in an attempt to increase his authority. The look on his face is convulsive, like he just swallowed something big.

"Gloria, don't you think he looks like he just swallowed an I-phone? making her my adversary against her will. I am on a roll now, and nothing can stop me; "is that an I-phone in your pants or are you just happy to see me;" I purr in my sweetest voice while glancing at the front of his pants at the same time. Do I imagine it, or did Gloria just stifle a grin? But before I can make sure, he barks, "she is fired; make sure she collects her paycheck and escort her out of the building."

My gaze darts back at his stern face, his eyes impatient. "Do you know my I-phone has a remote control? Let's go somewhere remote, and you can have control! Or, on the other hand, that's not my idea of fun." I trail off, clearly running out of steam.

This time I couldn't imagine it. His eyes narrow, and he shakes his head, his lips quiver, and he lets out a laugh, transforming his face in an instant.

"You should be on a show with Jerry Springer," he chuckled. "That was quite bold." I franticly search his face to see a hint of yielding, but once again, it is blank.

"You sound as if you are into him," I am clearly still in attack mode. He faces me; "you do realize I can't do anything to help you. The whole floor was present when your phone rang, and if I let it go, I would be the laughingstock of the staff. "Gloria," he turned to her. "Makes sure she collects her belongings and escorts her out of the building."

Smugly Gloria says. "Follow me." And yes. I have no other option than to follow her. Together, we leave the room. She stands guard over me as I collect my paycheck and belongings, and I leave the building dazed, holding a cardboard box. By the time I get to my car, I am fuming. It wasn't exactly the job of a lifetime or anything like that, no, but still, it was a paycheck at the end of each month.

I debate my options for a moment. Although I need to look for another job, there is no immediate rush thanks to a considerable inheritance my father left me some years ago and is firmly in the bank. Suddenly a sense of freedom rushes through me and creeps up. My anger is forgotten; I am almost light-headed with joy. It's abundantly clear what my next step should be: I will take a holiday, spend some of my cash, and just enjoy life. Hmm, what about a cruise? Shall we galls?

As I think of it, visions of sun-drenched beaches swim into focus together with cold Pina coladas. And just for the fun of it, I added some men in skimpy swimsuits. At night, I can dine with the captain wearing a new sexy low-cut dress or swim in the ships-pool in something that hardly covers me! And in the ship's disco, I may find some handsome, rich single male! But if all else fails, I can go to the ships computer room and try a dating room, and perhaps find Mr. Right there. I mean, how hard can it be to find a reasonably good-looking guy, who lives in a remote exotic location, travel there and spend the rest of my life with him? Oh, I know it has not escaped me that I am older than the average dating girl, but although I am 54, I don't look a day over 40, thanks to the facelift I treated myself to a few years back. I look confident, and smart with my carefully styled half long blond hair.

Hmm, warning bells start to ring! Didn't I recently see the Oprah show? What was the topic again? Did you watch it reader? A hot guy who lived in Nigeria who was a scam artist. One older lady dated this perfect looking English guy and fell madly in love, but it turned out he was Nigerian, using a photo of a male Caucasian model and pretending he was working on an oil rig; God only knows where. And then, when she was madly in love with him, he pretended to fly out to meet her. But on the way to the airport, somebody stole his wallet, and could she please send him some cash to buy another ticket? No way could he get a new credit card in time for the flight. And she, lonely sucker she was, would wire him the amount he asked for plus some extra so thankful that he travels to meet her. Needless to say, that when the money arrived, she never heard from him again.

Oh, OK, got it! Never send cash! At least, that is what I learned from the show! Hmm, so much for internet dating. For lack of a better idea, I better head to the travel agency across the street and look at some brochures.

Before I change my mind, I push open the door. Large posters on the walls of the travel agency convinced me I had made the right choice. Briskly I inform the lady who sits behind the desk that I want to go on a cruise, and she motions for me to take a seat.

"Where do you like to go, madam?" Now that's difficult; Nigeria is definitely out, but my knowledge of geography is somewhat vague, and I am having trouble thinking up country names with plenty of sun. My eyes flew to the posters; on one is a picture of a beach with waving palm trees and sun-loungers placed strategically at the waters- edge. In a crispy white suit, a good-looking waiter is serving invitingly looking drinks in tall, iced glasses with a tiny umbrella. I point at the poster, "there!"

"You want to go to Phuket?"

"Phuket?" I echo, 'where the fuck is Phuket?' "Is that where they serve the umbrella drinks?" I inquire somewhat timid.

The girl stifles a smile, "Yes, I believe so. It's in Thailand you can cruise along the islands. How long is your vacation?"

"A week or ten days," I muttered, clearly needing time to let Thailand sink in. Wasn't that far away?

"When would you like to leave?" The girl is undoubtedly efficient and, I deduct, is probably working on commission.

"As soon as possible."

"Now that narrows it down considerably," she answered, taking off her glasses. "We have a ship leaving in 3 days. You will fly to Singapore, and then a driver will take you to the ship. It leaves in the evening, and it sails along the coast of Malaysian and Thailand, and yes, it will pass by Phuket." She waves her hand at the poster, convincing me she is indeed a mind reader.

"After a few days, you will be transferred to a smaller traditional junk-rigged schooner and cruises the tropical archipelago from Phuket to Phang Nga Bay, visiting James Bond Island, the picturesque Sea Gypsy village, and more. the ship will make several excursions, to the limestone caves, or a dive in the Andaman Sea. Do you like to snorkel?" She rattles on, clearly taking no prisoners and taking a deep breath, but before I have the chance to answer, she continues. "Beautiful Phang Nga Bay's clear waters are famous for snorkeling and diving. And now she is almost drooling. "You can taste the delicious cocktails and try world-famous Thai cuisine."

"You make this an offer I can resist."

Efficiently she makes the arrangements, and I hand her my credit card, and she can't help a feel a sense of accomplishment. All I have to do is present myself at the airport counter of Singapore Airlines.

The Holidays

The next day is a mad rush of packing and unpacking and packing again, and locating my passport, a feat in itself since it has been a while since I traveled, and I have no idea what I did with the dam thing. Finally, when I am about to give up, I locate it behind the sofa. It is slightly worn, and after unsuccessfully trying to straighten it out, I put it in my travel bag, and tell the neighbors I am going on a cruise.

I lock my door and drive to the airport, where I quickly find a parking spot but am unsuccessful in locating a luggage cart. And I am forced to haul my oversized luggage into the terminal. Sweating and panting, I finally find a deserted cart and thankfully hoist my bags on it. After the heavy workout, I look around. Inside the terminal is what can only be described as a cacophony of noises.

My head is pounding, and I question the wisdom of my perhaps overzealous plans. I push my luggage to the Singapore Airlines' counters and wait in line for the self-check-in machines. They are new and intimidating, and the friendly staff of Singapore Airlines helps fumbling passengers. But for the life of me, I can't help wondering why they are called self-service-- machines- if they need staff standing by for help. Wouldn't that defeat the purpose?

The line for passengers who need help is long, and I decide to try it myself. I mean, how hard can it be, right? It takes me a while to work out where my passport goes and what side is up or down. I push a button, but nothing happens; frantically, I try again. But the only thing that happens is the machine asking: 'Please insert your passport.' In despair, I try to get it back and try again. But the dam machine won't let go. I tug and pull, wrench and yank but to no avail. Sighing, I admit defeat and look around me for help.

"Do you need help, madam?" Does a uniformed girl ask me with what seems like a condensing smile? She probably concludes that old tarts should stay at home and sit behind the geraniums, staring vacantly at space.

"Yes, please, the machine is keeping my passport hostage," I replied.

Efficiently she retrieves my passport, puts it back in the correct way, and checks with me if the name on the screen is indeed mine.

"Flying to Singapore?"

"Yes," I nodded.

She punches buttons for, I swear, a good ten minutes before she shoves a boarding pass in my hand and a VIP pass for the airport lounge in the other.

"You can go there", and she pointed at a counter, "you can drop your luggage of over there." Her tone has changed a tad when she notices my first-class ticket. Slightly flustered about the debacle with the passport, I queued up, forgetting I had a first-class ticket and could have taken the fast lane. After what seems like an eternity, my suitcases are labeled and disappeared on a conveyor belt. I am left with just my hand luggage.

After a long... long... walk, I reach Airport security. My bag seems to have increased in weight. Christ, what did I pack in their rocks? Jealously I looked at the other more experienced flyers that had the foresight to bring trolleys.

The queue reaches from here to Tokyo, and I wonder if I perhaps can jump the line somehow. A wheelchair with a young woman is pushed onto the priority lane, and I almost envy her as she is whisked through with considerable speed. Why didn't I think about getting a wheelchair? But wait! What am I thinking? I need to be disabled first, right? I shrug off the image of me in a wheelchair aside and agonizingly slow myself and the other passenger's inch forward. My bag is on the floor, and I kick it forward instead of carrying it.

Finally, after what seems like hours, it's my turn, and I am asked to remove my shoes/ jacket/belt and shawl. My bare feet curl up when they touch the cold floor.

An attended seeing my discomfort, hands me paper slippers.

Balancing on one foot, almost falling, I put them on. Hell, why don't they provide some chairs or something?

I open my computer bag, remove my laptop/iPad and phone and place them in one basket. My jacket, scarf/gloves/belt and shoes go in the next. My purse, passport/boarding pass, my book and handbag in yet another. Dutifully I finally donate all my dangerous chemicals, deodorant, lotion, perfume, and face cream that I packed in a clear plastic bag, not exceeding a certain amount, which I vaguely remember sufficing as essentials for an insect, a tiny insect.

Pleased with my endowers, I am so anxious to leave the intimidating area that I walk through the metal-detectors red light, praying I haven't forgotten to remove coins, keys and hoping the metal in my bra won't set off the alarm. Not fancy being strip-searched or worse, for possible hazardous items that may endanger my fellow travelers.

The woman behind the metal detector motions for me to step back and observe the NO-GO red light. My protesting that the light's practically invisible doesn't make an impression judged from her stern face. The light turns green. I step through the arc, feeling smug as I know I am not carrying anything dangerous.

'I get you now, miss,' I think just before the alarm goes off. What now? What can I possibly have that makes the alarm turn on? Mentally I go through my items of clothing, but I come up blank.

"Step aside, lady," growled what could only be prescribed as a Russian female wrestler. "Hands up, and please spread your legs."

I do what she wants, and the whole airport is watching as she frisks me; I can tell from the leery grin on her face she is thoroughly enjoying it. Not finding any apparent guns or bombs in my underwear, she isn't satisfied and grabs an electronic device and works it over my body, ignoring its loud pinging.

As I have nothing better to do, I look at the security staff that stares intently at their monitors for potentially dangerous items in my luggage that are a treat to the other passengers or the plane, like a chainsaw, a tiny pair of scissors or a nail file. And I breathe a sigh of relief when she concludes that I pose no danger, at least for now.

For once, I am lucky, and I am allowed to keep my items, without being reprimanded, for having the gall to forget to place my deodorant in the appropriate clear bag, like my last flight. Need I say it was taken of me. Resulting in me not refreshing for 24 hours, talking about a health hazard.

I retrieve my laptop; grab my phone, purse, jacket, iPad, and other stuff I wasn't even aware I dumped in the baskets but are mine.

My arms are completely full, and I want to leave the intimating area as fast as possible. But I am somewhat hindered by my way—to—big-paper-slippers. Wildly I look around for a table to stuff all my items back in my bag. The only table shared between 400 or 500 passengers is obstructed by a large piece of luggage from an overweight, heavily perspiring man, who mumbles something that sounds like... "huh, I don't know who put that in; my bag."

Slightly horrified, I watch him as he is escorted away by an armed policeman. Seizing the opportunity forgetting him instantly, I snatch the empty space and dump all my personal belongings on the table. Just in time, too, as the next bag is dropped on the table due to a new search. Quickly I shove everything back in my bag and try to zip it up. Grrr, that's the most challenging part; I re-arrange some items and try again this time; it closes, and with a thankful sigh, I pick it up and drop it on the floor, feeling that I am missing something.

Then it dawns on me, where the hell are my shoes? After a few minutes of frantically searching and yes, on my paper slippers which by now are torn and hang as rags on my feet, I find my expensive Jimmy shoe in a discarded plastic tray on one of the other belts. This is fast becoming a bloody nightmare.

"How on earth did they end up there?" I ask an equally puzzled security guard while I grab them.

"Are you sure you didn't put them there yourself, mam?" He inquired, sniggering. Suspiciously I come to the only conclusion I can and tell him in a syrupy voice, "I think somebody was going to nick them."

He shrugs awkwardly like he is caught out, "I don't think so, mam."

"Why else would my expensive shoes be on the other belt?"

"Er, hmm, I don't know, mam," he forces a smile, "I mean, who would leave this area without their shoes?" He persisted.

I look at him suspiciously, although he made a good point. I mean, have you ever seen anyone boarding a plane in paper slippers?

"Just as I am about to agree with him, a young woman wearing what looks like Calvin Klein jeans and that gorgeous jacket I saw hanging in a fancy boutique the other day shrieks.

"Hey, what are you doing with my shoes?" Her shoes? Is this some kind of sick joke? A new variant on how we can harass travelers even more?

"They are mine!" I protest, and I give a nervous little laugh.

"No, they are not!" She shrieked. "You are stealing my shoes!" Oh God, this gets worse and worse; now I am being accused of stealing shoes, which are mine.

"See?" Quickly I put a shoe on my foot. To my horror, it doesn't fit by a long shot no matter how hard I try. Panic sets in as it slowly dawns on me that they're really hers. And I feel like Cinderella's sister who is forced to chop off a toe. Gathering the remaining shreds of my dignity, I stammer. "Oh, sorry I made a mistake, but I have just such a pair, and as I couldn't find mine, I thought...". I trail off, feeling utterly drained as the mental picture of me spending a night in a holding cell and London airport pops up.

We have attracted quite a stir among the bored passengers, and they crane their necks to see what's going on. Everything has come to a standstill, and suddenly we are surrounded by guards with stern looks on their faces.

Somebody taps on my shoulder: Are these your shoes?" I turn around to see an attractive looking man in his mid-fifties holding my lovely shoes; I recognize them clearly by the tiny scratch at the front of my right shoe. Relief floods over me like a tidal wave.

"Yes, yes!" I shout, feeling buoyant. The crowd disperse as if by magic, clearly the excitement is over and disappointed, they stare ahead of them bored once more.

"Where did you find them?" I am almost swooning with relief.

"Somebody misplaced them, I think," he said casually as not to implicate anybody.

"Hi," he takes out his hand, "I am Mark, glad I could help."

"Silvia. "Silvia Smith, I say considerably lighter.

"Do you have time for a coffee?" he inquired.

I glance at my watch; hm almost two hours have passed since I arrived at the airport, and I have only just gotten through security; I still need to put my shoes on and walk to my gate, which, and I peer at the sign, is about a 15-minute walk away.

Quickly mentally, I calculate, coffee 20 min, walk another 15, hmm that's cutting it short, I muse, but on the other hand, he did find my shoes. Surely that needs a thank you, right? I concluded. "Sure, I have a little time." I mean what would you have done right?

"Great, let's go." I balance on one leg and manage to put on my shoes.

I grab my bag but, having forgotten its weight, almost keel over. Christ, I am getting too old for this shit, I think! Mark, observing my predicament, takes my bag out of my hand and effortlessly steers me towards Starbucks. Thankfully I sink into one of the deep armchairs and accept an iced coffee. Inside I can almost hear the sound of blissful silence. Relaxed, we chat; Mark is flying to Japan for a conference about robots, and eager to show him I have a sense of humor, I tell him that I am going on a cruise that serves drinks with umbrellas, which makes him smile. After only 10 minutes, he tells me he needs to catch his plane.

"Nice to meet you, Silvia," holding out his hand, "have a safe flight!" He scribbles his phone number on a napkin, which he hands to me, grins, and says. "Call me if you ever need somebody to find your shoes."

Disappointed, I see him go. I carefully fold the napkin and put it in my bag. I get up, gather my belongings and find my gate.

Boarding procedures for first-class passengers are almost over, and I show my boarding pass to a smiling stewardess that directs me to my seat. Sitting in my ultra-wide leather chair that doubles up as a recliner-bed with a glass of champagne, I can't help feeling pleased. And I am secretly tickled pink with my video entertainment screen that the stewardess magically produces from the armrest.

Then it's the turn of the economy passengers to enter the aircraft.

I enjoy the jealous looks they are giving me when they are eying my already half-empty glass of champagne, my extra-wide seat, and the complementary newspapers/magazines. No wonder they are flying cattle class with chairs that have barely enough leg space for toddlers.

After take-off, it isn't long before the same woman folds down my table and places a crisp white large napkin over it, serving me an entrée consisting of salmon, shrimps and tiny crackers, and I happily start munching. She keeps my wine glass filled, without being asked, and when I have devoured the last crumbs of the crackers, she takes my plate away and serves me salad and some sort of meat dish that is delicious.

"Fruit or ice cream for dessert, mam?" I chose ice cream not used to such luxury on a plane and briefly wondered what the economy passengers were having for dinner. The poor suckers probably had to buy their own.

The headrest, the excessive amount of wine and the recliner bed made me fall asleep and refreshed. I arrived thirteen hours later in Singapore.

After some curious glances by customs who aren't sure if it's really me on the passport, something I can't altogether blame them for, as I look more like a yet un-know-terrorist. Finely after a lengthy dialogue between officials, I am allowed to enter the country.

I grab my lovely new zebra-striped suitcases, easily located on the luggage belt, haul them in a cart, and step outside in what feels like Dante's inferno. Wildly I look back at the closed doors of the comfortable cooled airport hall.

'Holy shit,' I muttered. 'I travelled to a bloody sauna.' I am not sure if I can endure this kind of heat for a week. Within minutes, I am drenched, sweat pours into my eyes, and l search my bag for something to wipe my face. Thankfully I grabbed the only piece of paper I could find, the napkin with Marks telephone number on it, clearly forgetting. Drier now, I discard the napkin in the nearest bin and look around. While I am still deciding whether to step back in the cooled hall, I see a uniformed man holding up my name in bold letters standing next to a minivan. The decision is taken out of my hands, and I make myself known.

Helpfully, the driver seats me into the van and explains he needs to wait for two more passengers before driving to the boat. A somewhat older man with gray hair and a stoop enters and politely greets me. Silently we wait for the following passengers, who fail to show up after waiting more than 30 minutes. The gray-haired gentleman introduces himself as Dick Cabot, and we settle in some conversation, making it clear he is a seasoned traveler. He was not too bad looking if you go for that particular sullen outdoor look, you know: Dressed in a Calvin Klein shirt, but somehow, he managed to look slightly scruffy. It is beyond me why some men never look right even in the most expensive clothes.

His outfits looked a thousand times better on Indiana Jones that drive these hot flashy Land rovers. Now there is a delicious thought!

Where are they when you need them? They are more challenging to catch than bloody butterflies.

But when he started talking about stocks and bonds and how the financial world is doing, he has my full attention, not knowing anything of that world. At this point, it's possible that we together may embark on a whole new adventure. Is my search for my soulmate finally over? Alas, dear reader I had no idea how wrong I was, but bear with me shall we?

As it is, he turned out to be a wealthy English man and come to think of it. I find it very hard to remember why I started dating him in the first place as in due course, he turned out to be a real wanker. But let me start at the beginning. When we arrive at the boat, or more accurately the ship as I learn later, Dick mumbles. "A drink in the bar later, my dear?" Now that sounds like an offer I can't refuse and I nod. I can do with a drink. The moment we step out of the air-conditioned van, the heat blasts my face again. God, it's hot. So I decide there and then that if it isn't getting any cooler outside, I can always stay in my cabin for the entire trip watch TV and order room service.

We are directed to the gangplank, where a white-gloved steward steers me to the check-in counter, and I hand over my passport. A beautiful brunette with hair to die for studies my passport and comes to the same conclusion as the boys from customs earlier on that I pose no threat and hands me a form.

"Sign here please, mam, welcome on board." She pressed a button, and out of nowhere, a white-gloved man appeared. "This is your butler, mam," she says.

Holy crap! I have my own butler.

"Follow me, mam; I will take you to your room," he politely offered. Slightly bowled over, I follow him as he walks in front of me to one of twelve elevators. He presses for the elevator to arrive, and in awe, I take in the walnut paneled oak walls, gold buttons and large mirrors as the elevator smoothly rides us up. The door slides open.

"After you, mam," my butler smoothly said and stepped aside. Silently he glides in front of me—we pass several corridors with half paneled walls and lovely prints. Vases were holding lavish arrangements of flowers than stands on small, scattered tables.

The environment created is unrivaled and designed to put spoiled clientele at ease. When we arrive at the cabin, and the butler swings the door triumphantly open, and with a slight smile that plays around his lips, he awaits my response. I am stunned by the sheer luxury of the surroundings. Light blue raw silk curtains hang in front of the windows, allowing me to see a glimpse of the turquoise sea. And not only do I have a window with an ocean view but also a veranda.

"Wow, does the view come with the cabin?" I squealed. "That's freaking unbelievable." And dear reader it

is absolutely fucking gorgeous, I only wish you could experience this for yourself.

The butler, probably not used to such exuberant outburst, seems delighted with my exclamation, and he explains. "It's a private place just for you to breathe in the fresh air and sea the ocean swim by." He walks to the veranda door and unlatches it. I followed him out and looked at the sea with its unbelievable turquoise color. It's less hot as the sun is about to go under, and the sky turns from orange to bright purple into a dazzling pink. It's breath-taking! Tears well up in my eyes -if I only had somebody to share this moment with.

"There is a bowl of fresh fruits for you on the table," the butler interrupted my thoughts. "Do you want me to cut you some?" He holds an overflowing basket of lush tropical fruits in the air, and my mouth starts to water.

"I have a mango, please, and some pineapple," I am warming up to the luxury of being waited on hand and foot and forgotten my earlier sadness. I almost dance back inside.

He expertly busies himself with cutting my fruit. I watch him silently, thinking, this is so unreal. What happened yesterday was something out of a horror movie, but today I am being served by a straight-faced butler wearing white gloves who is cutting fruit for me.

This is fast becoming the best day ever! I clamp my lips together as I don't want to giggle like an idiot in front of my butler. 'My butler' I like the way that sounds. When I come back, my friends will ask me, 'how was your vacation?' I can casually say like it's normal, "oh, I had a fab trip, and my butler was the best ever.' Like I am accustomed to it, 'this one was so attentive and handsome.' And the jealous look on their faces will be my reward.

"What can I call you?" I asked, taking in his sleek appearance and his crispy white uniform. He looks about 45 years old, I guess and well preserved.

"You may call me Ben, mam."

"How many years have you been aboard, Ben?"

"Let me think about seven years before I worked for Lord Harry Cambridge, as his butler, but I like this better." He is warming up to the subject. "Sailing the seven seas has always been my dream. Let me show you around, Madam. Here is the bathroom," he opens a wood-paneled door, which has all the luxuries any spoiled guests may want. He shows me a selection of bathroom amenities and explains how to work the shower. Its well-positioned high-tech jets look more like something out of Star-Trek- flight deck than a shower. To tell you the truth, it's a bit daunting. Ben walks back to the bedroom and shows me the TV that is hidden behind a sleek panel. He flips it on, explains the remote control, and the blaring sound of a starving bitch complaining about something fills the room.

"I will draw you a scented whirlpool bath." He interrupted my thoughts.

"But first, let me get you a drink. He opens the fridge that is so cleverly hidden; I am heaving reservations about ever finding it again. Only armed with fierce determination and a GPS might do it.

"And while you freshen up, I will unpack your suitcases and chill your favorite drinks; can I start you off, mam? I can mix you a fine cocktail."

I want to pinch myself. Have I died and gone to heaven? Why have I never been on a cruise before? That was a serious oversight, and I vow from now on I will only take vacations on luxury cruise liners.

"Yes, please."

"What kind of drink would you like?" He persisted and handed me a cocktail menu. My eye scans intriguing names like Sunset cocktail (non-alcoholic), Hawaii margarita, a Cool Aid shooter, just to name a few. I settled for a Honey Deuce with honey/vodka/ raspberry liquor with crushed Ice topped off with a melon ball.

Efficiently he mixes my drink and hands it to me. I take a sip. It is delicious, cold, and refreshing, and because I am thirsty, I down in one gulp.

"You are a genius, Ben; you can run me that bath now; I'm a bit sticky from the trip."

He nods. "As you wish." He enters the bathroom, and I hear him switching on the faucets. After a few minutes, he enters the bedroom again, "I laid out your towels and your choice of fragrances. In the bathroom is a robe for your convenience."

Wow, he is good; I wondered how I was to come back after my bath- I couldn't very well come out stark-naked now, right? After all, he is staying to unpack my suitcases.

"Thank you," I smiled.

"Dinner is served at eight, but if you are hungry, I can order something for you right now. We also have an entertainment program, which ensures you don't have time to get bored. Our various personal trainers provide personal fitness plans. Or, if you like, you can join our Thai-Chi early morning, on the top deck. Many customers find it a great way to start the day!"

"I'll let you know, Ben," I smiled and disappeared into the bathroom. Randomly I open a drawer; inside are several packets of condoms discreetly tucked away. 'They may come in handy; I think. 'How thoughtful.'

The bath is full of warm bubbling water, and with a happy glow, I sink into the tub. Giggling, I pour more than a douse of bath oil in the water. I almost fall asleep until I hear the sound of the ship's horn blowing, signaling its departure. I glance out my bathroom porthole and see the dock slowly disappearing, and the journey has begun. The bathwater has turned frigid. As I pull myself up, well, let's say I tried; the oil I used earlier has made the bath so slippery it's almost impossible to get up. I resemble a two-year-old trying to get up from what has quickly turned into a tub from hell.

Every time I am almost up, I slide back down. At one attempt, I bang my head so hard on the side of the wall stars dance behind my closed eyes. I rub the sore spot cursing the pleasure-chasing fairies, God, my stupidity, my ex-boss and everybody else I can think of.

In despair, I yell. "Ben!!" Hoping he is still doing his duty unpacking my cases. Through the closed door, I hear his muffled reply. "Are you OK, mam?"

"No, I am not! I put too much oil in the bath, and now it's so slippery I can't get up."

Silence.

"Do you need help, mam?"

"Yes, please."

"Do you want me to find you your chambermaid, mam?"

'Hell? I have a chambermaid to? "Yes, please, and hurry the bath is cold," I yell. After a few minutes, I hear scuffling outside the door and some whispering.

"Hello mam, it's Mary mam, your maid. Is it OK for me to come in?"

"Yes, please. "Mary walks in, views the situation, and efficiently grabs a towel from the rack. "Lift your arms, mam, please," she ordered. Obediently I throw my arms in the air, and she slips the towel under my armpits. She is stronger than she looks and pulls me to a standing position without apparent effort, so efficient I suspect she has done it before. Then a thought enters my head, perhaps the staff provides liberal amounts of bath oil on purpose, ensuring themselves from good tips.

"Is all the staff trained to rescue slippery grannies?" I quipped before I could stop myself. She ignores my attempts at a joke. "Please be careful, mam. Step out. I will hold you."

Gingerly, I place one foot on the bath rug in front of the bath, then the second foot and I am rescued. Mortified, I thank her profusely.

"Will you be OK now, mam?" She asked, genuinely concerned. "You didn't hit your head now, did you?

"I am fine now, thanks, Mary; you are an Angel," admitting to nothing.

After Mary leaves, I need every towel to get myself oil-free. I rub my skin so hard it's turning bright red. I can't believe how silly that was; I can just see the headstone on my grave. Here lies Silvia Day-; starved in the bathtub on luxury liner.

With a critical eye, I grab the rope that hangs inside the door. It's the softest coat you can imagine, and lovingly I stroke the fabric. The hand-embroidered gold stitched monogram reads, Golden Voyage.

Oh God, perhaps I can nick this at the end of the journey. After all, I paid a fortune for this trip; I am entitled to it, I reassure myself.

Dismayed, I survey the bathroom with its mountain of towels on the floor and grimy looking bath. If I had not known better, you would think it was the first bath I had taken in over a year.

As there is nothing, I can do about it, I shrug my shoulders and walk into the bedroom, kicking off my bathroom slippers. My toes curl in the luxury carpet that covers the floor. The butler has left, but a small crisp card on the table reads; please ring the bell next to the door for service.

I open the wardrobe that takes up the whole wall. I am tickled pink when I see that my clothes are color coordinated by the wardrobe fairies. Why didn't I think of this? I mused. It makes picking out something to wear so much easier. I suck in my tummy and pour myself into the tightest black pants I own, and slip-on, against my better judgment, a pair of black high heels and apply makeup. As I look in the mirror, I must say I look stunning.

As my stomach rumbles, I grab a slice of fruit that Ben cut me earlier, it's delicious, but it doesn't quench my hunger. But from my limited knowledge about cruises, I know passengers can eat all day long, occasionally stop for shopping, then hurry back for more food, or sit at a bar and join silly games. So, I reckon I don't have to stay hungry much longer. Yes, I know it seems somewhat reckless not to watch one's weight, but I passed several gyms on my way to the cabin, so if I desired, I could exercise.

I leave the cabin; the way to the dining area is indicated and is next to the bar. When I enter the glitzy place, Dick Cabot, the man from the minivan, sits on a barstool. I can't help noticing that he is making love to his brandy, swirling it around in the glass, observing its color, commenting on it to the bar-tender and taking small sips from the golden liquid with a tremendously satisfying sigh, Christ! He made more noise drinking his bloody brandy than making love to me. Of course, when I didn't have that piece of information, I actually thought that it was sexy! How stupid can you get?

Casually I stroll towards him and take a seat next to him. "Hi."

"Hello, my dear, there you are," he greeted me in that refined posh English accent. "What's your sin?" I noticed he was drenched, in expensive aftershave.

"A vodka tonic, please." I grabbed my drink from the waiter, impersonating somebody in serious danger of dying with thirst and got it down in one gulp. Dick observes me with a tentative amused expression. Do I imagine it, or do I feel the ship throbbing with sexuality?

Several hours and drinks later, I still am not wiser about how he made all those millions. But this millionaire is definitely a future husband-to-be. He told me he lived in a large Scottish castle named Aubin Moor, which sounded mysterious and exciting. Later I learned it was a bloody, dark and depressing place holding creepy secrets.

"Another small drink?" Dick inquired. I knew that he was after me.

"I gave up on small drinks long ago," I quipped, slightly drunk, nodding vigorously.

Dick beckons the waiter who silently puts another drink in front of me, that I eye with the eager look which betrays the true alcoholic. The waiter, who looks at my face, disappears for a moment and comes back with a plate of assorted nuts that I eagerly gobble up, trying not to flinch at being caught. I knew drinking on an empty stomach was stupid. Dick, who observes me, gives a muffled snort of laughter, but I don't look up as I gulp my drink again; I swear one day I will stop

I check the time, it's almost eight, and the nuts have done little to quell my hunger. No wonder it's been hours since I had some food.

"Care for some dinner now?" Dick asked. Gallantly he takes my elbow as I slide off the barstool, and we make our way to a private dining room. It's lovely and intimate, with a beautifully set table and a large chandelier hanging over it.

Large candlesticks hold black candles that give the room some extra luxury. Gold plated cutlery lay next to the best China money can buy, and there are flowers everywhere. A waiter appears out of nowhere, greets us and hands us a menu. Without asking me, Dick orders efficiently in French for both of us.

"Don't mind asking what I want," I couldn't help saying, with darkened eyes slightly annoyed at his control.

"I thought you have expensive tastes that like to be surprised," he smiled.

He doesn't fool me with that fake smile, he knows what I am after, and I am appealed at being discovered. I try to keep up a bold front with light banter and jokes for the rest of the meal, but I am not sure if it is altogether believable.

We began with a delicious seafood entree with crispy crackers. My taste buds are bombarded with the flavor of the food. Duck in a red berry sauce follows the starter with delicately cooked vegetables served in small portions. Every mouthful holds surprises, and my earlier humiliation recedes. I decided that Dick Cabot, despite his age, was worth pursuing.

One evening during the cruise he told me over dinner that he lived in a small decaying Scottish castle named, Aubin Moor that was built on an island in the middle of a lake. This sounded mysterious and exciting. Later I learned it was more like a bloody mausoleum, dark and gloomy except for a few renovated rooms that had nice handmade furniture. The drawing-room was my favorite with its wonderful green and pink settees, high ceilings and beautiful paintings. The smell of intoxicating potpourri hung heavily in the air. The room had large windows with breath-taking views over the lake and woods. But I digress.

When I saw it for the first time, after driving the long and windy road leading to the castle, its size in the distance was impressive. On each side stood two rectangle towers, each with its own entrance. And in the middle of the building was a massive oak door. A narrow wooden bridge led from the land over a moat to the castle. After Dick parked the car, I almost ran to the building.

Thrilled I grabbed the brass knocker, just as a butler opened the door with a smile and spoke.

"Welcome to castle Aubin! After you my dear." Dick stepped aside to let me in and I noticed he was obviously very proud of the place, but once inside I tried to hide my disappointment. As I looked around, I saw a cavernous hall filled with armored knights keeping vigil.

Sad looking Victorian angels hung on the wall, and lit candles gave the entrance an eerie feeling. The flames in the gigantic fireplace cast dancing shadows on the walls, and seem to be whispering of misdemeanors, and evil crimes. And a gloomy feeling crept down my spine. Above our heads on the high vaulted ceiling hung a magnificent chandelier, that looked as if it could fall at any moment and crush us to death. I inhale sharply. My excitement in pursuing Dick is waning fast. No way can I ever live in such a mausoleum as this, I think. Dick, who is completely oblivious to my thoughts, raises an eyebrow and asks, his voice bouncing off the walls with misplaced pride.

"I bet you are impressed, right." Not waiting for an answer, he pulled a cord that hangs from the ceiling. Within seconds his butler arrives, accompanied by bouncing what looks like wolves in his wake. They ran to Dick, who affectionately takes time to pat them all down.

They are the largest dogs I have ever seen, and with their barking and tail wagging fighting for attention, they are a terrifying lot I mentally struggle not to flee the scene.

"Dogs? Giant man-eating dogs?" I croaked, my hands shaking as one of the dogs came closer. "Please, can you take them away? They scare me!" I pleaded in a trembling voice.

"Don't worry, my dear, they are not pit bulls," Dick explained. "They are pretty harmless unless you are a prowler, then they might rip you to pieces. Pat them so they get to know you." He gives a hearty laugh. I am surrounded by man-eaters that sniff my hands with suspicion and bark in a frenzied manner. Pat their backs? He can't be serious.

"Bloody hell I don't think so." My voice is a little strangled, and I step backwards. My immediate wish is to run back to the car, but I suspect that the dogs will shred me to pieces should I give in to that temptation.

"Welcome home, sir," the butler said, the respect in his voice genuine. "Ma'am," he nodded in my direction. Noticing my discomfort, he barks. "Down boys."

The dogs are obviously well trained, because, with one last warning look at me, they walk towards the butler, and follow him when he opens the double doors leading to the drawing-room.

"The fire is lit, sir, and I have laid out a small supper for you and the young lady. I will take the dogs to the kitchen. "Thankfully I throw him a weak smile, and behind his boss's back, he unexpectedly winks at me. Shakily I follow Dick into the drawing-room. And he struts to a small table that is set for two.

"Care for some light dinner, Silvia?"

I nod and sit down, and Dick pours some red wine out of a crystal decanter for us. "Cheers, may your stay here be a happy one." He smiled.

I take a long gulp; the wine is delicious, and images of the terrifying dogs recede. I place the glass carefully on the table and taste the hors d'oeuvres that are delicious. After the wine follows champagne that he pours into long thin flutes, their bubbles tickling my nose. In my bubbly haze, I think I might get used to this until I hear far away the barking dogs. That works like a cold shower, and I resolve that if Dick wants me, they must go. I am clearly still in denial about my possible girlfriend's powers to be.

The following day after breakfast, Dick meets me in the assembly hall where, he explains, his ancestors used to receive guests and disgruntled farmers that complained about their taxes. Despite the roaring flames in the gigantic fireplace, it is unsuccessful in warming the place and shivering, I walk towards it. "Sorry for the cold. The central heating is not yet connected, although all the groundwork is done."

I can adjust to the cold, although adjusting isn't my strong suit, but for a moment I wonder if he is really worth it. I shiver and get even closer to the fire thinking probably not. On each side of the fireplace oversized leather armchairs that look decidedly uncomfortable reside. And the forlorn armored knights look just as miserable as they did last night and still give me the willies. It doesn't take much imagination to expect the shadow of a ghost to appear at any time.

On a small side table lie several books, and still nervous about the possible reappearance of the dogs, I pick one up. Stamped across the cover, I read:

'How to recognize the predators in your life! 2 million copies sold.' No wonder he is still a bachelor. I gulp. He probably spends his days reading tales of female temptations and tricks! Before I can dwell on the title, Dick is already out of sight, and I hurry as fast as I can after him, taking care not to slip on the polished black and white squares of the marble floor.

"The castle dates back to 1791. It has eleven rooms, nine bathrooms, and fourteen fireplaces. It's been in my family all this time!" His voice booms of the walls. "It has also been used in a famous movie. I'm sorry I can't remember the name, but it will come to me. My uncle left the estate to me, and it was love at first sight. I vowed to restore it to its previous glory, but as you can see and it's going to be a long and arduous process. However, the downstairs is done." And he waves his hands around the hall observed by the gloomy knights. He takes a deep breath and continues. "We took great care to preserve the frescoes, fireplaces and ceilings. I currently employ an army of tradesmen, stone cutters, masons, painters and carpenters. You may recognize the various mosaics in the halls come of course from Italy! And the tapestries on the walls were restored in France. Plumbing and rewiring came next. But the first thing we did was to replace the roof as all the beams were rotten and the shingles broken. A massive undertaking, as you can imagine!"

I am unsure how to respond to this flood of information, so I silently climb the worn-out grand staircase. I hadn't been upstairs and because of the massive renovation currently underway we had slept in one of the downstairs bedrooms that

I thought still required restoring. Hm, but after hearing Dick's raving about the restorations I came to the conclusion I wasn't on-par.

"We have not yet replaced the carpet-runner on the stairs, as the tradesmen trample all over the house."

I let the adjective we slip by, nod and proceed warily, but because I feel some kind of response is required of me, I make an effort. "It's a significant improvement." Like I had seen it before. He is silent. He is probably aware of my antagonistic feelings.

I climbed higher trying to relax, but I couldn't help my heart going into overdrive when a foul stench hit my nostrils, and I felt an ice-cold hand closing around my throat. Without warning lightning flashed, followed almost immediately by the roar of thunder, and I jumped half a meter in the air. Had I not held on to the railing, I would have fallen headfirst down the stairs. In shock, I look up and see a shrouded figure floating above the landing looking at us with his hands stretched out. Brilliant! That's all I need, a ghost! I let out a bloodcurdling scream. Why am I not even surprised? Hadn't I felt the dark powers of this place from the moment I stepped inside?

"What's wrong, my dear?"

"I thought I saw a ghost! Is your place haunted?" My voice was shaky. He doesn't immediately reply, then responds. "It's an old house possibly, err, hmm." He clears his throat. "Yes."

That's it. I vow to leave on the next available train. All the uneasiness I felt earlier rushed back. It's time to take off my get-rich-quick-goggles. 'Deluded old fool, I think.' Although I remember he had been charming when we first met and even brought me small gifts. But come to think of it, if a rich guy brings you small gifts, it's a sure warning sign. He does not intend to spend his fortune on you, girl! That should have been an indication, but I can be very blind or dim-witted, especially when I think I am in love. Weary, I rub my head.

"Why didn't you tell me before we travelled here that you had ghosts?"

"I gather you don't like ghosts, right? Dick said as brightly as he can. Although he isn't fooling me.

"Too bloody right, I don't." I hissed. He defiantly throws a glance at me, then shrugs his shoulders. "Come dear, let's proceed. Look, there is no ghost, see?" Against my will, I look up, and sure enough, there is nothing. Reluctantly I place one foot in front of the other even slower this time, ready to run down if the Ghost reappears.

It doesn't.

When we reach the top of the landing and step into the gallery, I cautiously look around. Paintings of more deceased aristocratic ancestors greet me with somber looks. Although the paintings, draperies and furniture gave the hall back something of its former glory, they do nothing to remove the spooky ambiance.

Dick walked to one of the windows and threw open the shutters. As the light streams in trough rain-streaked windows, I get a better look at the elegant, delicate Victorian chairs that line the walls, upholstered in old pink velvet on exquisite gold painted legs. Wallpaper behind each chair depicts gorgeous hand-painted flamingos in vibrant pink and white standing in a shimmering aqua opaque lake. Whoever had painted them was a true artist. It was beautiful.

Several carved French chairs upholstered in white velvet made a stunning addition to the hall. On the old oak floor lay a big hand-knotted Persian carpet. Adding extra elegance to the room with its faded colors. Pity somebody had partly covered the rug with plastic to protect it from laborers, I guessed.

"This hall will be used for elegant dinners or dancing once we are finished," Dick's voice boomed out. In silence I walk around touching a chair or a piece of artwork standing on one of the wall tables.

"Be careful," Dick warned. "The porcelain pieces are priceless."

Quickly I replace the delicate golden swan with its craned neck that I am admiring on the sideboard. As I don't want to be responsible for murdering it. Turning around I give my attention to several closed doors, leading off the gallery.

"Can we look inside?" Pointing to a closed door. Dick explained he couldn't show me the rest as work on the bedrooms was underway, and he didn't want to disturb the workers. I half expected him to climb to the second floor to continue the tour, and show me possible skeletons in various closets, but thankfully he didn't. Instead, he turned around and we headed downstairs.

The following week Dick mostly ignored me and I spent most of my time relaxing in the oak-paneled library, sipping a whiskey, and reading a book. Living with the sod wasn't too bad, as it was a life of leisure. In that respect he met all the husband requirements besides being rich. Several staff kept his home impeccable, and his housekeeper made sure there were fresh flowers in every room. Breakfast was served every morning in the conservatory, with plenty of fresh fruits and homemade jam.

There was also a billiard room and a fabulous old-fashioned kitchen with gleaming pots and pans that made my hands itch to prepare food. I boasted I could cook my way into any man's heart. Unfortunately, I was banned from entering the kitchen after cooking him an excellent spicy curry, thinking he would love it. But to my surprise he took one bite and started yelling it was too hot.

"Bollocks," I muttered. "I am sorry. I didn't know you were so sensitive to spicy food." Unfortunately, he was still too busy rinsing his mouth that he couldn't or wouldn't acknowledge me. I felt a bit like the wicked witch of Eastwood, and the atmosphere after that incident became a bit chilly. I was beginning to understand why he still was a bachelor. What a pig. It was impossible to tell where I stood in his order of importance.

Where shall I begin. Oh yes. Of course, sex did not happen often. When it did it was preferably in bed with the lights out and a few sounds as possible.

A wham-bam thank-you-ma'am, kind of thing. And did I mention he always insisted I have a shower first? Like I was unclean. I always felt faintly insulted. What is wrong with a woman's body anyway? I shower every day, in fact, sometimes twice a day, nothing too dirty down there! It was not that he wanted me to wash before performing oral sex. No, I should have been so lucky.

At least that would have made showering understandable, but as it turned out, he didn't believe in that either. But, like so many other men, he had no objections when oral sex was performed on him. Whenever he could, he literally waved it in front of my face. Also, the use of condoms was not for him. Of all the stupid things I did, this was probably the most ridiculous. At the time, I thought of it as an investment in the future, giving him what he wants in the hopes of marriage. The result was that I almost ran to the shower after sex to get rid of any trace of him. Nothing worse than dried-up sperm in your underpants.

The few times we had sex the *normal* way, I did not even have time to blink my eyes during foreplay. It was that short. Another thing Dick didn't believe in. Can you imagine with a name like that, how could you not believe in foreplay? The great O was often an illusion, but if I were fortunate and desperate enough, I could manage a tiny orgasm.

Once I was really turned on, I got up and fetched my vibrator. I mean, I knew he wasn't going to last long right? Oh, boy, was that a mistake. He seriously objected to my using it. Clearly, his manhood was under attack, so to appease him, I put it away.

I should have known what kind of guy he was, of course, when I first laid eyes on him; there are always tell-tale signs that give it away.

It turned out that Dick was, in fact, a lazy slob, the only man I have known that was capable of falling asleep behind the wheel of his car while waiting for the traffic lights to change to green! Things came out in the open when I found out he actually took the car to go to the post office around the corner and told me he hated exercise.

After several weeks of getting to know him better, things turned sour. Let's face it they hadn't been all that great to begin with, but I could at least pretend to myself things were ok.

It went something like this. After breakfast he says, "would you care to see the gardens?" Without waiting for an answer, he walked outside. It's not easy to walk in my shoes on the gravel, and I need to tread carefully, I swear under my breath, wondering what it would do to my expensive shoes. Finally, after what seems like an eternity, we come to a rose garden.

"These are pink phlox, and purple Veronica" Dick explained.

I know very little about gardens, but it's breath-taking, and in awe, I walk through a myriad of flowers competing with their vibrant colors.

"The grounds are meticulously laid out by season and reflect..." Here, he stopped as an old Porsche drove up. The car stops, and a woman gets out. She makes getting out of the car into an art form with her understated elegance, and her tight skirt never rises too high. On her amazing looking long tanned legs, she wears six-inch-high Louis Vuitton stilettos, obviously not worn for comfort but to draw male attention. Just looking at her made me feel awkward and underdressed. Her heels click on the road until she gruffly stops to pat the dogs that come running when they hear her car arrive. I can only hope the dogs are too busy to notice me.

As she walks closer, I see she is far older than I first thought, has applied too much makeup, and is wearing false eyelashes.

"Hi, Dicky baby," she purred with pouting lips, kissing him full in the mouth, making it clear she has her mind set on him. This isn't the scenario I planned when I agreed to come here with Dick. I take a step backwards; I need to regroup. She rattles something off in a language I do not understand, and Dick nods a few times asking her quick questions. They both completely ignore me.

After a few minutes feeling like the wicked witch, I have had enough and introduce myself.

"Hi, I am Silvia."

She ignores my outstretched hand and instead shoots an inquiring glance at Dick, who clears his throat, looking startled for a moment. Hell, has he forgotten I am standing right beside him?

"Silvia, this is Mercedes. She lives nearby. Mercedes, this is Silvia, eh hmm, a friend." She barely looks me over, but her contempt is all the more evident.

"Where did you get those shoes, at the recycle store?" She asked, glancing down. "They are very unusual." All my muscles tensed when I looked at the skinny blond in her Armani skirt and cashmere sweater. I take a quick breath and ask in a syrupy voice:

"Did you by chance stand in front when they dished out the emaciated looks?"

Her eyes shoot daggers, and she breezes past me and mutters. "Where did you find her, Dick? In the gutter?"

At that point, I contemplating gross bodily harm to the bitch, whose lifelong compulsion it is to stay thin. But then I think, hell, isn't that enough punishment?

At that point, Dick foreseeing bloodstained heels intervenes.

"Shall we step inside, ladies and have a glass of wine?"

Thankfully the skinny one is temporarily distracted and grabs his arm like he is God's gift to women and gives one last triumphant look to me.

Dick, with his trophy on his arm, turns around, leaving me to follow them, mind you at a safe distance from the over-exuberant dogs. As he steers us towards the drawing-room, we pass the billiard room and the old-fashioned kitchen.

Dick pours us a healthy amount of deep red wine in crystal glasses, and I ignore Miss Starving Africa, who keeps up a steady banter in the same foreign language obviously intended to shut me out.

I look around. The walls are lined with heavy bookshelves, holding costly antique books. If you like dark rooms, this is for you, but on me, it's wasted. In the vast fireplace burns another malevolent fire. Perhaps it was my imagination, but did the crackling flames like in the hall whisper of past misdeeds by the owners of the castle? The whispering voices are so real it makes the hair stand up on the back of my neck. Is it my imagination, or do I see the earlier ghosts floating by? But before I can fully process the imagination, I hear the echo of distant screams, which scare the living daylights out of me. Before I know what, I am doing, I jump out of my chair.

"What was that?" I shouted and gripped the back of the chair in blind panic, trying to control my breathing. Do I imagine it or do I hear the sound of heavy chains rattling? I let out a scream. Startled Miss Starving Africa and Dick look up. If I hadn't had their full attention before, I sure as hell have it now.

Dick gets up from his chair and, with a concerned look on his face, pats my back. "I think Silvia sensed something; some people do." He whispered.

"And what exactly did she sense?" Inquired Mercedes, while giving me a cold stare. How I dare to interrupt her tête-à-tête with Dick, who strides over to the fireplace, positing himself in the middle.

"Rumor has it that there is somebody killed in this room." He explained to Miss Skinny," Without a pause, he lowers his voice. "It's believed my great-great-grandfather murdered a young boy," he turned towards me. "Did you hear the sound of shackles and chains by any chance?"

I nodded, unable to speak. Dick was silent, then gathered courage.

"Some say the young boy was murdered here and placed behind the fireplace by my great-great-grandfather, who swore his servants to secrecy."

"Why was he murdered?" I asked.

Dick looks uncomfortable and clears his throat. "It's said he sexually abused the boy who then demanded money, or he would expose his dirty secret."

The mental picture of some old geezer doing some possible ass squeezing in public was too funny for words, and I gave a nervous giggle. By way of an excuse, the eerie atmosphere must have made me slightly hysterical. I must have babbled something because Mercedes looks at me, her lips in a sneer. "A boy was murdered here. Do you really think that's funny? How stupid are you." She mocked.

Her voice works as if in a cold shower. As much as I hated to admit it, she is correct. The boy paid for it with his life, and it is not a laughing matter. Dejected, I am silent, staring into a vacant space. That's it! I knew these old mansions were evil. Who would want to live here? Certainly not me, I think.

"But here, I am inconsiderate boring you with the gruesome details of my past ancestors. Let me pour you ladies some more wine!" Dick is trying to defuse the situation. Humanity never fails to amaze me. Here was a guy who was proud of his heritage earlier on, and now as something unsavory comes to light, he falls apart. At that point, I realized that there was no sign of any vitality or energy in this relationship. My millionaire had surpassed all the other losers I had dated. And I knew beyond any doubt he had just failed the husband-to-be test. Mercedes was welcome to him lock, stock and barrel, shackles and chains, in this case.

Faith Healer

(New Title Carrot -Man)

One lunatic relationship I remember happening years back was a guy I met sitting next to on a train. 'Has that ever-happened to you dear reader? Falling as a brick for a stranger, who dazzles you with his gorgeous blue eyes? Well, it happened to me, let me tell you how I temporarily lost my sanity shall we?'

He was of average height and not particularly good-looking, with his clothes slightly rumpled, but this was due - he explained - to the fact that he had been traveling for days! I found him adorable!

And I fell madly in love with him there and then. It seemed like it was a love meant for a lifetime. Little did I know that this love for him would become an obsession and almost destroy me. If I had had any clue, I would have had second thoughts and switched seats. In the beginning, he impersonated the perfect boyfriend, and I could tell, just by looking at him in bewilderment and wonder, he was going to be around for a while. I honestly never loved another man more than him.

He had something extremely compelling and sweet around him, almost feminine, and he made me wonder that I was perhaps a lesbian. After getting off the train, a few blissful months followed. He was a bit vague about his profession, but as he always seemed to have enough cash in his pockets, I was not too concerned about this lack of information. We were blissfully in love, did all the things lovers do: walks around the park holding hands and whispering sweet things to each other, the stuff other people hate when uttered in their presence. I was ecstatically happy and carefree.

The sex was mind-blowing, and we made love in every conceivable place and position. I felt this time I'd truly found my perfect soul mate, not realizing the power of good communication is just as crucial as having stimulated sex organs. As it proved, this was a serious oversight.

He had moved in with me shortly after we met, claiming he had no place to stay at the moment as he was in "between" houses. I had at the time no inkling of the fact that, in reality, he was too stingy to spend his cash on something so mundane as a house.

My mad attraction for him made me forget everything I believed in and held true! Even after discovering that he was a vegan in the first week we met, I usually have no patience for these species. I am a firm believer in the survival of the fittest, and as such, we need to sustain ourselves with meat to stay healthy and strong. But in him, I found it amusing and even a little exotic! This is a sure indication of madness on my part. My mad attraction for him made me forget everything!

Of course, I could have for- seen problems when found out, he sometimes only had-as he called it-a 'fruit week.' He consumed tons of the stuff and advertised the fact by farting non-stop. It still beats me up why men have absolutely no qualms about openly farting. It's a disgusting habit.

As it was usually my habit to copy my boyfriends' various peculiar eating habits, I learned some things and did not succumb to the same temptation. Besides, I am a fervent meat lover and felt that I would go totally bananas after one fruit day. I knew I could not possibly survive on orange peel and apples!

The disapproval look on his face was almost comical when he saw me consuming a thick juicy steak the first time he took me out to dinner, making me feel very uncomfortable. I seemed to be doing something seriously wrong and had me squirming in my seat. His disapproving looks took away my appetite, and after a few bites, I shoved the plate away and ordered a salad.

That had his instant approval. His eyes lit up, and the look he gave me was warm and intimate. I could feel myself melt into a puddle beneath his feet.

Let's face it, I was too smitten by him to even care about what food I ate. After he moved in, I was careful not to show him I occasionally devoured a salami sandwich in the kitchen which sinful pleasure, such was my madness, making sure to brush my teeth afterwards to get rid of the smell.

Eventually, my secret meat love came out when my craving became just too strong.

Each time I thought about the meat, I salivated and had to lick my lips to keep from betraying myself by drooling. Finally, when I couldn't suppress the temptation a day longer, I caved, bought and cooked myself a steak liberally, dousing it with garlic and drenching it in butter, making my mouth water in anticipation. I made his usual boring salad and put both dishes on the table. His incredulous look when he saw the meat made me giggle nervously.

"What's that?" He inquired, pointing at my steak, grabbing it and carefully shielding it away from me, "you are clogging your arteries, and I can't allow you to eat this."

It took me only a moment to recover. As fast as I could, I grabbed my plate and tried to wrestle it away from him. For a moment, we were both fighting over ultimate plate-control, and, as I was clearly more motivated, I won.

"Don't eat that crap," he pointed a stern finger at my beautiful steak that was slowly oozing blood.

Ignoring his insane demand, I was careful to keep my plate out of the reach of his grabbing hands. Now that I was once more in possession of my food, I had absolutely no intention of not enjoying the steak till the last morsel.

I cut off a large chunk of meat and slowly-perversely-placed it into my mouth all the time, looking provocative at him, just to see his reaction. The taste of the half-cooked garlicky meat exploded my taste buds into a pure mouth orgasm. I gasped and could not suppress a groan of delight.

"That disgusting," he yelled. "You did that to annoy me," he was right, of course. Let's face it. I just realized the happy months were over; he was getting on my nerves. And I noticed I enjoyed aggravating him. Slowly I ate my steak, savoring every mouth-watering bite. He turned away and sulkily ate his salad, glaring at me from time to time with pure venom in his glance.

Finally, in a bitter haughty voice, he said. "I am not sure what your game is, but let me assure you I am not amused, in future please eat this... this" ... pointing at my blood-drenched plate, "this dead cow in the kitchen."

When I heard his words, I almost choked! Opening and closing my mouth a few times, I finally croaked. "Excuse me. I believe this is my house. I can eat whatever I like, so please shut up, you righteous bastard!" Clearly Indicating the shields were off.

How dare he sit on judgment on me! That's it! The honeymoon is definitely over! Realizing in an instant why I had been feeling unhappy for several weeks now. The reality was, he was restricting my life with stupid rules and commands, stifling my personality! And I went along with it! No more! I vowed. He was fast becoming a pain in the proverbial butt. And it was not just his eating habits that were grating my nerves. There was something much more serious going on. A few weeks after we started living together, a phone call came for him, as it turned out it was from a patient. It was then that I learned he was a 'healer of sorts. If he placed both hands on a sick body and softly rubbing the affected area. The pain would (or so he claimed) would disappear as by magic.

Afterwards, Greg would present them with a bill that was way out of proportion, without asking whether or not they could afford to pay! He always told me that I had no notion of their suffering and what they were going through and would gladly have paid twice the amount he charged them, just to feel better.

However true that may seem, it did nothing to alleviate my anger about him asking absurd amounts of money for his *healing*.

His whole profession mystified me, knowing I was far too pragmatic to be lulled into what I felt was his false sense of *reality*. In turn, he accused me of being 'acrimonious, childish and not sharing his beliefs!'

His reflection of life was totally different from mine and often made me feel inferior when I didn't share his views about his spiritual *New Age-crap* of peace and love. Holy shit. 'I hope dear reader you aren't fooled by that crap.'

He *meditated* for hours on end, demanding utter silence in the house as it destroyed his concentration. Claiming he needed tranquility and serenity, abhorring my use of the phone or the radio, it had him screaming in rage when I forgot about his 'golden rule.

Obviously, he had difficulties controlling his aggression. Mediate some more? Perhaps until you see blue in the face? I love playing my stereo loud and often dance to the music. But that was no longer possible, and I could not help resenting that I was subjected to his strict new regime in my own house. He would first ask me in a disapproving voice if I could stop the music. When I hesitated, he would become angry and start slamming doors for a while.

And when that no longer satisfied him. He would be arguing trying to convince me by 'babbling' incoherently about the meaning of the universe-our mystical auras-destiny-and why they had to be on the same plane until he made me want to yell in frustration.

He didn't like anything better than to tell me about the true meaning of our suffering and why we had obscene beliefs in pure materialistic pleasures (meanwhile, he was perfectly content to fill his bank account riding on other people's pain). His double standard was disturbing, and I had no idea how to get through to him.

He always told me of his need to cultivate or magnify his sense of love for the divine by focusing on his beloved esoteric deity. Thereby-he said-creating sparks of a spiritual memory that had been lying dormant within him.

(What the fuck is he talking about? I more than once thought). Do you know?

He claimed that he gained power over his thinking and behavior by meditating that enhanced his self-understanding and self-acceptance. Needless to say, I had absolutely no idea what he was referring to.

He further claimed that this would overcome any behavioral problems, such as anxiety, hyperactivity, and aggression. Sarcastically once asked him if it would also overcome his greedy capitalistic mind. After looking at me. A soft glow came over his face- And, and he admitted that he was having some problems with that part of him.

Not only was he a *healer* he also had many customers that came for his special Tarot card reading. Are you familiar with this?

It goes something like this.... place obscure looking cards on the table that depict horrifying images, turn them over, telling your viewers in a softly equally horrifying gloomy voice...

'This card is one of death! And here we have -Ace of spades-, four of devil.' And..., making a show of dramatically pausing: -'Ah, -Judgment! -The spirit of Eternal Primal Fire! Impending significant changes.' His almost orgasmic sigh made me aware that was the card most sought after.

He slowly drove me crazy, plus the fact that he was a smug, arrogant bastard about lots of other things too! I swear he made me drink, anything to forget how unhappy I was. Just because I did not meditate, he had an uncanny knack for making me feel like an idiot. It made me realize that we didn't have a future together–as we didn't share sharing one thing. However, getting rid of him was almost impossible and proved to be a real challenge.

"I want you to move out!" I started one evening, brushing the table clean in one gigantic swoop of his Tarot cards, observing them detachedly as they fluttered slowly towards the floor.

The week had just come to an end, and, as it had been a terrible week of constant arguing and bickering, I had enough. I poured myself a glass of red wine, took a large sip, and walked close to him, holding my glass.

"Now it's not for you to be separated by your wine for more than a foot, is it?" He inquired sarcastically. "And what on earth do you mean when you said you want me to move?" Switching from attack to quizzed mode required no effort.

"I stayed up late last night playing poker with your Tarot cards. I got a full house, and four of my friends died. Consequently, I picked a fight with the Joker, who informed me there was Energy, Force, Happiness and Optimism, lacking from this house"!

"Yes. I did pick up one or two angry vibes from you", he said. "Not sure why, though!"

"You are the most arrogant, ridiculous, preposterous, conceited person I ever had the misfortune to live with, and your halo is in desperate need of polishing," I informed him.

"I am tired of you fucking with my brain. The spiritual believes you hold mean only one thing to you, but you are too stupid to see it!"

"See what?" He asked, dazed, throwing me a hurtful look in the vain hope I caved. I am not impressed, I had seen it all before, so I was not going to be persuaded to let him stay this time. He tried again. "What is the problem, love?"

"It is immoral and wrong what you do to all those sick people, Greg." I told him for the hundredth time.

"I have to help them," he was pleading now. "They depend on me."

"And you depend on them," I yelled again. "You are perfectly happy to relieve them of their hard-earned cash. Sometimes they have barely enough money to see out the end of the month, why can't you help them for less or for free? See how well off they are before charging them a ridiculous amount of money!"

"By now, it is clear that you do not share my beliefs," he told me coldly, ignoring what I said.

"Too bloody right I'm not," I yelled again. I can't help myself. By now, I am a screaming bitch-I loathe myself but know I no longer have a say in the matter. Either he'd go, or I'd go, period. I look at him, shrugging my shoulders.

"I want you out! Preferably today."

"Fine," he said. "Obviously, I cannot work in these circumstances. It lacks the right atmosphere, and the peace within is notably absent. I wondered why my last patient did not respond well to my touch, but now I know!"

By this time, I am seriously contemplating the concept of murder. How dare he accuse me of being a bad influence on his healing powers? Of all the gall!

It was true that the house's atmosphere has changed because we do not see eye to eye. My memories of the good times that we spent together are blurry. I can't accept his callous behavior, and I know I am not good at hiding my discontent. It must have shown, hence the difference in atmosphere.

"It is always about what you want, but what about my needs? You move into my house expecting me to bow to your wishes and in doing so make it impossible to be myself!" I hear myself whining. "What don't you understand about *You Move Out*? O-u-t-of- my-h-o-u-s-e!" I spell it slowly, making sure he listens! I swallow hard. I am on the verge of crying. What is happening to me? I must be exhausted and realize my lover is rapidly becoming the object of all kinds of smoldering, hateful feelings, and I am helpless to stop it.

"You have to give me time to find another place," he retorted. Judging correctly, that I was serious.

"Why can't you leave today," I asked him. "It's not like you have a whole house to move!"

"I feel bad vibes coming from you," he told me. "Perhaps you would like me to place my hands on you, just to soothe those irritations you are obviously struggling with?"

He is talking to me in this crazy language, one that I am unfamiliar with.

"How come you don't even want to understand me a little?" I repeated this despondently.

"I am trying," said Greg in a shockingly mild voice. "But it is not easy for me."

"You have changed since we first met."

"Changed?" I queried. "Changed how?" I fell into his trap way too quickly.

"I mean it," said Greg. "You condemn me, and I believe you do not value the way I choose to lead my life. I suggest you change your way of thinking and your character."

This is not going according to plan! I'd expected him to be upset or even angry, not this "holier than thou" attitude, and to make matters worse, he has the nerve trying to calm me down by placing his hands on me "Do you know what I am feeling?" I asked him again.

"No."

"I feel sadness and resentment coming from you."

"Why?"

"Because my life is not the same as yours, I find it impossible to understand you; we do not share the same ideas or even come close!" I told him. "You are always judging and finding me wanting; I can't take it anymore."

He looks disappointed as if it was the first time, he heard this bizarre comment from me!

"I find it impossible to believe in your ethereal, spiritual New-Age crap!" I stepped it up a bit.

"Well, that's brilliant," he said despairingly, "Perhaps I should try my powers on you, see how you respond". And moved towards me. This was the third time he volunteered his hocus-pocus healing on me.

"Hold it! Back up, Mister!" I stepped away and walked out of the house, having no desire to be *healed* I swore to God never to let anybody stay in my place ever again!

Five weeks later, he still hadn't moved out, claiming he couldn't find a proper place! Bull!

There were many places I knew he hadn't even bothered to look, and finally, taking matters into my own hands, I looked in the papers for a suitable place.

After two days, I found an ideal house for him; it even had a small garden to build his 'Shrine' in, a Thai spirit house that was now standing in my front garden, much to the amusement of my neighbors.

Every morning he paid *Homage* to the Spirits that probably rented the place from him, I thought perversely. He, placed fresh flowers and soft candy in the mini shrine, making sure the birds were having a field day. I paid a month's rent, packed his meager belongings in a few boxes and moved the whole lot to his new premises. Then I called a locksmith to change the locks on my front and back doors and prepared myself for the moment he came home.

When he finally drives his flashy looking immaculate polished Mercedes up, I brace myself for the upcoming confrontation.

He gets out, and I bite my lip waiting for the moment his key enters the lock, finding myself holding my breath. He takes out his key, inserts it into the lock and turns. Of course, it doesn't budge, and he tries again. Finally, he rings the bell. Impatient, loud, and insistent.

I think about not answering the door at all, but the persistent ringing drives me crazy-surely, he knows I am inside, with my car parked in front.

"Why can't you ring once?" I asked furiously, flinging open the door, letting my temper get the better of me!

"What is the matter," he wondered. "My key doesn't fit in the lock."

"That's because I have changed the locks, Greg. This is no longer your house, and I found you another place to stay. "You are no longer welcome here."

I told him his new address and handed the key to him. "The rent is paid for the month, and" I pause for effect, "have a good life."

"I thought you loved me," he said slowly.

"I did," I informed him. "But our relationship is too difficult. I can't handle it!"

He shook his head in disbelief. "If you love me, how can you shut me out of your house?" He muttered. "Are you not even going to discuss it with me?"

"No! This is my decision, and it is final. All of your things are in your new place."

And with that, I slammed the door, praying he didn't spot the tears in my eyes. I hear him slowly retreat to his car, opening the door and starting the engine, and with a soft purring sound, it fires, and he drives off. I feel a strange mixture of relief and searing pain shooting through me. For months afterwards, I lived in a fog, having neither objectives nor goals. Getting up in the morning was a drag, as I was merely existing. I was floundering, suffering from sleepless nights, exhausting me so much that I finally took sleeping tablets. Thankfully they put me into oblivion for a few hours at least, although I knew that only time will heal...

The Ikea whisperers

A few months later, I met my new boyfriend in, of all places, yes, Ikea: He was an Ellen's friend. Let me fill you in, shall we? Suffering from Stock-shop syndrome, my friend Ellen and I were thrilled when they opened an Ikea close to the town we live in (the nearest one was in London, 3 hours away by motorway if you were lucky.) Overjoyed, Ellen and I drove to the glitzy new Ikea on opening day. That that was a stupid idea became soon imminent. Huge crowds waited in front of the blue and yellow building, which didn't seem to move as quickly as we had hoped. We parked the car expecting to find a possible shortcut for customers with a family card. Alas, there wasn't. To pass the time, I read the billboards. One read:

'No entry without a working GPS! Keep your phones charged at all times. Families are advised to stay together. Ikea is not responsible for lost husbands and kids\or grandparents.'

Not used to such frivolity from Ikea, we laughed. Somebody must have a sense of humor. We queued up and accepted water bottles attentive Ikea staff handed out in the scorching sun. However helpful the team was, they panicked when customers began to look for toilets assembled or not. Finally, after 2 hours of waiting, we entered the building. Our spirits perked considerably because we still had a few hours before closing to cruise around.

   We were welcomed with a free IKEA bag, balloons and friendly faces, and we eagerly picked up the catalog, the block note and the free pencil. Unfortunately, a smartly dressed staff member informed us they ran out of complementary GPS devices. This information didn't unduly worry us. We had visited Ikea's before and were primed to follow the yellow lines, hopefully preventing customers from getting lost in the maze! It speaks for itself that we experienced Ikea shoppers had the foresight to bring cookies and a change of underwear because visiting Ikea can easily take the whole day. Savoring the moment, we eagerly looked around. Taking in the drug called Ikea, excited kids lined up to enter the ball pits. Unable to wait. What they hoped to find there remains a mystery. Treasure at the bottom? Or possibly reach the other side of the world if only they dove in deep enough? Who knows?!

   But whatever the attraction is, one can't deny that Ikea's greatest achievement is to lure in customers that look for a bit of free time from their kids for a few hours. Knowing fully well that once the customer is inside the store, very few walk out with nothing!

I walk closer to the ball pit and press my face against the glass, looking at the happy faces of the children, and wonder for a moment if Ikea has ever lost a kid in the sea of balls. Momentarily worried, I look around for warning signs, 'Keep your head above the balls at all times! Or: Ikea is not responsible for lost kids!' Not seeing any, I deduct that kids were not left behind other than on purpose.

My stomach growls, reminding me we had no lunch. "Let's go to the restaurant first; I am hungry. I can't wait to taste the meatballs," I said to Ellen.

"I heard they have new vegetarian balls, the Gronsakbullar" Ellen answered, who is a bit of a health freak. "It's Ikea's first step towards a healthier and more sustainable ecosystem. I want to try them, and, in the meantime, I am saving the planet as well." She added rather smugly.

I am rather vague about how she would achieve that by eating, no doubt, tasteless veggie balls, so I didn't answer.

"Apparently, the balls cost 50 cents less, which is always a bonus," she droned on.

I instantly forget Ikea's favorite balls, veggie or not, as I observe an Ikea newbie couple in front of us, nervously pointing to the serene yellow lines and arrows that would direct them relentlessly throughout the store. Looking at them, I could tell they were blissfully unaware that soon they would bash each other's brains out when attempting to assemble their flatpack dresser with drawers... and think, if they succeeded in the assembly quest, they could survive anything life throws at them. Poor sods, they had no chance in hell! Briefly, I wondered if there is a clinic that handles Ikea-related trauma!

But I digress.

Did you know Ikea has its own language? Not fluent in it, we held firmly on to our Ikea dictionaries, which we consulted now and then. But for some reason, they proved utterly useless when I asked the staff where I could find the Ypperlig. My pronunciation was probably wrong because the assistant asked for an article number. Sighing, I try it with another product, the Faithfull. But as it has, I didn't score with that product either. I tossed the dictionary in the nearest gray Ikea KNODD (bin) and cruised around at leisure, slowly edging towards the restaurant until I felt a blister coming on. Damn, I knew wearing new shoes was a mistake! I head for the nearest bathroom to take off my hose and investigate. From previous experience, I knew the bathrooms were far/far away, and stopping by the occasional showroom toilet didn't help. When I located a working bathroom, I was highly uncomfortable and seemed to have developed a limp.

I entered one of the bathroom stalls, took off my nylons, and sat down. I looked at my heel from my elevated position and saw that a huge blister had popped and left a gaping wound oozing water and blood. And came to the undeniable conclusion that I didn't need a tiny plaster but more like an ambulance taking me to a bloody emergency room. My hand went into my handbag and came out with a sanitary napkin that I occasionally wore to stem unwanted urine when I was in danger of laughing too hard.

It sure was big enough, but how to fasten it around my ankle without losing it in one of the Ikea ails? Think how embarrassing that would be.

In despair, I eyed the object. I went through my bag again and came up with a pair of scissors that I used to take the napkin apart. After fiddling with it for an eternity, I finally applied it to my blister and had enough material to tie it neatly around my ankle. Only one problem left. I couldn't get my foot in my shoe, but as I couldn't very well walk on bare feet through the store, I had no choice. I folded the back of my lovely heels to serve as a sandal, and exceptionally pleased with my endeavors, I exited the stall much more comfortably. Nearby, I heard somebody being violently ill. Poor thing, Ikea had obviously caught up with her. Another woman was standing at the washbasins with tears streaming down her face and a rolled-up hanky in one hand; sobbing became an instant source of my interest.

"What's wrong, dear?"

"I can't find the exit, and I have been hunting for hours", she sniffed -showing she was incapable of the yearly survival of the fittest contest. A nearby skinny blond laughed nervously, apparently finding the crying lady a source of amusement. But I suspected she probably struggled with the same lost- in Ikea-emotions.

"I thought this was supposed to be fun," the crying lady wailed.

I took a step closer, intending to give some comfort, but at that moment, an Ikea staff member came in. And whisked her out so fast we didn't even have time to say goodbye. Mm. I didn't recall this being mentioned in the Ikea brochure.

However, I couldn't dwell on it too long as Ellen waited in the restaurant. And I couldn't wait to tell her about the blister-sanitary pad solution. When I entered the restaurant, I looked dismayed at the man sitting across from her at the table. Their heads were close together, and they were laughing. I wondered who he was and why I didn't know him. As I approached their table, they both looked up.

"Hi Silvia, let me introduce an old friend of mine, Bob. We just ran into each other. He finally left his wife and required some furniture for his new place because she cleaned him out. Bob, this is Silvia, a good friend of mine."

Bob got up from the table and grinned. "Nice to meet you, Silvia. Today is my lucky day. Not one but two beautiful ladies help me with shopping. Why have you never told me you have this delightful friend?"

Looking at his handsome, chiseled face, I felt myself tingle with a long-forgotten spurt of pure lust. Ikea would light up if it only could harness my sexual surge. He seemed nice, but scarcely audible danger knocked on my mind as I observed him. It went something like this!

Knock-knock.

"Er, excuse me? Can I have a word? remember, more than once, your choice of men left something to desire?"

"What now? Don't disturb me!"

"Yes, I understand you are in lust, but please take things into perspective here."

"Leave me alone!"

"Don't tell me later. I didn't warn you!" My subconscious growls.

"Shut the hell up."

"If you looked at the slightly longer repercussions, you see what I mean!"

"What is it to you anyway?

"Well, for starters, I have to pick up the pieces if you fall apart again. Remember what happened last time? Do you? Do you? You were a blubbering wreck for eight months!"

"Mm."

"I am sick and tired of you throwing your body at every Tom, Dick and Harry. Do you copy?? It has to stop, and it will now, be a good girl and tell Ellen you want to go home!"

"Sorry, can't do it. Have you seen how utterly sexy he is? Are you blind? And he seemed to like me, didn't you notice? No! It's you that should shut up! Go!"

Silence-

My thoughts are interrupted when she turns towards Bob and says. "Because you have been moping around forever, getting over that silly bitch, your ex-wife!" She snapped at him, clearly annoyed. "You know how I feel about her!"

Do I imagine it, or do his eyes turn a shade darker? But before I have time to dwell on it, he seemingly shrugs his thoughts away. "Can I treat you, ladies, to a lavish tree-pound Swedish meatball lunch?

We followed Bob to the counter, where he bought three Ikea meatballs dinners and paid for them. Ok, I grant you it's not the gourmet dish of the month, but the simple meal tasted good, and we joked and laughed while we ate.

The rest of the afternoon we spent together picking out furniture for his new house. He was chatty and friendly, and I totally forgot the warnings my brain had given me.

"I never knew shopping in Ikea was so much fun," he said.

"Ah, the shopping is easy. It's the assembling that's the problem. Have you followed the short course that Ikea offers its customers?"

"Short course?" He lifted his eyebrows and looked quizzical at me.

"Yes, where you and your partner learn how to assemble various pieces of furniture. If you succeed without screws or pieces of wood leftover and... haven't smashed each other's brains in, they give you a relationship diploma because it's as solid as a rock."

He listened to me with interest, and his hearty laugh was my reward. And when he asked if he could see me again, I foolishly gave him my phone number. After that, we started dating. He was just as charming as when we met at the Ikea restaurant, funny and attentive, and the sex was good. Unfortunately, when we ran into his wife in town after two weeks of dating, she threw a hissy fit when she saw us together right in the middle of the street. He looked almost apologetic to her and reassured her that it was nothing. Long story short, he moved in with her again. That was the end of that wimp.

Blue-Stocking Spinsters

Bluestocking spinster is the latest derogatory term my mother has come up with for me. Let's clear its meaning up, shall we? Bluestocking is an 18th-century word for a woman with literary and intellectual interests. Spinster, of course, refers to an unmarried woman, usually one beyond marriageable age. Often, she looks after her elderly mother or father. As a result, she usually has either a poor sex life or no one at all. Let me tell you, to most people, they are social outcasts. According to my mother, who is 93, I fall into that category. She keeps telling me that it's a shame I have not been able to find a husband.

After the nasty break-up from Tarot man, or as I now prefer Carrot -man, one and a half years flies by. Everybody I know is either married or divorced, and because of that, they think they are qualified to give me advice. And did I mention my mother and sister, who still have partners? They are the worst and relentlessly tell me what I should do. They have told me to crawl back to Carrot Man more than once. It has taken me a long time to regroup, and painful memories still sting. I still carry residual anger at him. Although I had prepared myself mentally before getting rid of him. I kicked myself a thousand times.

Why hadn't I done it sooner? How could I have missed seeing what a narcissistic jerk he was? I mourned the loss of my dreams, not to mention the passion we shared. As a result, I bought all the self-help books I could, and they all agreed that keeping active and busy was the best medicine. I jogged for miles until I was exhausted. It was the only thing that made me go to sleep. During the day, I kept myself as busy as I could. In the end, I was glad I did stick it out and had not caved. My body has vague memories of sex, telling me it's time to move on. I called my friend Jane who is like me, a single happy go lucky spinster/cougar, albeit with four grandchildren. I asked her if she was currently seeing anybody. Much to her chagrin, she confessed that her sex life was like mine, sexually barren.

"Perhaps we should outsource finding a boyfriend." She volunteered. "Or why don't we go and find a professional sex worker?"

"Isn't that a bit intense?"

"I don't think so", she replied. "Men do it all the time."

Although I was slightly shocked by that deliciously wicked thought, when the conversation got on to more solid ground, I became more and more intrigued. At the end of our one hour talk on the phone, we are both convinced that the only thing left for us is finding some man and paying him to have sex. Men do this all the time, and they don't seem to have a problem with it, so why not us girls? As it turned out, Jane had made some enquiries about the possibility of hiring an escort previously and had done a lot of research on the subject. Once she had set up a date but at the last minute had chickened out! I told her I would give the matter serious thought and get back to her. The idea of a warm, gorgeous hunk appealed to me. Even if I had to pay him!

Once I made up my mind, I started the male-hooker search myself. But pinpointing an agency that caters for a woman's needs isn't as easy as it sounds. First, I looked in the yellow pages, but after fruitlessly searching for half an hour, I gave up going out and buying a newspaper. I wasted another hour going painstakingly through all the seedy sex ads for men. God, they must really not be getting any at home. Could they all be single if the massive number of ads were any indication, promising desperate men every possible delight? Or do their wives and girlfriends not give them any? I find it a mind-boggling possibility to think that most men that use the services of prostitutes are either married or have woman friends. Wouldn't that dent the relationship if their partners found out about it? I shrug, toss the paper away and consult Mr. Google himself. I recently bought a fiendishly expensive I-phone and didn't have time to figure out all its functions. So, I decided to ask Siri.

"Hi Siri, can you help me?"

"What is your name?"

"Silvia."

"What can I do for you today, Silvia?"

"Can you find me a gigolo?"

"Interesting question. Why do you want one?"

"Because I need one!"

"I can find you one in Thailand. Does that help you?"

"No! If you can't help me, why are you called an assistant?"

"To make your life easier!"

"So? Why don't you?"

"Don't expect me to do all your dirty work!"

"If you don't answer me, I will ask Alexa!"

"Good things come to those who wait!"

"But I don't want to wait!" I wail

"Don't wait for me to light your fire if you have your own matches, if not buy a lighter."

"Well, that is bloody useful," I slammed the phone on the table. What a useless twat! Back to the drawing board. I finally managed to find the information I was searching for in a Girly magazine. The ad reads Male Escorts for hire! Can be taken into town. Full options!

Full options that sounds intriguing! Does that mean they will fulfill all sorts of naughty fantasies a girl might have? Another fascinating bit is: 'can be taken into town'. That sounds like the agency provides their clients with some leash, as though for a puppy. 'Oh, by the way, ma'am, here is the leash. Keep it nice and short! Don't let them get any ideas about straying or becoming distracted'. While I am conjuring up delightfully unrealistic pictures of my escort in a sexy swimsuit with a collar and leash around his head, I smile and boldly go where no woman, at least no one that I knew of, had gone before and dial the number. This was an itch I had to scratch.

The Beauty Parlor

The lady answering the phone from the Escort agency was used to desperate women and efficiently took care of all the arrangements. Mr. Escort would be waiting for us in the lobby of a hotel about two hours' drive from London, and she would book the room for the weekend. Would I please be as kind as to please give her my credit card number? The amount she quoted for the weekend took my breath away, and more so when she told me that it was only for the escort plus the room. Food and drink were extra and would also be put on my tab, plus all other expenses that we would incur. Although it was more than I had anticipated, I was so much into the idea that it did not pose a real hindrance, stopping was not an option

If only Jane could join me, I thought, it would be nice to have somebody around to share the experience, so I called her back and explained I had already booked everything. She agreed she would make similar arrangements. I knew Jane had no financial difficulties, as her late hubby left his massive portion of his estate to his devoted wife by obliging her to die

The next day we spent grooming and getting ready for the evening, beginning with a trip to the beauty parlor, usually not a place where I go every week.

I am led through the torture chambers, viewing left and proper ladies with blistered faces, and I feel a doom coming over me. I should have fled the place, as a sense of doom came over me.

Once inside the treatment room, an attendant tells me to strip, gives me paper knickers to wear, and leaves the room. Shivering because I'm nervous and cold, I don my clothes and wear paper knickers. Self-consciously I wait with my hands crossed in front of my boobs. Every instinct tells me to flee the salon and possibly the country.

The beautician orders me on the table draped with a crisp white linen sheet. I feel like the proverbial lamb led to slaughter, and I start to make a run for it. I grab my clothes, and just as I am stripping the paper knickers away to replace them with my French silk panties, Jane comes in and shoves me back onto the table. Meekly, I stay and look around me. The salon owner tried to bring a Zen-like atmosphere into the room, judged by a giant wooden Buddha head on the wall that looked serene at my almost naked body. Having traveled to Thailand, I am almost sure he isn't allowed to see naked female bodies. Before I can voice my concern, crappy new age music fills the room. The tranquil surroundings are l waisted on me as I feel more like a trussed-up chicken, ready to be cooked! And to top it off, out of the blue, the sound of gently flowing water makes me want to pee instantly. Bloody hell, who's stupid idea was it to put in a fountain, for God's sake, why? I growl, my nerves screaming. And just as the need for a bathroom becomes stronger, the lights dim, Jane comes in and mummers in a soothing voice meant to relax me.

"You are in good hands. This place isn't called a Wellness center for nothing."

Hmm, I am not sure that's true, and my worst fears are confirmed when two beauticians resembling monsters from an alien planet eye me. Telling me with serious faces, they would start with a facial, then something they called light resurfacing, detoxing exfoliating and various other treatments that I can't recall.

"Please close your eyes, mam. I will do your eyebrows now. This may be a little unpleasant."

A little unpleasant was undoubtedly the understatement of the year as she tattooed a permanent eyeliner above and under my eyelids. That alone deserved a place in the Guinness book of records as humanity's most painful beauty procedure. But as it happened, I spoke too soon.

My eyes were shut and swollen from the excruciating tattoo of the perfect eyeliner. What is wrong with using a pencil every morning? I thought when they administered the procedure with a needle! After my ordeal ends, a sympathetic looking maid offers me a glass of water.

"Water? Hell no," I can summon just enough energy to croak. "Get me a real drink, will you." The speed at which a whisky arrives makes me believe that such requests were not uncommon.

As I sip my whisky, which is oddly soothing, the most cheerful of the beauticians says. "It's time to remove the hairs on your face, but don't worry, we use our exclusive string method!"

I gasp! Hair on my face? String method? Do I have hair on my face? Where- where? My hands fly to my face, but all I feel is smooth skin. I am affronted, and I have no qualms in voicing it.

"Hair?" I yelled. "Hair?" I repeated for good measurements, "I have no hair on my face!"

She replied. "Yes, you have, mam. They are soft, but still. You don't want any hair on your face!"

"What does that mean string method:" I inquired apprehensively. "Are you going to tie each hair with a string and pull it out? Wouldn't that be rather time-consuming? I mean, think of the knot alone. How difficult must it be to tie a knot around soft short hair? I will still be here till x mass," I babbled at that point beyond reason.

After they are done, my whole face feels like I have been outside in the sun for about 48 hours non-stop, and I am too terrified to look in the mirror at the bits of skin that must be hanging down. Probably, flapping up and down with every step I take.

Next comes a body wrap with a seaweed massage. Hmm, it sounds not too bad, I think innocently, until I feel the burning heat scorching my tights.

Need I go on? The hot wax on my legs to get rid of more unwanted hair was administered in a steady flow, where it slowly cooled and then swiftly removed in one quick movement, Which had me screaming every time at the top of my lungs. But the most embarrassing moment came when she ripped off my paper covering and started discussing the bushy half gray jungle that grows visible between my thighs.

Shocked, she gasped. "Really, mam, this au-natural look is so out! Modern men don't want to claw through all that hair to find your privates. No, they want women looking like newly born babies."

"Babies?" I echoed, coloring it slightly. "Since when?"

"Babies," she confirmed. After some inquiries from my side about how they thought they would make me bald, she told me she prefers laser, but I need several treatments for a lasting effect. Bloody hell, my heart sinks when I look at my bush and consider if they were going to do hair by hair, I need to stay overnight, so I opt for a simple shave. The beautician looks a bit disappointed. "What about wax madam? It lasts much longer before you have any re-growing hairs. Let me show you. I am back in a jiffy." Briskly she strides out of the room.

I breathe a sigh of relief after the sound of her disappearing tapping heels, but alas, it is only too short. After a few minutes, she enters again carrying a tray covered by a towel, and assures me I am going to love the result.

"Spread your legs, mam", she ordered. And embarrassed, I moved them an inch.

"No, mam, please spread your legs so that I can do my work." Admitting defeat, I spread them as wide as possible, enough to make any boyfriend drool. Effectively she brushes the hot wax over one of my vaginal lips. As the heat of the wax hits me, a shudder goes through me, and I yell. "Holy shit, that hurts." Wildly I push her hand away from the now throbbing area. "What the hell are you doing?" I shout, "stop!"

"I can't stop now, mam; I need to remove the wax," applying a calm voice. She puts a strip of paper over the wax and, in one mighty swoop, rips the wax and hair away, resulting in my yelling so hard I swear they can hear me in the street.

"Goddamn it, woman, I told you to stop."

Unperturbed, she produces a mirror. "Look, mam, don't you love this look?"

Look? Do I have to look in a mirror now? Why? I never look at my vagina in a mirror, never! Why should I start now? But the expected look on the beautician's face is my downfall, I overcome my fear, and despite myself, I look at my vagina, which looks ugly red and swollen. "What is this?" I croaked. "Men like this look? I find that hard to believe. Why have I never heard of it? Then it occurs to me that it must be all the porn flicks guys watch -where all the girls have hairless crotches. Seriously cheesed off, I flop back on the bed, the fight taken out of me, my energy drained and vowed. "I never will I go through this again."

"You want to leave it like this?" The beautician asked in an incredulous voice, looking uncomfortable. "We have to do the rest. You can't go out looking like this."

"I can't?" I wondered out loud. "Why ever not? It's not like everybody can see it." Then reality strikes me, didn't I have a date tomorrow with Mr. Escort? "Dam, dam," I swore, I couldn't show up with a half-bald pussy. Resigned, I let her finish her torture, screaming every time at the top of my lungs when she rips off the wax. After 30, excruciating minutes later, she hands me the mirror again, and I even manage a little laugh, as I am true as bold as a baby's bottom and apparently every man's wet dream. But I must say after the initial shock wears off, I rather like the change, except for the irritating burning that lingers for the rest of the day and which I hope will wear off before Mr. Escort proceeds to have sex with me.

"It's time for your deluxe organic spry tan, dear," Miss Torturer announced.

"Spray tan?"

"Yes, your body is very pale and uninteresting, but don't worry, we will give you a healthy bronze looking natural tan."

"Healthy looking tan? How the fuck will you do that? I don't have time to sit in the sun today! I murmured.

"In our deluxe spray-tan machine. Follow me!" She answered and opened the door. Meekly, I got up from the table and followed her buck-naked, at, at this point I was beyond caring. After all, she had just seen it all.

"Please put the robe on, mam. We have to walk through the salon."

"Er, hmm, sure," thankfully to be spared further humiliation, I slipped into the robe she held up.

In the tanning area, she tells me to step into the cabin, and take off my robe. I slide the warm thick robe off me and squeak. "Hell, it's cold in here. Can't you heat the place?"

"No, mam, this is the optimum temperature for spraying on your tan, and aren't you the lucky one? We have a new machine, and the drying time is only 15 min," she purred. She pushes me to the back of the cabin. "Please, mam, legs apart and keep your arms away from your body, and put the goggles on. We don't want the chemical to come into your eyes."

I do as I am told, and without further ado, she points the nozzle at my head. The icy blast that hits me is unexpected and careless, and the full blast of color hits my nose and mouth, leaving me gasping for air.

"Shit," I yelled. "Will this ordeal never end?" Shivering in the cold, I let the tan dry. Then it's time for my hair and make-up. I dressed and stepped into the hairdresser's salon. After 3 hours in the chair, I look in the mirror; the transformation is complete. Is this me? I feel my body expanding in relief, almost squealing with excitement. Mirror- mirror on the wall. Who's the sexiest of all?

"You look beautiful now, mam; quite a transformation. My attendant sounds triumphant, as though she has pulled off a miracle, but I guess they have from their point of view.

Everything comes together to about a month's salary, beauty does not come cheap, and I realize that this isn't going to be a regular thing; or soon, I will have no money left to buy little luxuries like food. After Jane and I paid, we both went to our respective homes to pack a bag.

http://www.rent me a guy.com

The next problem starts when I can't decide what to wear for the date? Meeting? Encounter? Hell, how would you even classify it? Not coming to a conclusion, I turn my attention back to choosing an outfit, which is nail-bitingly difficult. Let's go through my closet, shall we? Are we going for the sophisticated dull, subtle prints first!? NO? Boring? OK! OK, you are right. I want to look trendy yet fashionable, and you made a good point not to go for the neutral black and, white. OK! what's left? Ah yes, the sporty look? Oh? You don't like that either? What are you saying? That look can only be pulled off by teenagers? Dam! You are right again, that's out too! What was I thinking suggesting shorts and a top? Nah! Okay, we got it now, thank you! Sexy it is...! Great.

But wait a moment! Why on earth would I like to give my escort a sexy look? I mean, I am hiring him, right? Looking sexy certainly, isn't a requirement? But on the other hand, he better be good-looking! Why hadn't I thought of that before? And I almost panic at the thought. I take a few deep breaths and realize I am behaving like an idiot. Of course, they wouldn't send ugly guys. Let's look at this logical. The agency clearly can't send a bald chunky man! They soon would be out of business. I breathe a sigh of relief. Phew, dodged a bullet there!

Glad we have come to a mutual decision, dear reader, I take a step forwards, grab a dress that is at least two sizes too small and slip into it. Or, more to the point, I say I tried to slip in, but for some reason, I get stuck halfway. Why wasn't I built like a model and have a sexy-size eight? And survive on one carrot and six celery sticks a day? Achieving that emaciated look I am envious of, you know what I mean, right? At the best times, I always was at least a couple of pounds too heavy and could easily be used as the key-note- speaker in *weight watchers. *

Out of the corner of my eyes, I see your disapproval look, and I take off the offending garment. Then I spot the designer jeans hanging right in front of me that I bought several weeks ago but haven't worn it. It hangs next to a pink angora top. How could I have missed it? It's perfect! I grab it and see your look of approval. Well done! Mission accomplished. I breathe a sigh of relief. I take off the dress and put my reader's choice on, ah! Now we are talking! That looks much...much better and pleased I leave the bedroom.

Jane and I were supposed to meet our escorts in the hotel lobby at six. The drive would take approximately two hours, so we left late afternoon, as we didn't want to arrive too early, giving our *dates* the impression that we could not wait for them to ravish us.

Let me show you Jane's sleek new Mercedes, with its luxurious white leather seats, who's only purpose in life is to embrace. I dare you, sniff the expensive leather seats! And tell me you aren't jealous. It's nice, right? It never excites me, as it conquers dreams of yachts and private jets. I think I could seamlessly fit into the world of money.

After we entered the car, Jane switched on the ignition, and I confessed I felt a bit apprehensive! But rather pleased we hadn't backed out at the last minute. And look at us! We positively looked the part. Even our outfits matched the color of Jane's car. The drive was uneventful, and two hours later, we arrived at the glitzy hotel.

Taking one last long look in the mirror so nicely provided by the manufacturer who knew what a woman requires in a vehicle. We took a deep breath and walked into the hotel.

I see you looking around the hotel lobby dear reader, trying to find our dates, it's crowded, and nobody pays any attention to us. At first, we couldn't see any men that fit our description of what male escorts should look like. Unsure of our next move, we came to a standstill and surveyed the room. Two guys get up from a couch and walking toward us.

I am sure had you been there, you could have heard the thudding of my heart that was loud... really loud. When the men were close enough, the tallest of them said:

"Hi, you must be Jane and Silvia," I am Steve, and this is my friend Dan;" they shake our hands, and after a minute or so, we figure out that Steve was my date and Dan Jane's. They looked us over and didn't blink an eyelid, undoubtedly used to pleasing grannies in their sixties.

"Now let's get acquainted," Steve said, "do you ladies want to drink something?"

The first glass of Chardonnay went down exceptionally well, and any reservations we had vanished as we effectively polished off the bottle between Jane and me. Being pleasantly high, Jane contemplated whether or not we should order another bottle. But considering why we came, we decided that it perhaps wasn't the right decision. No doubt we would not be able to remember much after two bottles of wine, not to speak of how we would feel the following day.

The men ordered a beer, and I noticed they were very moderate with their alcohol intake. Too much would probably severely ruin their performance. Recalling my previous experiences with drinking men was of any indication.

Once, after an excessive amount of alcohol, one of my boyfriends had trouble getting it up... It was a highly upsetting event because he gave me a slightly wounded look, so you knew he wasn't to blame. What a wanker! I can't even remember why I went out with him (another one). What was it with men and me?

"You girls are ready for some fun?" Steve asked, rousing me up from my memories.

Jane sweetly asked, "what do you have in mind?"

"Just come with us. How about some hot tub?" Steve asked. "The rooms have some great Jacuzzi's. You girls will love this."

"Say no more," Jane responded, "lead the way!"

When we descended the elevator, I saw an immaculately uniformed guard standing in front of the club. Whose sole purpose in life seemed to keep the riffraff out. Picture him, will you? He looked us over with the eye of the true connoisseur and obviously knew our *dates* and did nothing to stop them from entering.

Jane, who followed the two men closely, could enter the club unhindered. But after giving me an insolent look, the guard stopped me, looking me squarely in the eye asking; "Something for the doorman, mam?" in a derogatively, slightly inquiring voice. While taking the liberty of looking me up and down.

'Shit, more frigging quid's;' this one knew why we are here; I think. I dig my purse out and shell out some loose coins. The look on his face doesn't make me proud when I hand them over, and

I realize I have just made an enemy for life. Well, you can't win 'em all!

As soon as we enter the club, the luxurious surroundings take my breath away. And listen! The sound of soft music flooding over us seducing us. I take a whiff of an alluring scent that fills the air that elicits a strong sexual reaction. Water streams from the palms of a large copper Buddha fountain, and the gentle whisperings of the flowing water are soothing and peaceful. The carpet it's standing on has a rich auburn color, and my heels almost get caught in it. You must admit that the walls decorated with Gold and black hand-painted wallpaper- are exquisite. Exotic birds and bamboo wild but at the same time peacefully and tranquil.

Against the walls are several plush sofas covered in fake fur tiger (or at least I hoped it was fake)? You know what I mean. But don't let me digress...

Swiftly Dan opens one of the ornated doors, the Jacuzzi is the first thing that I see, and it's already filled with warm soapy water looking very inviting. And from the corner of my eye, I see Dan steering Jane to the next room, and I smile at her.

Now I want you to take the room in. In every little detail, deep red rose petals float on top of the bubbles... On the edge of the bath stands a silver tray holding a bottle of champagne with two glasses! And the seductive voice of Barry White fills the room from invisible speakers. I have died and gone to heaven! I barely suppress a purring sound. When I still admire the opulent surroundings, all of a sudden, I notice Steve has removed various pieces of clothing and is as naked as the day he was born. I can't help but notice his well-proportioned body and am suitably impressed. As nothing seems to be happening, I am unsure how to proceed; Steve must see something on my face and walks toward me.

"Come," he said, taking me by the hand. "This you are going to like, I promise you." And in one fluid motion, he lifts me and puts me in the Jacuzzi, clothes, hair, makeup, etc. It's so unexpected I start giggling uncontrollably.

The warm soapy bubbles are pleasantly erotic. And the soft light was intoxicating due to the music, and not to forget the amount of wine I had polished off. I spend a couple of minutes just enjoying the sensation of warm water that is soft and soothing. Steve, I should say naked Steve. In the meantime, seemingly out of nowhere, he produced an air mattress that floats on top of the water. He jumps in the bath, slowly opens my jeans clasp, and unzips it. After I wriggle out of it, he unceremoniously dumps my wet jeans on the floor and removes my bra and panties.

Dear reader, it's time for you to close your eyes! He lifts me on the mattress without apparent effort and admires my bald pussy. And for the first time that day, I relax. The warm water that laps around the air mattress is comforting, and my spirits soar even higher. Life seems good, and the memories of the house-of- horrors-beauty-salon recede fast. Life is certainly looking up now. I am so relaxed I don't even notice that a maid comes in to pick up my wet clothes. They would miraculously reappear a few hours later, freshly laundered and ironed. I lean back with excitement because Steve has somehow positioned himself behind me and started nibbling my neck. "Relax, baby, he whispers."

Shivers of anticipate tingle through my body, and he slowly starts stroking my neck, shoulders and the top of my boobs.

"I will give you a very nice massage first," he whispers. "Why don't you climb on the air matrass and turn around so that I can stroke your bum."

I do as he tells me. He moves over and takes one of my feet in his hands, kneading and stroking. Taking my toes in his mouth and sucks them one at the one. Jeez! That feels good! I almost purr, deliriously happy I have rented him for the whole evening and not just for an hour. After what feels like ages, he takes care of my feet, calves, and tights and skillfully avoids my crotch. My desperate go-to-pussy-area wiggling does nothing to deter him from his given course. By now, I am so turned on. It's easy to let him be in complete control, and I go with the flow!

Slowly he continues stroking my inner thighs, down the smooth surface of my knees, across my calves and then to my ankles and feet - then back again.

"God: You are good,' I moan, noticing that my nipples are rock-hard.

"Turn around," he commands and whispers, "you are hot!" His voice is sensual and warm, just like the water and makes me forget he probably tells the same thing to all his clients. His knowing touch, gentle caresses and particular wickedness are my downfalls, I need an orgasm, and I need it fast, and as I can't wait any longer, I start playing with myself to get some satisfaction.

Steve catches on quickly, his finger tracing the outline of my lips, and I open my mount to suck on it. My boobs are stimulated by a hand other than my own. And I start moaning a little as my fingers move faster. Now, his hands are at my breast, gently squeezing and tweaking my nipples. I flinch, knowing my orgasm is very close.

"Come," he whispered in my ear. There is a lot more where it comes from."

My whole-body sparks at his voice. His tongue is now flicking my navel. Argh! That is good; the agency has to be applauded for its selection. He moves and takes my nipple in his mouth and gently sucks. That's all it takes. With a deep satisfactory grunt, I explode. Long shuddering ripples went through my body repeatedly until they gently subsided.

"Wow" That was great," I whisper. I hadn't foreseen the evening to start by fingering myself to a climax, but what the hell, I was the boss, right? And now I will have sex with Erotic-rent-me-boy- I smirk at the thought. This was a great, please the hell out -me-evening, and not do-what-boyfriend-wants-you-to-do" shit. The idea is exhilarating and frees me of any inhibitions I may have had.

For the first time, I understand why men go to hookers, because they do whatever they please, with no need to pleasure their hookers.

Girls, I recommend www.Rentmeaeroticguy.com for some evil pleasures. Steve was worth his body in Gold. As good as the agency promised and didn't let me sleep for a minute.

The following day, we are lying lazily side by side, me slightly sore from the evening's pleasures and looking at the sun that had just come out over a clear cloudless sky: its reflection seen in the hotel's pool. I look around the lovely hotel room and know this date has ended; I kiss my erotic-rent-a-guy on the lips and whisper in his ear.

"If you ever want to repeat this experience, it must be for free because I can't afford this too often."

He laughs, swings his well-proportioned body out of bed and walks to the bathroom. I quickly dress, grab my purse, takeout a 100 pound note and place it on his jeans. It had been an expensive date, but oh, boy! Had it been worth it.

Will Married Men Leave their Wives?

It was Xmas time, and once again, I was in love or was it lust? Hmm, I am not altogether sure, but what I will never forget is the first time I met Martin. His words were like sweet tranquilizers, mysterious and exotic. A friend of mine introduced us at a party, and it went something like this:

Silvia said. "Don't look now, but there is a man who has been ogling you all evening." This immediately perked me up from the somewhat apathetic state I was in.

"Where," I hissed, swiveling around, almost straining my neck. Mind you. I was somewhat unbalanced because I had consumed various alcoholic beverages. He was standing in the middle of the room. I look at him, taking in that he is tall, slim, good-looking, and well dressed, sipping a casual glass of champagne. With his neatly trimmed gray beard and mustache, he looked around 55. The sum-up of his assets was a purely automatic response.

Just when I was done assessing, he turned his head, and I almost doubled over, feeling like a giant bowling ball thumped me in the stomach, and I could barely suppress the urge to float over to him.

"Wow! He is gorgeous," I whispered to Ellen, feeling apprehensive, unsure if I would escape this one unscathed.

"Do you know who he is?"

"Sure," she said. "It's Martin Gain; he is the head of the large bookstore around the corner two blocks away. He inherited the store from his uncle when it was still small. He expanded it, making it the success it is today part of many franchises."

I opened my mouth to say something, but she motioned for me to be quiet. "Look," she hissed. "He is coming our way, but remember he is not also gorgeous but also very married."

In an instant, the need to be witty and intelligent vanished. Now, if there is a warning, I don't need to hear it is that one. And I decide to leave. I swivel around and head for the door. I almost managed to make my escape when I tripped on the opulent high-poled carpet and broke my heel. "Dam," I swore. "I knew wearing these shoes was a stupid mistake." A strong male hand grabs my elbow and prevents me from making a complete ass of myself.

"Didn't your mama tell you not to go down for a man in front of an audience?" He smiled.

My heart starts thumping, pull yourself together, girl. I glare at him, ready to retort with an angry response, but when I look at his face, I see genuine concern with a hint of amusement and humor in his remark. The thin smile I produce can't hide the annoyance I feel about the broken heel. After all, it was his fault.

"Do you have any idea how much these shoes cost?" I snapped, not wholly won over yet.

"I never question a woman's motives paying a king's ransom for the pleasure of being uncomfortable," he quipped and chuckled. "You need a ride home. The car is parked nearby. By the way, I am Martin Gain, and you are...?"

"Silvia Smith." Do I sound slightly breathless?

His eyes crinkle up as he looks down at me. "Shall we?" He grabs my elbow, and his firm grip makes it impossible for me to resist. Besides, I have no car, no shoes to speak of, and I am curious to know more. Later I wondered why I didn't remember dating married guys was a serious health hazard at any time. He leads me through the door, and I toss caution aside against my better judgment as my curiosity is sparked. He hands the door attended a ticket who hurries away only to come back driving a shiny Porsche. He hops out of the car and hands the keys to

Martin, who tips him handsomely, judging by the attendants' faces.

Politely he opens the door for me, and I sink lower than I had anticipated into the leather seat. My skirt rises and exposes my shaven pubis. Hell, he must think I am a slut. Mortified, I pull my dress down and wait for his response, but I hear only a slight chuckle. He asked me for my address, and after a light, flirty conversation, we arrived all too soon at my apartment. I step out of the car, clasping my purse tightly; shall I ask him to come in for a drink? Adapting a stony expression like I don't care whether or not he accepts my invitation, I ask hurriedly. "Do you fancy a coffee?"

"I thought you'd never ask," he answered cheekily.

Slightly nervous. I open my purses, take out my key, and insert it into the lock. That evening I made a good candidate for winning the getting-laid-fastest- award. Although the sex wasn't all that good, as he obviously wasn't familiar with the word foreplay. He just dove in. When he exposed my hairless crotch, he purred. "Wow, you have been a good girl!"

"A good girl? Have you any idea what I went through to look like this? How would you feel if somebody first put boiling wax on your balls and then, in one swoop, ripped it off?" I inquired.

Judged by his pained expression, I could tell he wasn't familiar with the experience. But I forgot everything when he kissed me again. We had several dates after that, for understandable reasons, always took place in hotels or my apartment, until he asked me to go with him to a small seaside hotel for the weekend. I wasn't sure what he had told his wife, nor did I care. He had a congress to attend until I found out, and I was left alone most of the day.

Things turned sour when he came back after he had concluded his business. I wasn't sure what started it off, but he claimed I had misplaced something. Perhaps I did, perhaps not. Honestly, I couldn't remember anyway. Even if he was right and I was wrong, does it matter? Well, it did, as it resulted in a big argument. Sounds familiar, doesn't it? I am sure you have been in a similar situation. It went something like this.

"What did you do with my papers on the desk?" Pointing to it.

"Well?" he inquired sternly when I didn't immediately respond.

I swallowed and immediately felt I had done something wrong, except I couldn't recall anything.

"I haven't seen your papers or removed them, honey. Are you sure you brought them with you? Perhaps you left them on your desk at Godzilla's place?" I couldn't help adding.

I agree that was foolish, but he was always calling his wife *Godzilla* and I saw no harm in repeating it.

He throws me an icy glare. "Your statement is uncalled for. At least, come and help me find them."

A pent-up rage rises through me. What the hell? Who does he think I am? The missing papers, detective? I get out of bed, hanging on to my dignity, only clad in the panties I had put on earlier, hoping for some fun. But after looking at my lover's face, that hope vanished instantly. He is leaning against the bathroom door, arms folded with an arctic look on his face. I edge towards him as I feel a flicker of alarm when he glares at me.

"Let's not fight, darling," the haste he steps away from me is almost comical. It was clear you-are-to-blame-for-the missing-papers-time. He told me in great detail why he thought I was to blame and was not satisfied with that. He kept pushing it down my throat, just in case I didn't know.

After listening to him for about 30 minutes, my hand edges towards a steel vase without knowing exactly why. My grip tightens, and for a brief moment I am tempted to throw it at him. And only as the grimy yet satisfactory picture of his skull exploding goes through my mind do I stop myself.

"What the hell is wrong with you?" I finally managed. My voice cracked under strain; I couldn't believe this was happening. He was so wonderful and attentive when we first met. I had felt like a kid with a new toy, but now the toy lay broken at my feet, and I wanted to kick it so hard it would land on the moon.

"You are insane and in serious need of therapy!" I yelled at him.

That stopped him for a moment, but it turned out it was only so he could catch his breath. Oh boy, was he unstoppable. He informed me precisely how this upset affected him, his body and his sleep.

Of course, it affected his bloody sleep. He was so busy raving and ranting he hardly had time to pause for a moment and relax enough to lie down and sleep. No, he kept pacing up and down between the bed and the bathroom, all the time cursing under his breath, shit this, shit that and how this fucking situation affected him, and why he wouldn't be able to go to work the next day. The statement of that last remark eluded me, being a stickler for responsibilities myself. A little sleep deprivation wouldn't stop me from going to work.

Of course, it never occurred to him what his insane ramblings did to me or how it would affect our future relationship. All I wanted was to go back to London, but the fact that we had arrived by car-his-car complicated matters a bit. It was getting late, and I had lost my earlier appetite. All I wanted right now was for him to shut the fuck up, but he never did, and utterly knackered I did not even realize this was the typical behavior of a narcistic jerk.

Morning came, and I headed to the bathroom. My gaze drifts towards my soon-to-be ex-lover sitting in a chair asleep. Even in his sleep, he looks stunning. What a terrible waste that there wasn't a normal human being inside. I wonder how his wife coped. She probably was ecstatic the moment he left. I thought sarcastic. He woke up when I opened the bathroom door.

"Good morning," I tried

"Get dressed; we leave in 10 minutes," he barked, clarifying I was still the scapegoat.

Silently we drove back to London, where he dropped me off on the corner near my workplace and drove off without as much as glancing back. For the first time this weekend, I relaxed.

The next few weeks passed, and no word from Martin. He undoubtedly found another woman and had completely airbrushed me of his life as I had never been there. My humiliation was complete. When was I going to take control of my life? Hasn't the experience with rentmeaguy.com taught me anything at all? 'Let me repeat it galls Never date a married guy or a narcissistic jerk, you will end up losing your sanity or the will to live.'

A few weeks later, Jane rang me inviting me to a naughty ball masquerade somewhere in the middle of London next Saturday, and everybody was supposed to dress up naughty. I was a little confused about the word naughty and ball together.

"Is everybody supposed to come naked and have sex?" I inquired in a puzzled voice. Jane laughed.

"No, silly, you only dress naughty."

Interesting notion, "you mean to go as a nurse or," here I paused. I had clearly reached the end of my naughty fantasies.

"We can go dressed in fur coats with nothing underneath, but this seems a bit drafty in the middle of winter." Warming to the subject, she babbled:

"Let's discuss hair and costumes, or rather their lack," Jane answered, giggling.

As I was determined to be no doormat, we decided to go as SM bitches, dressed in black leather and carrying a whip. I must say, hiding behind a mask and being in charge appealed to me. Jane took me to a shop that rented costumes. After trying on several outfits, I looked at the amazing transformation in the mirror. The woman was staring back in the mirror I had never seen before. She wore black skin-tight leather pants that had taken me ten minutes to put on, worrying me how I was going to pee. Every intimate detail of a woman's anatomy was clearly visible. I couldn't get my eyes off it, and I wondered what it would do to the males in the room. Jane looked at me, amused; "Oh boy, all the guys will be salivating when they see your camels' foot."

"Don't you think we are too old to pull this look off?" I asked, looking critically in the mirror.

"No, stop worrying!"

She had chosen a short black skirt that only just covered her bum. She opted for a thong underneath; her large breast barely covered by a tiny bikini top. We looked like two professional hookers.

"Let's go and paint the town red!" She announced with enthusiasm.

In the car, we discussed how we would control the evening. For once, we weren't going to grovel for the pleasure of touching a guy's dick.

"God," I rolled my eyes. "This will be fun."

The moment we walked in by magic, we had the immediate attention of all the males in the room. We sure were a sight, wearing our sexy black costumes with long flowing blond hair and black face masks. Out of nowhere, a man dressed as a pirate appeared with two glasses of champagne.

"I died and gone to heaven." The pirate sighed, his eyes nearly popping out of his head when he openly ogled our boobs: "Which girl is going to be mine tonight?" He asked, looking us over with naked lust in his eyes.

"Let me be clear and explain the rules to you," I said slowly, raising my eyebrows, making eye contact, and looking him over carefully while slowly sipping my champagne.

"If you so much as dare laying a finger on my friend or me, I kick you in the bollocks," deliberately waving my whip in the direction of his crotch. The incredible transformation of him shriveling right in front of us was highly amusing, and we managed to keep a straight face only by sheer magic. As on cue, we turned around, leaving the would-be-suitor nursing his battered ego. The moment our glasses were empty, full ones appeared before us, and we lost count of the amount of alcohol we absorbed. It was incredibly noisy, and drones of people in various stages of undress walked past us.

In need of fresh air, I headed for the back of the room, stepped out on the patio, and leaned slightly dizzy against a pillar, closing my eyes. When I opened them, I looked straight into Martin's eyes, steamroller-abusive-were-are-my-papers-Martin.

"Hello," quit a transformation, how extraordinary, he said slowly, looking at my crotch. "Did you get my messages?"

Messages? Did I get his messages? Hell no! I am slightly drunk, but not that drunk, but I know he never sends me any messages.

"I thought you pressed the eject button on me, shouldn't you head back to wifzilla?" I inquired sarcastically, turning around. That was too much for his ego, he grabbed my arm hard, hurting me, and I realized this man has an unpleasant, perhaps even dangerous, streak.

"Listen," lowering his voice, he hissed. "You were once mine not too long ago, and if you tell me, you behave and say sorry, I might take you back!"

For a moment, I am speechless. What an egomaniac asshole! Then as by instinct, my whip strikes him in the face, leaving an angry red welt. His hand flies to his head to inspect any damage, his eyes spitting pure venom.

"Bloody bitch," he roared, giving me such a dirty look I almost cave, but then a sense floods back in me. "You will never grab me again," or I will call your wife and tell her about your little escapades," I yelled.

"You wouldn't dare," he hissed back, grabs my upper arms and pulls me sharply towards him.

"Fuck you," I yelled and started struggling, raising my whip again.

Approaching footsteps come closer. He lets go of my arms, "you wouldn't dare!"

"Well, you wouldn't take the chance, would you?"

And with that bold statement, I walked back inside, feeling his eyes burning a hole in my leather outfit. Shaken about that nasty encounter, I grab a drink from a passing waiter.

"Are you all right, madam?" He asked; "I saw that guy gave you a hard time."

"Yes, he was, but I am alright now. Thanks for your concern. That's very nice of you."

He blushes. God, he is young. I wonder if he is old enough to shave. "How old are you?"

He tells me he is seventeen. He is adorable and looks very innocent, and I can't resist the temptation to ask. "Do you have a girlfriend?"

This has his stuttering. Suddenly a wild desire to have sex with him takes hold of me. But of course, he is way too young, and the thought of running the risk of getting arrested works as a cold shower.

"Why am I always dating losers?" I muttered instead, displaying all the signs of a drunk telling a bartender their life story. "I tried many times and always end up with jerks or morons."

"You have to trust your instincts." Waiter boy informs me, or if that fails, you can always buy a Robosapiens."

"A, what?"

"A male robot almost humanoid. I saw an ad in a robot magazine. They are amazing, mam. Nobody would know they're not human." He gushed and told me some more details. I am silent, wrapping my head around the concept.

"Does he really look human?"

The boy nods. "Wait a sec," he told me. "I'll try to find the magazine for you. It must be around here somewhere," and he shoots off, only to return triumphantly a few minutes later with the magazine. It's a highly glossy magazine with an iron robot on the front cover.

"Christ, I hope he looks slightly more human," I remarked.

"Oh, yes, he does, look!" He opens the magazine and springs a picture of a tall, good-looking guy. For a moment, I am speechless. "This is a robot?"

"Yes, and he does everything you want."

"Everything?"

"Yes."

I stare at the picture. Good God, is this a robot? He looks so real! Does he have a penis? A hairy chest? Can he cook? Or clean? Can I take him to mommy and introduce him as my boyfriend? Al the questions tumble through my mind at once. In awe, I stare at the picture. The boy reads my mind because he says:

"Nobody knows he is a robot unless he tells them, and sometimes he wonders himself."

I shake my head and check the calendar for the date. This must be an April Fool's Day joke. Then I see the date on the cover of the magazine. It's a week old. Well, so much for that theory.

"You can take the magazine, I have read it, and there is a website, see?" And he pointed out the web address.

I must be seriously mentally ill to even contemplate the thought of pursuing this. This...this... toy? I start laughing hysterically and realize that it's partly due to the alcohol and the encounter with Martin. Out of its own accord, my hand grabs the magazine.

"Some women are so into their Robosapiens; they even marry them." Good luck, madam," and he returned to serving drinks.

I try to find Jane, but it's impossible in the crowd. I text her that I am going, grab a cab and head straight home. In the taxi, I lean my head back and let the conversation with the waiter go through my mind, it's hard to diminish, and I plan to write the robot company an inquiry letter.

>Silvia Smith
>
>Hammily Avenue 2 /a
>
>Flower dale
>
>Phone: 004419807645
>
>Email: silvia@yahoo.com
>
>To whom it may concern,
>
>Yesterday when I looked in a magazine, I came across your advert for a Robosapiens, so please tell me how much it cost, there was a 6-figure price in your ad, but surely that can't be right?
>
>Can you add some more information about the Robot, please?
>
>Does he like dogs? I need him in a hurry, and please send him over as soon as possible.
>
>Best regards
>
>Silvia

Cognitive Robotics Group

Kings Boulevard 211/217

Queens green

NYC 4389

Fax: 0044134657833

Phone: 00441346 8776

Email. robotic@hotmail.com

Dear valued customer,

We regret to inform you that the Unit GX42 you inquired about is not available at this time due to high demand, but recently one of our older models became available. The Unit was returned by his owner, who preferred a dog. Our Robots are highly sought after, and many of our customers would go to great lengths to acquire one. However, when we looked at our list of impatient customers, your name came up. At your request, we can add an extra faithful chip, free of charge.

Here is some more information about the Unit:

The UNIT FQGC-O1- 747 is an intelligent, interactive robot designed to react and respond like an actual human. His behavior is the result of training (not programming).

This Robosapiens is the first affordable, intelligent entertainment humanoid of its kind and carbon-based.

The Robot learned from its creators, by copying their actions.

And is equipped with sensory perceptions hearing, vision, and feelings that enable him to utilize rapid acquisition and re-acquisition of sensor-motor couplings.

The Unit FQGC-O1- 74 uses a neural processor to perform any human task flawlessly. Our stride is to sell our customers an almost Human Unit they can relate to. After a short time, the client often forgets the Unit is an artificial life form and becomes attached to him. In some cases, Robotic marriage is not as uncommon as one should think.

The Unit copes with unforeseen situations and noise variations. It adapts remarkably well, even under the most challenging circumstances.

Instinct Software adds dimensions of "motivation" and "well-being."

Unlike our other Units, the O1-747 is an autonomous brilliant human like being.

He speaks two languages English and Spanish. And something that is called the Basic Alien-robotic leplex 11. Our department is currently studying the possibility of adding the popular Venus language.

The Unit has the ability of near-perfect Communication and problem-based learning is expected to solve almost any problem that can come up. In order to stay on top of things he update's itself constantly. (Unlike human males)

The Robot is equipped with infra-red motion detectors (PIR) that enable him to perceive any treason's activity. Which by no means perfect, allows him to locate and/or recognize potential trouble sources.

Note: 1 We send regular updates to all of our customers when new chips come available.

Note: The Robosapiens is a non-smoker. Should he start to smoke, alert us immediately, and we will terminate him. The Robosapiens is made to create a capable, affordable male companion.

Last but not least – the First Law of Robotics is, of course applied Robosapiens are incapable of hurting any humans, or for short, Ro-human-block (RHB)

We sincerely hope that this information will help you make up your mind; please let us know soonest if you are interested in this special offer.

Best regards

Mark Stein

Customer support Sales Director

Silvia Smith

Hammily Avenue 2 /a

Flower dale

Phone: 004419807645

Email: silvia@yahoo.com

Dear Mr. Mark

Thank you for your kind offer of sending me a second-hand unit. However, I insist I want the unit XG42 that I initially saw in your advertisement, and a second-hand unit may be full of viruses. Kindly reconsider.

Best regards (also to your staff)

Silvia

Cognitive Robotics Group

Kings Boulevard 211/217

Queens green

NYC 4389

Fax: 0044134657833

Phone: 00441346 8776

Email. robotic@hotmail.com

Dear Mrs. Silvia

We once again inform you that the XG42 that you want is not available. You may not know it but manufacturing such highly technical units is a delicate and time-consuming process; currently, we only make ten such units a year.

As we have presently 250 customers waiting in backorders, simple calculations state that you would have to wait 25 years before a unit could be delivered to you.

However, this special offer on one of our top-notch models will not last. Please be so kind as to reply within three working days if you are still interested.

We have added some additional info on the Robo, that we hope will make you up your mind. At your request, we added a photograph.

Robosapiens- Chemical Analysis

Elements: Robo-man

Symbol: CB Carbon-based

Anatomic: 7'27'2 in length curly short hair.

Mass: Currently 200 pounds, but due to isotopic fluctuation, this can vary.

Occurrences: Pi (Precious Individual) Rare

Physical properties: Anxiety when faced with travel/ (TR) and (BS) beer-shortage

Chemical components: CUKGS Currently un-know glowing substance

Storage: Keeps best when stored under 30 C ideal temp 15C

Uses: Companion, carrying heavy loads, candlelight dinners, kisses

Interchanging parts won't work

Warning: Extreme cases of snoring can occur

If you have any questions in the meantime, we have 24-hour staff on standby to answer all of your questions and give technical support.

Best regards

Mark Stein

Customer support Sales Director

Silvia Smith

Hammily Avenue 2 /a

Flower dale

Phone: 004419807645

Email: silvia@yahoo.com

Dear Mr. Mark

I told all my friends I ordered a companion unit from you, and they are all coming to my house to meet him. I guess I have no other option than to accept your offer. He doesn't sound too bad except for the snoring part.

Please make sure he is clean and ready for instant use. I don't want to disappoint my friends.

Best regards

Silvia

P.S I forgot to ask if the unit has a name and a manual.

Bye now

Silvia

Cognitive Robotics Group

Kings Boulevard 211/217

Queens green

NYC 4389

Fax: 0044134657833

Phone: 00441346 8776

Email. robotic@hotmail.com

Dear Mrs. Silvia

We are delighted that you have accepted our offer for Unit FGGC-0 1- 747 (one of three). I am sure your friends will be thrilled. As is our policy, you will be billed after the customary period of 1 year. For your convenience, we have enclosed a manual and a sales agreement. Kindly sign the contract and disclaimer and mail it back to us

Being of sound mind, I (state your name) hereby agree to take care and reject the right to sue the pants off the idiot who made this Robosapiens. Any injury, real or imaginary, incurred while under my control shall not be held responsible to the Cognitive Robotics Group.

This particular FQGC-01-747 Unit (short for fancy a quick game of chess) was developed in our research labs to meet the requirements of discerning customers, requiring a humanoid type unit capable of delivering great satisfaction to its owner/caretaker/lover.

It is a male type Unit, equipped with all the usual functions, which will be described in the following sections.

Due to high demand, we could not ship a brand-new unit, and therefore a second-hand model was dispatched. However, we believe this has certain advantages because, for example, the Unit is programed to learn from different situations and environments and adapt accordingly.

Also, much less time will be necessary to train the second-hand experience unit in some respects (See later notes)

The Robosapiens comes with a lifetime guarantee. Please take your time to read the basic installation and instructions when he arrives.

Best regards

Mark Stein

Customer support Sales Director

Silvia Smith

Hammily Boulevard 211/217

Flower dale

Phone: 004419807645

Email: Elsa@yahoo.com

Dear Mr. Mark,

Yesterday the Robosapiens (I call him Paul, didn't like Peter) arrived at my house. I am absolutely delighted with him, all my friends will be green with envy, he is not only very clever and good looking, but he also does the dishes, takes the garbage out, takes me for a long walk and seems to like me.

He does not need to bond with other Robosapiens. This is great as my other male companions always spent time with their beer-drinking buddies and would not come home until they were pissed.

I did send him out to do the shopping, and he came back with the right products and not only that he brought me flowers, and in the evening when I came back from work, he had cooked me a gorgeous dinner with candlelight. And what's more, he let me hold the remote of the T.V. without a nasty fight.

However, there is one small matter I would like to bring to your attention. So far, the Unit has not asked for sex. When I asked about it, he told me he needed time to get acquainted with me. Have you any idea how long that will take? I hope he isn't gay.

P.S. Can you give me your private phone number?

Regards to you and your staff

Silvia

Robo Comes Home

The novelty of having the Robosapiens in my house in the last weeks is wearing off. We slept side by side. He kisses me goodnight and falls asleep immediately, heavily snoring like my previous boyfriend. Not sure why the manufacturers haven't taken that imperfection out, silly buggers. I hope it is a defective sensor or chip, and make a mental note to call Mark, the sales director, to ask him about it.

I have some additional questions as Robo-man has not made any advances toward me. So much for! We-have-the-perfect-male-companion-for-you-shit, the sales manager promised. It only shows my willingness to believe in improbable stories; I should have known better. I must suck if not even a daft Robot wants me, dam. What's wrong with this crazy Android? This should be the ultimate- intimate-sex-fairy-tale story of a lifetime, but so far, the story has taken on a surprising twist. It has been more like a sex-on-shoe-string-tale. Perhaps my expectations were too high. Maybe Robo-man needs time to adjust. But as usual, I digress. Let me fill you in. He arrived four weeks ago in a big truck that offloaded a box that read:

CARBON-UNIT -OPEN WITH EXTREME CARE!

The delivery guy shoves a piece of paper under my nose, clearly wanting my signature, waits until I sign, and then hands me an envelope.

"Please read this, Mam," he said. "I will wait and unpack the article for you. Please call me when you are done reading, and in the meantime, can I use your loo?"

As you can understand, I am not too happy about him possibly stinking up my bathroom, but I can't see how I can politely refuse his request. He must have seen something in my face because he volunteers additional information about the nature of his business. "I will be in and in and out."

I direct him to my pristine bathroom and tear open the envelope that reads in big, bold letters:

READ INSTRUCTIONS BEFORE OPENING

HEALTH WARNING: The Robosapiens is heavy since their mass and weight depend on their velocity relative to the user.

HANDLE WITH EXTREME CARE: This product contains a maximum amount of life force that is electrically charged. Some particles are volatile and may move at warp speeds of a hundred million years.

ADVISORY: There is a minimal but not non-zero chance that time-warping can occur, resulting in Natural Deselecting. The product may spontaneously disappear from its present location and reappear at any random place in the universe, including other solar systems. The manufacturer will not be responsible for any damages resulting from this untimely event.

IMPORTANT NOTICE TO PURCHASERS: the entire universe, including this product, may one day collapse into a so-called black hole. And the existence of this product in that universe will be guaranteed.

UNIFIED THEORY DISCLAIMER: The manufacturer may claim that this product is 4-dimensional. However, there is no substantial evidence suggesting the Robosapiens exist in a fourth dimension, or for that matter, in any other dimension.

WARNING: When and if the Robosapiens is wrongly exploited, space- warps and time -velocity may occur in its vicinity. If that happens, a timeline breakdown of all major events will occur.

The manufacturer will not be responsible for any damage and inconveniences that may result from this untimely event. This product may attract every other piece of matter in the universe. Should it accidentally come into contact with anti-matter, annihilation of the entire planet will occur. This product may display mood changes or any other physical reaction near high-tech hardware, such as a washing machine or vacuum cleaner.

ULTIMATE DISCLAIMER: This product may contain a bonding link to a parallel Universe. Therefore, its adhesive power to the owner/caretaker/lover cannot be permanently guaranteed.

HAZARD WARNING: Law of Probable Dispersal may spontaneously come into effect when the aspects of essential observations rather than philosophical theories come under severe scrutiny, and de-fragmentation can occur, resulting in Synchronized Transposing:

IMPORTED CONSUMERS-NOTICE: Law of selective gravity can and will apply; when the Unit losses gyro motor control, objects consequently start falling and will do possible damage.

PUBLIC NOTICE AS REQUIRED BY LAW: Any use of the Robosapiens, in any manner whatsoever, will increase the chaos and disorder in the universe of the owner/caretaker/lover.

The consumer is warned that this process can ultimately lead to turmoil and possible insanity.

ORGANIZED CHAOS DISCLAIMER: Chaos in the Robosapiens can erupt from lost objects; He may get irritable, fidgety or downright confused when things appear to be in a neutral state called light-warping or invisibility.

On a scale of the whole universe, the chances of this ever happening to the Unit are infinitesimally small. However, scientists have discovered that specific Units attract this phenomenon.

The Mother of All Disclaimers

This Unit does not present any male; all rights reserved. You may not distribute this other than for use by the OCL and all of her associates. Do not take the product with milk or food. You may not make a profit from it or publicize it without written permission from God. Please do not put the Unit in a microwave or dryer.

Do not fold or bend. The Cognitive Robotics Group is not liable for damages due to use or misuse. If defects are discovered, do not attempt to fix him yourself but bring him to the nearest dealer. Keep away from sunlight. Chessboards, ex-wives, or soon-to-be ex-hubbies do not subject to direct sunlight. Batteries are not included. Do not break the seal if you do not intend to use the product. The Unit is made from 100% recycled carbon-based electrons and magnetic particles; no animals were harmed in manufacturing this product. Do not store in a confined space or subject to intense heat. Must be over 18. When overdose on the Unit, do not induce vomiting, but consult your nearest hospital and seek medical help instantly. Do not drop the Robo into a volcano or a swimming pool. Disclaimer! Does not cover hurricanes, lightning, tornado, tsunami, volcanic eruption, earthquakes, floods, and other Acts of God. Room service or any meals are not included. Military use of the product is not covered. Tripping on moonlight walks over stray dogs and or seashells are not eligible for any claim. Divorce and/or marriage and body odors do not qualify for restitution. Discontinue the use of the Robo if the following occurs.

Confusion

Insanity

Weight gain

Pregnancy

When you realize you are smarter

Irritation

Sweating

Sleep deprivation

If you contemplate suicide

Overdose

Smoking

Holy shit, when I finish reading the unpacking instructions, I go into an acute panic. For a moment, my heart stops, warnings? Advisories? Pregnancy? Confusion? The mother of all disclaimers? The credibility of the Robot-boys is in grave danger. They omitted this data when I acquired -Mechanical-Pete. Excuse me, Paul.

My stomach starts churning, and I break into a cold sweat. I am convinced somebody has made a mistake and sent me the wrong instructions by accident, more suitable for an Alien from a faraway Galaxy than a suitor-to-be. My instinct to bolt kicks in, and I slowly reread the instructions again, my eyes scanning the first few warnings.

The second time reading, I found them pretty funny. Somebody with some humor has gone to great lengths to write detailed disclaimers to cover the company's ass if something goes wrong.

While I am busy settling my mind at rest, I see that the delivery boy has returned and is standing next to his truck. He grabs his toolbox, extinguishes his cigarette, and casually walks toward me. I can't help admiring how his jeans cling to his hips and his oozing masculinity. I had been too preoccupied to notice him before, but I am sure making up for it now.

"Hello, cutie," I wink at him, and he looks at me. He is not sure if I take a Mickey. He is so occupied with this struggle he trips on the pavement, stumbles and only just recovers.

"Hell!"

Composing himself, his vanity wins over his embarrassment, and he grins back. I see him looking at my boobs, wondering if today will be his lucky day. I smile. It's certainly tempting, and if I weren't so curious about unpacking Robo-man, I would have taken the chance to get to know him better.

"Can you help me open the crate?"

"Sure, Mam, it will take me about 20 minutes. Why don't you wait inside? I'll call you when I am ready," he said.

I walk inside without knowing why I feel apprehensive and nervous. I pour myself a coffee sit down and close my eyes. I must have dozed off and woke up because the phone rang.

"Hello?" My voice was slightly sleepy.

"What have you been up to, girl?" The friendly voice of Ann boomed out.

"Has your Robot arrived yet? Let him know immediately that you are the boss would be best. I always say the sooner they know it, the better, have you? Let him know you aren't as sweet and innocent as you appear!"

"Well, yes, he is here," I tried to cut her off. "The driver is unpacking him. Thanks for your advice, but I think I check him out before saying anything. Listen, I have to go now. Thanks anyway. I'll let you know how things develop." With that, I hung up the phone and walked outside. The delivery boy has opened a side of the box and carefully drags a large packet out.

"So, what do we now?" I asked anxiously. "Will he start working immediately, or do you have to kick-start him or something? Plug him in?" That sounds silly even to my ears.

"Don't worry, as soon as all the wrappings come off. He is automatically activated when he comes in contact with direct sunlight."

I walk towards the large packet and randomly start ripping away the plastic bubble wrap, layer after layer, until only one piece of plastic still clings to him, showing me the outline of his bulky frame, and I hesitate.

When I finally pull the protective plastic covering of Robo-hero, it's love at first sight. My mouth opens, and I feel a sudden urge to kiss him. Trying not to react and keep a cool head, I register his broad shoulders and golden tan; I can hardly breathe. It should be illegal for a male to be this handsome.

"Hello, Robo-delicious. Get up and glow," I softly welcomed him, hearing myself purr. "I have decided to name you Paul." I added huskily.

His eyes fly open and immediately lock into mine, and I go right away into a drug-induced-semi-conscious– euphoria. I suck my breath in as I look into his beautiful eyes and notice his full lips that I want to sink my teeth in. The sight of him makes my knees go weak, and I can barely contain ravishing him, but for some reason, I don't want to include this on my multitude of sins list. I suspect a washboard stomach underneath his trendy clothes. I love his sleek appearance and broad frame. And can't stop gazing at him as he slowly takes off his designer's sunglasses and squints in the glare of the sun that's too bright for him after being cooped up in his trunk.

"Hi," is his first word. "Nice to meet you, "I am your Robosapiens, and it is my pleasure to serve you. And if you like to call me Paul, that will be my name." His gazed moves over my face with obvious interest. "Did you read my Manuel?"

"Eh... well, technically no," I dodged huskily. "But I read the unpacking instructions. I didn't want to damage you."

At that point, he chuckles. I can feel him watching me; it's way too sexy to see how his eyes never waver from mine.

"I am waiting for the Manuel-angels to explain it to me," his heartily laughed at my wittiness is my reward.

"What's your name?"

"I am Silvia."

Can I imagine it? For a moment, he seems surprised. Did I imagine it? I hope it isn't because he expected to hear his previous owner's name. After all he was returned to the factory. He runs his hand through his immaculate hair, looking lost for a moment. My eyes travel down to his chest, which is visible under his open shirt. The mass of dark chest hair he shows has me drooling. I can barely remember my name, hell!

"I hope I don't have to use the warranty on you soon!" I whisper, barely audible, for the lack of something else to say. He ignores this and scrutinizes me with such intensity that I'm starting to feel self-conscious. Have I forgotten to wear a vital piece of garment or anything?

"Can I ask you a question?"

"Sure," he casually took off his jacket and threw it over his shoulder. His eyes are opaque, and I have the urge to drown in them. I struggle to keep my voice neutral and concentrate.

"Silvia... Your question?"

My face pricked when I stammered. "As I am now the Fairy of Robo-land, can you kiss me?"

He looks confused for a moment, then comes closer, cups my face with his hands and fits his mouth over mine, filling it with his taste, but as soon as it begins, it ends.

I stand there, that's it? That's what he calls a kiss? No tongue? For a moment, I am baffled. I look at him; he is the epitome of all males, and he kisses like that?

"I hope that doesn't count as your final score!" I croaked. As a sense of gloom sets down on me.

He doesn't respond, his hand is stroking my back like he is feeling my anxiety. I calm down somewhat and marvel at how handsome he is in an urban, rugged way. And not as I feared all-Iron-plated and technical. You know, he looks more like a big, rugged teddy bear, with his now slightly disheveled wavy hair that I want to run my hands through.

The thought that I own that hard-rigid body and, in theory, can do all sorts of naughty things is exciting, and I swallow suddenly, inexplicably nervous. This-is-just–what-the-doctor–ordered! I decide. The wait is finally over, and I hope this Must-Have-Toy will never expire on me. I conclude that I should be able to handle a mechanical toy, after all I am ingenious and resourceful. Boy, I don't know it yet, but oh boy! Was I wrong!

"Tell me where the kitchen is," he said in an authoritative voice, shaking me out of my musings. Does he want to go to the kitchen? Now? My mouth falls open, that's the last thing I expected, he can cook too? Slightly dazed after the kiss, I point him in the right direction, and he starts rummaging through cabinets and drawers, finding several food items I'd forgotten and that were expired. He looks at the cans, growls, and says in an exasperated voice.

"Do you have anything I can cook that isn't going to kill you?"

I inspect the discarded food items riddled with unimaginable life forms that could kill me at any time and look back at him. He stares back silently, waiting. After a quick look at him, I pass him a can of tuna, which is only slightly out of date, and says, "there is mayo in the fridge."

"OK, let me make you some lunch. Does a low-fat tuna salad with cream crackers and chocolate ice cream for dessert sound good?" He asked.

Holy shit! I gaped at him. Mirror- mirror on the wall. Who is the slickest Robo of all? It seems we have a winner, and I peek at him through my lashes as he busies himself. Then he turns around, glares at me, and scolds me. "You should be more careful what you eat; this stuff could kill you easily."

"I have applied for my witches' brew exam," I reassured him, slightly sarcastic. Did I misread him or did his arrogant male side show up?

"What does that mean," he asked unperturbed, raising an eyebrow.

I keep my face impassive and reply. "Just waiting for the cauldron to arrive, I'll be all set to poison all my past lovers I'll have problems with."

He slowly digests the information, clenches his jaw, and answers.

"Do you always joke?"

I nodded, suddenly feeling like a fool because he sounded like a man, not a robot, and mumbled. "Well, if you don't want to know the answers, don't ask."

"Ok, point taken, now eat!" He eyed me warily, sighed, handed me my plate, and I sat down, wolfing down the simple but deliciously tasting food. He is a master if he can whip this up out of a simple can of tuna. Then surprisingly, before I could stop myself, I asked. "Why did your previous owner return you?"

He stops what he is doing, his eyes burn into mine, and his lips press into a hard line. "I rather don't want to discuss this right now," he answered in a clipped voice. I gape at him; again, he seems not different from any other man I've dated.

"What happened to; 'I am your Robosapiens, and it is my pleasure to serve you?" I hissed, seriously pissed off.

His eyes scorched through me, and my euphoria about the tin man evaporates rapidly. He doesn't answer my question. Instead, he asked. "How many lovers did you have exactly?"

"That's none of your business," I answered haughtily.

Fast as lighting, he moves toward me, grabs my arm, and his eyes drift from my face to my boobs and back, giving me a curious look. My knees suddenly feel wobbly, and I have the urge to smile. When I do, he unexpectedly gives me a devilish smile. His lousy mood has vanished. The tension between us is over, and I breathe a sigh of relief. He leans towards me, grins wickedly, and with one eyebrow arched, he asks. "Would you like me to run you a hot bath? You seem to be jumpy; the hot water will soothe you!" He purred still with that incredible smile.

I am silent digesting the hot bath offer.

"What are you thinking about?"

"Nothing much; I just thought I saw Santa walk through the kitchen." I shrugged.

He laughed out loud, and suddenly I was deliriously happy as he grabbed my hand and said. "Please, show me around your home."

I flush with pleasure as I remember he is mine and mine alone, and my breath is shallow as I show him around my modest house. He doesn't talk but seems to take all the details in.

"The house is just like you; I like it."

Just like me? What does that mean, I wonder? Is it good or bad?

"Don't worry, it's good," he smiled again, and now I was convinced he could read my mind.

"Where is my room?" He asked.

His room? Holy crap, I had not prepared a room for him, as I was under the impression, we would fuck our brains out every night. For a moment, I am at a loss for words, then my ownership chip takes over, and I reply curtly, only managing not to waver my voice. "You will be sharing a room with me."

"Is that what you desire?" he asked softly, in an almost hypnotic voice.

"Yes," I whisper again. And swallow hard. Where has my voice gone?

"I am all yours: if you so desire," his thick voice against my ear is intoxicating, and I tremble. His hand rubs my back, and his breath is hot against my neck. He smells delicious, a heady mixture of male and some expensive lotion. Pure pleasure shoots through various body parts, and I almost swoon.

"Later," he murmured, later I will serve you."

I shallow, heat is surging through my loins, and I clench my thighs together, and for a brief moment, I wonder if I can, by clenching and unclenching, achieve an orgasm.

"Come, let's go for a walk." He commandeered, shaking me out of my reverie.

A walk? I want sex, but I wonder how to get it through him without being too forward. Hm, I never had to beg a guy for sex, not even at my age, and I am certainly not going to start right now, I decided. I grab my coat and step outside. With his lean body, he moves quickly and strides next to me. When I think he isn't looking at me, I register his impressive muscles and broad shoulders. I am so deep in thoughts I fail to see a hole in the ground and tumble headfirst towards the pavement. He reacts instantly and catches me before I make a fool of myself.

"That was close," he murmured, with both his arms around me. "Are you always this clumsy?"

Clumsy? I am not clumsy, just distracted by his raw male strength. Male strength? With difficulty, I reminded myself that he is a Robot.

"Please," I growled. "I am fine let me go."

"Anything you say," his voice was smooth as silk, and we finished our walk-in silence. Once back in the house, he informs me a trip to the supermarket is imminent for cooking dinner. I hand him my credit card and the keys to my car, with instructions on where the supermarket is, which is unnecessary because he is equipped with a GPS. He curtly informs me, and almost relieved, I watch him drive off. When he comes back, his arms are laden with food items. He smiles and disappears into the kitchen, where he starts cooking.

After another delicious meal, he notifies me that he needs to rest. Hoping that's a euphemism for sex, I walked excitedly in front of him to the bedroom, swinging my hips seductively. When we enter the bedroom, he unbuttons his shirt and quickly strips, totally unperturbed by me watching him with raw, unbridled lust in my eyes.

His naked body mesmerized me, and I ached to touch him, but to my dismay, he turned down the bed, stepped in and instantly snored when his head met the pillow. With an open mouth, sexually frustrated, cursing the hormones racing through my body, I head back to the living room, turn on the TV and watch an old episode of a James Bond movie, mentally comparing Paul to Roger Moore. Unsure of the winner, I finally head for bed, and as I unsuccessfully push my Robo-man out of the way to make room for me, my last thought is that I feel somehow cheated.

The following day, I wake up to the delicious scent of coffee and sizzling bacon, and somewhat dazed, I wander into the direction of the kitchen, wondering why he hasn't 'served' me. It's humiliating, and as I ponder several reasons, I press my hands against my throbbing head. When are my-sex fantasies-becoming a reality?

Robo-stud has been in my house for a week now and spoils me. Each day he proves to be a gourmet chef and, on top of it, an exciting companion. And although we continue to sleep in the same bed, to my great disappointment, he still hasn't made any advances toward me. We are like an old married couple who are very comfortable with nakedness after many years. When I think he isn't looking, I gape at his pecks whenever he stands in front of a mirror, flexing his muscles. Sometimes when he sees me watching, he asks me to touch his arms to feel how hard and toned his muscles are, and although he hasn't gotten a fat belly, I can see he is still holding it in. I find it adorable and funny at the same time. Did I buy a vain Robot? Boy, they sure weren't kidding when they said they gave their Robo-studs human qualities. I laugh out loud and can't wait to introduce him to my friends in a few days, hoping they will turn green with envy as he puts Adam to shame.

Apart from being vain, he is an exciting purchase. He loves talking, and I listen to him spellbound. He is brilliantly witty and clever, making me feel like I want to run off with him to Vegas and marry him. And apart from my sexual needs, he takes excellent and attentive care of me. He teases me and makes getting to know me into an art form. Once when I was going over some bad memories, I made sure they didn't show. Or so I thought. His eyes were on me when he quizzically volunteered: "I have just what you need; I brought some crunchy chocolate cake with nuts on top, don't worry, they are low in sugar." He got up and started rummaging in the suitcase he had brought with him when he arrived and triumphantly took out a small packet wrapped in foil. He opens it, breaks off a small piece of cake, and holds it to my lips. The gesture is so sexy, and I practically melt.

Obediently I open my mouth, and he slowly slides it in. The texture of the cake is just right, fluffy and tastes divine. The crunchy nuts are fresh, and when I bite on them, my taste buds explode in my mouth. If this is the reaction, he provokes by giving me a piece of cake, I know I will seriously be in danger of dying during sex.

Or...if he keeps this up, I will be soon as fat as a ball, and he can roll me into my car, and I will not even care about sex. I feel the loud pounding of my heart beating. Perhaps he only wants me when fat? Ridiculous! I divert my eyes and try to come up with some remarks, anything to break the hold he has over me, but the only thing I can come up with is a giggle.

To hide my embarrassment, I close my eyes and images of lazy, sun-drenched beaches swim into focus. It's a warm sultry lazy day, and I feel a gentle breeze on my almost naked body and sense a presence close to me. Robo-man is stretching lazily, and I have the urge to snuggle closer to him. I stretched out my hands to stroke his back. The images are so strong and powerful that I almost feel his skin's texture under my hands, I know it isn't real, and instinct tells me I have to press the delete button to erase the erotic image my befuddled brain is wishing for. I shake free and try hiding my confusion with difficulty, but somehow, I must have projected my state.

"You are daydreaming?" He inquired quizzically, his impression friendly and candid. He smiles, alluring and seductive, and oh, boy, my doubts about this project vanish instantly. If this is a mistake, it's the best mistake I have ever made. I smile back, but inside I am still a bit apprehensive.

"Are you ok?" He persisted.

Slightly ruffled, I covered up my temporary lapse of sanity by testing him.

"Yes, I am fine was just kissing a frog," I muttered.

He laughed. "And? did he turn into a prince?"

"I decided to have his legs for dinner," I croaked. It's an effort just to speak. "With a cream garlic sauce."

His chuckle is my reward; the atmosphere is heady. I am basking in his warm glow, feeling like I won this month's catch.

"You have quite a sassy, smart mouth on you," his eyes were glued to me. I nod, unable to talk.

Every evening he makes time for me, we sit hand in hand on the sofa watching movies, or we talk, mostly about me. I babble and rant on and spill my guts on how I grew up, my hateful school days, weight gain and losses, my disastrous relationships, the lot.

As on cue, he grabs my hand and whispers. "I would have liked you fat too."

Warmth flows through me, and I gulp and am seriously in danger of ending up as a puddle at his feet.

My amazing too-good-to-be-true-boyfriend doesn't care about an extra pound or two. And although he doesn't realize it, he just passed the perfect-boyfriend test with flying colors. He is undoubtedly proving to be an-essential-no girl can do without.

For some reason, I can't phantom why; I need to impress the hell out of him, and a few times, he laughs outright at my flippant narrates that color each story bubbly and outrageous.

One evening after the movie ended, he grabbed my hand and asked. "So, what do you want me to do?"

I stifle the urge to tell him what I think he should do now and more than once. But I can just contain myself, and I am tired of rejection. I have learned that when I show my desire, he whispers. 'Later.'

He smiles again, alluring and seductive, I smile back, but I am still a bit apprehensive inside. He slightly frowns. "What's wrong with you today?"

Dam, he is good. He even picks up my mood swings!

"What do you want?" He pressed on.

As I don't want to appear like a sex-starved-crazy-woman about to jump his bones, I smile back, shake my head and say confidently. "Nothing much, just wondering when the milkman is stepping by."

At my answer, he looks quizzical, leans against the wall and reaches for me. I find thinking challenging as he wraps his strong arms around me.

"From Santa to the milkman? What do they have in common?" He asked.

Unaware that I am projecting my frustrations, I blurt. "Both are known to deliver overrated illusions."

Dumbfounded, he looks at me. "Can you give me an example?"

I realize I have conveyed something I didn't want, and I try hiding my discomfort. I sit down, and fiddle with the remote control, which seems to have acquired a life of its own, as the case flings open and the batteries fall out, scattering them all over the floor and under the seat. And realize I have been handling it perhaps with too much tension.

"Bloody hell," I muttered in my breath. I know it's a stupid thing to say, but my mind is blank.

"Come," he grabbed my hand. "You are way too tense and twitchy. Let me give you a massage."

A massage? Boy, another one? I can't remember when I had so many massages, hot-stone, relaxing–Thai-massage, Shiatsu-a Japanese variety, even healing massages. He is familiar with all of them. Yep, those Robotic boys have done their homework when they put their software in him. I try to pull myself up. This is the time to be bold. After all, I couldn't look more brainless if I tried. Forcing myself to ask, I open my mouth. "What about a sexual massage."

He looks up, the grin on his face is unexpected, and my heart starts to thumbs, aargh! This is ridiculous. Am I falling for this mechanical penis? I examine my hands, hiding my discomfort, but there is no fooling him. His grin would get even more significant if that were only possible. Mortified, I had to get away from him. I quickly turned around, and in my haste to get away, I heavily banged my toe against a cabinet. My heart plummets, and I start yelling and swearing uncontrollably; that's it. I will return Robo tomorrow and ask for my money back, forgetting I have yet to pay for him in my haste. From now on, I will start dating the old-fashioned way. Shit, shit, I am as tense as a rubber ball.

"Ok, so no massage," said Paul, unperturbed by my embarrassment. "Relax," he grabbed my shoulders. "You need to learn to be patient," his smile turned me to instant mush. To hide my discomposure, I do the only other thing a woman can do and run my fingers through my hair and flick it from right to left to left. My hair is a warm golden blond, with some darker strands, the results of a month's salary at an excellent hair salon, and the effect isn't lost on him.

"Today, your hair looks lovely," he said softly. If he continues this, I will dissolve into a puddle on the floor at his feet, the happiness his comment gives me doesn't fade, and my pleasure intensifies. I stare at him. His face is warm and friendly; I am not sure how he did it, but his comment on my hair instantly transforms my mood, and I meet his intense gaze. My heart is hammering when I look into his bedroom eyes; they will be my downfall. He is standing so close to me that I can smell his cologne, and my breathing quickens. As I breathe in the delicious heady scent, the rush of joy surprises me—what a fantastic long-forgotten feeling. I realize I am in danger of falling in love with Robosapiens. Hmm, perhaps I should rethink this. My sanity warns me, how can I love a piece of wire? Mind you, an excellent selection of wire, sure, but even so...jeez... This is a mess. The shock of the discovery is a bit too much, and I open my mouth, but nothing comes out, but a slight croak..." err...hm."

"I want to run away with you," he whispered. "To the sea and just look at the view."

"Hmm, wasn't that a popular song at one time? Suddenly I realized that Robo's manufacturing boys had worked months, possibly even years, uploading his memory banks. He probably has a vast repertoire of responses for every occasion that crops up. The sobering thought works like a cold shower! He is still making small comforting noises, oh how easy it is to be seduced by his silken voice, and I lose the rational trail of reasoning about his possible-data-bank -responses. Paul's steady brown eyes are still on mine, and suddenly, my eyes water. With his thumb, he brushes the tears away and kisses my cheeks. The electric jolt that shoots through me takes me by surprise. His strong hands are on my back, stroking and are oddly soothing. What am I going to do with this electrical-jammed-packed wired–alien? And why doesn't my body listen to my brain? I find him incredibly sexy. Beware; I hear a small voice inside my brain. When something seems too good to be true, well, you know the rest. Now all I have to know is –HOW-TO-DO- this mysterious Robo-man! Suppressing a groan, I try to remember anything in his Manuel about his sexual responses that I should have read. I had only superficial glanced at it, of course. I mean, who reads the manual when you buy an appliance? I realize that perhaps that was a serious omission. I need to make amends and look wildly around me to see if the Owner-Manuel is within reach. For once, luck is on my side, and I spot it on the coffee table.

"Excuse me," I stammered. "I need to go to the loo." And, with that, I break free of his gaze, grab the Manuel, and lock myself in the bathroom, hoping against hope there is a quick, easy way to know the ins and outs of this mysterious non-metallic-Robo. Quickly I scan the pages until I find what I am looking for.

Social and Sexual Interaction

*T*he *FQGC-01-747 Unit is programed for social and sexual interaction with the OCL. It is designed to ensure satisfaction for even the most demanding and spoilt OCLs.*

For example, a G-spot chip locator (GSCL) will eliminate the need for any ugly and lengthy poking. We believe such a locator is currently not present in most humanoids as we did an extensive survey and after evaluating the raw statistical data, we concluded that 100% of the male-population lacked this basic knowledge.

What? Oh boy! Thrilled I read he has a G-spot chip locator. Yippee! My mind immediately wanders. The phrase currently not present in most male-humanoids is an understatement if I ever heard one. Indeed, none of my partners ever mentioned or demonstrated their knowledge of the so-called pleasure spot. Wow, this is a hell of a sales pitch! Happily, I read on.

The new fat-line shaped phallus is carefully designed to provide everything necessary for sexual functions.

We found that most women preferred this model over a long thin phallus. The probe device which we have fitted is, we believe, better than in previous models. However, we are constantly looking for ways to improve, and suggestions are welcome.

(Note: Once the virtual stimulation reality program is activated (automatic) and once firmness is achieved, the Unit's instincts chip (BIC) takes over, and the body part that is designed for just such an event starts functioning.

What's this? Welcome to Fantasy Land? He seems to have a unique combination of three synergistic functions: a probe, a G spot locator and a top-of-the-notch penis.

It is starting to look more and more like I hit the jackpot! *Thank you, God!* I prayed silently.

Sure, I know where to find the G-spot, but for Tinman to know is certainly a bonus; I had only discovered it myself some months back, after reading about it in Cosmo Girl, and had explored it for hours on end. I had no idea why it had taken me so many years to hear about its existence and why I needed to learn about it from a magazine.

Why couldn't they teach this in schools in reproduction classes? But I guess it is, forgive the pun, virgin territory. Nobody ever told us about G-spots or even female orgasms. Just the birds and the bees bit. Of course, we thought we knew everything there was to know about the subject and sat in class giggling and joking.

"Are you all, right?" Tinman knocks on the door and brings me back to the present. I wonder why his automatic response chips aren't functioning. I sit on the loo and look at my options. Only one thing to do; I must find out if all his bits are working.

"Sure, I am fine," I hollered.

I unlock the door and step out, avoiding his concerned gaze. Slowly I walked upstairs, determined to try my female powers on him by wearing something low cut and sexy. He follows me into the bedroom and watches me like a hawk as I struggle with the zip on my jeans.

"Let me help you." He comes closer, reaching over, and smiles in a way too sexy a manner. Do I imagine it, or does he brush his hand deliberately against mine? Hell, if I wasn't turned on before, I am now.

Warmth runs through my veins when he removes my jeans in a tantalizingly slow fashion, exposing the lace panties I wear underneath. I am unable to move, trembling as the pulsating between my legs grows stronger.

He tugs at my shirt, and I feel the dampness in my panties; my nipples grow hard and are visible through my shirt. My whole body is throbbing.

Expertly, he removes my shirt and lets it slip to the ground, and quickly unhooks my bra. I realize he is well instructed in the art of undressing. There is no dithering or unnecessary fumbling.

I am clad in knickers and shiver in anticipation. My breath comes in short bursts as he slowly and deliberately strokes my body. Is this the result of the learning chip the Robo-boys have installed? That thought dampens my desire a bit.

Where the fuck has, he learned this? Ah! Of course, didn't Mark say he had a previous owner? Damn, damn, damn. Visions of him making love to his previous OCL distract me. A searing pain goes through my body, and I realize I am jealous!

I screwed up my courage and asked him. "Where did you learn this?" He kisses my shoulder and starts nibbling at my neck. "Be silent and enjoy!"

He continues caressing my bare flesh, and ripples of desire flow through my body. I forget everything! Holy crap! He is worth every penny.

I need to know if all his *automatic stimulation chips* are in working order. Even if it kills me I have to find out. My hand moves of its own accord to the front of his jeans. The hard bulge I feel is startling and I start rubbing him through the fabric.

With each stroke, I make his bulge more visible. For a moment, neither of us moved. I ache for him to kiss me. He raises his hand, and his thumb trails the outline of my mouth that seems to have a will of its own as it slowly opens, and I suck on his thumb. His breath is warm on my cheek, and his other hand strokes my neck. My heart pounds when he lowers his mouth to mine.

The kiss that follows is hot and sizzling, and our tongues intertwine. I open my eyes and look into his, waiting for him to devour me, as his hand tugs at my knickers. He looks at me. I do not imagine it - his smoldering eyes are hot with passion.

"Lie on the bed face down. I will be back in a sec," he whispered and returns. He is carrying a bottle of sweet-smelling massage oil in his hand and sits himself on the bed. He puts some oil in his hands, warming it between his palms before he puts them on my back.

"You are going to enjoy this." He is practically purring and starts stroking my bare back. Oh God, this feels good. It's too wonderful to resist.

I groan as he softly strokes and kneads. His skillful hands feel like heaven, and he takes his time. A long time, kneading my tense shoulder muscles until I am so relaxed, I am practically putty in his hands.

His hand goes to my lower back, reaching the waistband of my knickers. He gently tugs them down and as I wriggle out of them. He pours an extensive amount of oil on my backside. I slowly melted. God, he is so skillful and inventive. I allow him to touch and penetrate me with his fingers in a way none of my previous lovers have ever done. I start shaking and moaning with desire, and after what feels like an eternity, he finally allows me to orgasm. It is so powerful I almost passed out.

"Holy shit!" I gasped when I finally found my breath. "That was quite something!"

"Have I not made you happy?" Paul frowned.

Is that a glitch in his software? How could he not know that I just felt the earth move? I prop myself up on my elbow, not caring that I am naked and slippery with oil, and my sheets will never be the same after today. Slowly my passion is ebbing.

My face is still flushed. Do I imagine I see a pulse throbbing in his neck? No, of course not. He doesn't have blood streaming in his veins. Hell, he doesn't even have veins. I correct myself and flop back on the pillow.

"Come here," I said smiling in gratitude. "Let me do the same to you."

He looks at me for a moment, then turns around, retrieves my discarded shirt from the floor and hands it to me. Hell, seriously? He wants me to cover my nakedness.

Slowly I put on my shirt, unsure what to do after the apparent rejection. My chest hurts with tension, and I absent mindedly rub it.

"Sleep a little. I am going to cook you a wonderful meal." He smiled down at me.

"Sure," I mumbled, uneasily.

Then, unexpectedly, he winked at me.

"Don't worry about me."

"Let me give you some pleasure too," I begin again, but he turns around.

"I don't want to discuss it right now, perhaps later," and leaves.

Slowly I sink back against the pillows confused. Why doesn't he allow me to play with him and give him an orgasm too? It's this how it's going to be in the future?

Perhaps I should have been more persistent. What man would refuse pleasure, but then I remember he isn't a man but an Android. Damn, damn. A temptation free android, so technically, I am asking myself irrelevant questions.

How can I forget he came off a conveyor belt? I need to read the manual again, to see what I need to know about his responses. Quickly I scan the pages and find what I'm looking for on page 29:

Cerebral cortex programming

We come to a complex subject that concerns the cerebral areas of the FQGC-01-747 Unit. We must state that the Unit's operation in this area is not always prone to scientific analysis. We have found in tests in our laboratories that some results may be unpredictable.

So, the OCL would be well-advised not to subject the FQGC-01-747 Unit to over-rigorous analysis or questions, but rather allow operations to take place and let the Unit perform in ways it finds acceptable (assuming of course that these occur with the OCL's own preferences!).

However, by and large, the FQGC-01-747 is programed to display the usual sorts of humanoid-like responses. So, for example, the Unit will take great pleasure during SSI functioning and fuel renewal processing, not to mention playing a good 30 games of chess once a day.

The Unit may display some sorrow if absent from his OCL for long periods. This is where the loyalty chip comes into operation. The Unit currently has the chip activated, so prolonged absence from the OCL contracts sensations of loneliness in the FQGC-01-747.

Well, he seems to be motivated enough, according to the manual. I wonder if he needs a replacement chip or something equally vital. At least, I hope it's something as simple as that.

I suddenly realize that I might have bitten off more than I could chew. The urge to discuss these new developments is pressing, and I have to call or email Mark right away.

Cognitive Robotics Group

Kings Boulevard 211/217

Queens green

NYC 4389

Fax: 0044134657833

Phone: 00441346 8776

Email. robotic@hotmail.com

Dear Ms. Silvia,

We are delighted that you are satisfied with our product as I stated before, we took great care in selecting this fine U*nit*.

We regret to hear that the Robosapiens is yet to have sex with you. However, when you read the Manuel, you will find that the Robot needs some time to adjust to the Care Keeper Owner/Lover of the moment. (We use the abbreviating of OCL).

(Notification: The Robosapiens doesn't assimilate rapidly.) Only after a concrete and mutable connection has been established with the OCL.

At the request of our customers, we have a fateful chip implanted as male humanoids always seem to want intercourse with anything that wears a skirt.

Give the Unit reasonable time to adjust, and we are full of confidence that the matter will be resolved soon.

The *Unit* may suffer from a little temporal distortion. His dilutetium crystals may need replacing.

And no, currently, we have no gay *Units* in our production. If the problem persists, we can try to modify him, and please keep us updated.

As you requested the number of my cell phone is: 173-ROROBOSAPIENS feel free to call me day or night.

We at Cognitive-Robotics Inc. sincerely hope that these instructions and specifications will be a helpful guide. The *Unit* has proven to be a valuable and stimulating companion to any OCL who would like to interact with him. The Unit has been carefully programed, and while by no means perfect, is designed to bring pleasure and stimulation to the owner. It can be a sensitive *Unit* and may even malfunction from time to time. But if treated with respect, you too will be treated with respect. Summing up, we feel that you have made a wise choice in your purchase, and we hope you will enjoy many years of (relatively) trouble-free operation.

Best regards

Mark Stein

Customer support Director

The Pin Code

When I wake up, I am not sure what's in-store for today. I have a nagging suspicion it will be another endurance test. I needed some answers and decided to consult Siri, my personal assistant from Apple. If she doesn't have an answer, who will right? After all she gave me sound advice before, and I am confident she will do the same today. I pick up my phone, and I ask,

"Hi, Siri, how are you today?"

"Hungry for knowledge Silvia!"

Hmm, that doesn't sound promising. I need knowledge, not Siri. I try again.

"Siri, can I talk about sex?"

"If you don't mind, I rather not."

Siri, I need Paul to make love to me."

"Why don't you Google that or ask Alexa?"

I stifle the use of a four-letter word.

"Siri, what do you think is the meaning of life?"

"I don't know, but I am sure there's an app for that."

"Siri, can you give me some advice about my boyfriend?"

"OK, I will give it a try, although I would rather be reading a book."

"Siri, can you please advise me. What should I wear to attract him?" I am pleading now.

"Well, you should shake off obsession and wear clothes that are more age appropriate for starters."

I gave up! Today Siri is in her usual unhappy mood and getting helpful answers out of her is like traveling on a train without wheels. You very soon get nowhere. Perhaps Professor Google who seems to live inside my laptop will help me. I type in my question.

"Why is it that my robot doesn't want to have intercourse with me?" I didn't have to wait long before I have my answer.

"He probably has erectile dysfunction! Or he is afraid you think his belly is too fat or his penis is too small."

"What? I yelled. "You've got to be fucking kidding me, right?"

"No, I am not kidding!"

I will try again. This time, I type

"What is the best way to address men's problems in the bedroom?" The answer was swift.

1. Do not try seducing him! It will only stress him out.

That straightaway raised a new question. Can a robot be stressed?

2. Do not wear overly suggestive items of clothing. He will only feel pressure if you do.

3 Do not question him about why he doesn't want sex.

The list of do's and don'ts goes on, and nowhere does anybody come up with a real solution, except that all men between 40 and 75 will experience some kind of erectile dysfunction. Fuck, what a useless piece of information! I felt his erection, so that isn't the problem. I realize I must be the problem and I need to know why. I unlock my phone and consult Siri again.

"Siri, do you think I am ugly?"

"All the evidence I have supports answer in the affirmative! So yes!"

"Bitch."

"I love you too Silvia!"

I sigh, switch off my phone and head for the shower. WTF. Fuming, I shower, dress and head for the living room. I have a suspicious feeling I probably will end up embarrassing myself again. How much easier it would be if Tinman was human.

What was that old saying again? Something about paying the right price. Or was it, everything has a price? Or do you get what you pay for? Well, sure as hell, this one had a hefty price tag, in more ways than one! Sighing, I muse that what once was the easiest thing is now the most difficult. This is going to be an endurance test, but I am not sure if I want to wait around long enough for a satisfactory outcome! Why is the Android playing havoc with my emotions?

While I am still thinking about it, I spot a bar of my favorite chocolate on the table. How did it get there? I can only conclude Roboman left it there for me to find, just as I am feeling puckish. How sweet! A warm feeling embraces my heart. Thankfully I stride to the table, grab the bar, rip the wrapper off of the chocolate and wolf it down. The snack sticks to my tongue, and I quickly wash it down with some leftover wine from the previous evening. It's a disgusting combination, and I almost choke on the sticky stuff.

OK. Leaving the chocolate for me was sweet, although it almost caused my early demise, but is it enough? Sure, he is kind and thoughtful, but is there a real man inside? Wait! What am I thinking? A real man? He is a bloody robot! I shake my head, questioning my stupidity. I need a drink and walk to the liquor cabinet. Pouring myself a stiff drink, I contemplate my options. The whiskey is smooth and soothing and goes down remarkably well, so foolishly I take a second and then a third glass in quick succession. I start to feel dizzy and float away on a cloud where robots don't exist and men, all men, want me. They drive Land Rovers and smell sexy in a musky way. Tipsy I dream on, seeing myself and a gorgeous man eating a beautiful meal in a perfectly romantic setting with soft candlelight and seductive music. This is followed by a sensual massage. Here my dreams come to an abrupt halt, as I suddenly remember the failure of the previous massage.

Hmm, this is bad. Back to the drawing board! Perhaps a bath together? Because it stands to reason that the proximity range in a bathtub must be the right setting for intimacy. My fantasies are running away with me as I conjure up hot soapy water and me playfully blowing bubbles and licking the water out of his belly button. This is usually an instant hit with a regular guy, but a nagging doubt that it will work on Tinman can't be altogether silenced. I think, wait! Damn! He is a Tinman. I can't just plunge him into the water! I break out in a sweat. I am a bit vague about electricity and so on, but I am sure I heard somewhere that water and electricity aren't a perfect mix. Suddenly I remember the movie with Mel Gibson and the hairdryer that fell in the bath. I shudder. I most certainly don't want to wake up in the hospital the following day or worse, not wake up at all! OK. Got it! No playing in the bath with Robo! I almost roar in frustration!

This Android-Robo-stud is fast in danger of becoming a pain in the proverbial ass! What now? Should I resign myself to having no sex for the rest of my life? For a moment, I fear I am having a black-out! Calm down, girl! How can you even consider a life without sex? Did I think for a moment that reducing my almost non-existent sex life even more would be satisfactory? The stomach-churning thought works as a cold shower. Then suddenly, I am disturbed by the unusually loud voice of my Robo.

"Damn it," he shouted. "What did you do with my pin code from the bank? I can't find it anywhere!"

"Pin code?" I echoed! Does Robo has his own bank account? That's impossible! It must be mine! I mean, let's face it, the boys from Robotics can't have sent me a robot with his own bank account, right? Did he forge my signature for joint custody of the account? And is his intention to empty it as soon as he can? Mind you, there isn't too much left, but I still want to hang on to what there is! I break out in a cold sweat. My head is spinning, and I realize I am in a state of confusion! Not to mention a soon-to-be impoverished state! Before I have time to react, he continues loudly.

"Hell, and damnation!" He strides into the room where I am sitting. The anger on his face is almost comical, and I say it in a soothing voice.

"I haven't touched it! Can't you remember where you put it?" That turns out to be the wrong thing to say! It's only adding fuel to his burning fire. Turning towards me, his arms wave wildly in the air as he squints his eyes, shouting even louder.

"How often have I told you I don't want anybody going through the papers on my desk? Huh? Can't you do me this one courtesy? I have asked you a million times not to do this! Is this too much to ask? Really? I have asked nothing of you, and you do this to me! Do not touch my stuff! Ever! Why can't you leave it alone when you tidy up! Can you tell me why you need to do this? Can you? Can you?" He repeated with venom.

I am speechless for a moment. Has he asked me a million times? When exactly? In another life? Then it strikes me! He is confusing me with his previous owner! Damn! Stunned for a moment, I don't know how to respond.

Wasn't it only yesterday that the same thing happened with Martin, the married guy? Well, he also had a previous owner.

Vividly I remember his ravings throughout the night when he misplaced his papers in our hotel room. Was I in for a similar experience? Is there a missing-papers virus going around? One I am unaware of? My head is starting to hurt, and I hold it with both hands.

"Please stop"!

He paid absolutely no attention and barked. "My pin code, please! Can I have it back?"

I realize the cheerful romp I thought we were going to have won't materialize soon, and I decide I have only one option left! respond in kind in an aggressive manner.

"Where did you get a pin code in the first place? Is it from my bank account?"

"Don't be ridiculous!" He snarled. "For your information, robots come with a limited amount of money in a secure account so that we can be independent."

"Independent?" Now I am getting angry. "Why on earth do you need to be independent? I bought and paid for you!" Although that last bit isn't strictly true, he does not need to know that.

He ignored my attack, and he fumed. "It arrived a few days ago. Where did you put it?"

"I told you I have not seen it or even touched it!"

This is an argument I am not going to win, and I decide to ignore him until he calms down. Unfortunately, it doesn't work! He is very insistent. Repeatedly telling me how he can't trust me and why is it so difficult for me to leave his stuff alone. And why am I so evil!

Over and over until my head is spinning. From cute Robo-boy, he has turned into a mindless devil! What does he think he will accomplish? That I suddenly as by magic produce his stupid pin code? I walked to a chair and sat down as I ambushed. My head feels it is about to burst. I have a throbbing headache, and I am starting to feel sick, probably due to the excessive amount of alcohol I consumed before in a such a short time.

I have to throw up and quickly run to the bathroom and vomit until I have nothing left. Weak and miserable, I hang over the toilet bowl, smelling my own vomit. Finally, when the gagging has stopped, I flush and wash my face at the sink. By accident, I look in the mirror. God! I look terrible! No wonder I can't get a real man.

Feeling sorry for myself, I drag myself to the bedroom and crawl into bed. Falling asleep is impossible, as Roboman is still mumbling and babbling incoherently about missing pin codes and inconsiderate girlfriends and OCLs. Every so often, he yells, swears and shouts. I have no clue what he wants to accomplish, but it isn't working, whatever it is. Finally, I drift off, but not for long, as he comes into the bedroom, obviously bored with being ignored, shakes my recumbent form and says: "Can you promise me not to touch my stuff again? Ever? Can I trust you enough to do me this small favor? Are you my friend or my enemy?" He towers over me, frowning. It's obvious he expects me to recant and eat humble pie!

I groggily sat up, the effect of alcohol still befuddling my brain. I look at him. He is even more handsome in his rage. His hair is messy, and I ache to run my fingers through it. For a moment, I am tempted to grab his hands and humiliate myself. But then his following words swiftly kill of my cuddly feelings.

"Of all the stupid things you do this must be the worst. Interfering with stuff that isn't yours!"

Stupid? Do I do Stupid things? What idiocy is this? His fury is palpable. Why on earth is he acting so dramatically? The boyfriend from hell is now living inside my house, and I have nobody to blame other than myself! That's it! I have had enough!

Sweetly I say. "Gosh, you are such a drama queen! Thank you for correcting me. Luckily you don't have to search around for a second opinion about my character. Has the thought occurred to you that perhaps your pin code is together with the VCR manual you misplaced last week, and they are out painting the town red with your money?"

The look he gives me is intended to reduce me to an amoeba, but I am starting to enjoy this, and nothing can stop me now.

"You know," I said casually. "When you make too much noise, I will take you to the scrapyard and sell you, weld you into a piece of art and put you on the mantelpiece! Who needs a crazy android with serious anger control issues anyway?"

He opens his mouth and closes it again. Did I get through to him? For a moment, he stands still and looks at me, then he turns around and disappears into the next room. The sound of silence is pure bliss. I pull up the bed cover over my head and fall to my Immense relief I fall immediately into a deep sleep.

When I wake up in the early morning, I notice Roboman is lying next to me, but his incoherent babbling is still going on! I perked up my ears, trying to make out his mumbles. Is he still going on about missing pin codes? Or possibly something more interesting like former owners? What's that? What's he saying? Then clearly, I hear the word devil! A few minutes later, after some gentle prodding, I have a sentence: "All women are Devils!"

His tangible manifestation of hostility towards women is out on the table! His previous owner must have been a difficult bitch! Or was she? Perhaps the real problem is a faulty chip! Having witnessed his rage last night when he was totally out of control, how could it be anything else? Why did he get so angry about the pin code anyway?

I am more convinced than ever that I should have tried to find out the story of his previous owner. Did she have the same problems as me? Mark from marketing omitted to give me that piece of must-have data! Mind you, I didn't ask him but still... why did she return him to the factory? I mean, if he is as good as Mark claimed, she would have kept him surely?

My feelings of empathy are certainly with her. Having gone through last night, I certainly don't want to be around to witness his uncontrolled rage a second time! Where is his good behavior chip? Is it malfunctioning? Or does he even have one? Damn!

Time to check the manual to see if there is anything in there I have missed. When I locate it, I go to the index and find what I am looking for on page 23:

DISCLAIMER: *(Mechanical zero object-locators, although functional, are not precise enough to automatically locate objects.*

Although extensive dynamic mapping is stored in digital images, the Unit has a problem locating objects in time and space. Things can disappear at regular intervals. This can also apply to an impressive amount of computer files or papers. Currently, the FQGC-01-747 will find objects in the last place he looks!

The manufacturer is not responsible if objects never re-appear.

Note: locator placers (LP'S) can solve this problem by inserting a small chip, that when activated, will emit a strong beep, Effective range of 750 feet. Or the Robosapiens can just ask the OCL (owner-caretaker-lover) where the objects are.

Hmm. That is interesting–a *locator* chip. He certainly seems to need one. Reading that the Robosapiens can just ask the OCL where the missing objects are explains a lot. He is programed to ask! But does this have to be in such an unpleasant manner? I make a mental note to call Mark from Robotics to ask. Perhaps I need to take my robot to the workshop and get several problems fixed. I leaf through the manual to see if there anything else of interest I should know, and I read: Compliance Devices

The Unit comes with a new positron brain feature, an embedded behavior control (BC) individual coding, and a custom build compliance design (CD). These are all digitally controlled.

These, of course, were built in after compelling requests from consumers.

(Note: as this is a relatively new intelligence characteristic, we didn't have adequate time for extensive testing so that some bugs may occur.)

Did that say compliance? Doesn't that mean that when I asked him to stop his shouting, he should have? Some bugs may occur,

I read… some? It's more like a bloody plague! OK! Time to call Mark.

I retrieve my notebook, find the phone number from the Robotics boys and dial the number! First, I get a busy signal, and I redial. Busy again! Damn! I dial again and an automated voice informs me that the number I have dialed is not in service! OK. In my haste, I must have dialed a wrong number. One day I must learn how to be patient. With trembling fingers, I dial again, and I hear:

"The number you have dialed is not in service!" I feel a panic attack coming on. What the hell is happening? Is their phone out of service? Or is their company bankrupt? A thousand questions race through my head, and I have no answer for any of them! Dial again! I hear the same infuriating message and break out in a cold sweat. Suddenly I seem to have developed a breathing problem. Calm down, I tell myself trying to control my breathing. Slowly and carefully, I dial again and just when it starts ringing a hand comes up from behind me and takes the phone out of my hand. Mr. Tinman asks in a stern voice "who are you calling?"

Now, this puts me in a spot. Shall I be bold and tell him? Or shall I make up an excuse? While I bite my lip, trying to decide, he asks: "Did you find my pin code yet?"

Stunned by his merciless persistence, I open my mouth several times, but no sound comes out. I am sure I must resemble a fish close to dying. Unsure how to handle the situation, I take a deep breath, turn around, walk outside, and get in my car. My hand trembles slightly as I reach for the ignition key. Then the soft sound of the purring engine shakes me out of my lethargic state.

In my haste to get away from the house, I pushed the gas pedal almost to the floor. The tires squealed in protest.

After driving for almost an hour, I have calmed down somewhat. I stop the car and look around. Where am I? I see a family walking nearby. Mommy is pushing a pram, and daddy is walking the dog, and I feel a sense of acute jealousy springing up. Everybody else seems to be doing OK. Why am I not? I have tried almost everything, and now am faced with this new debacle. I am sure it's exactly that, another failure. Back to the drawing board, or in this case more like the factory, to return him and get a refund. I turned the car around, and calmer I drove home, only to find he wasn't there. «

I assume that he is probably out playing chess with the other addicts in the park. That's another thing I am not happy about, coming to think of it. In theory, he should have provided some income to sustain himself, but so far all I have seen is that he likes to play (literally).

Chess in the park. Playing games on the PC. Facebook, Twitter, Second Life. Chatting to people I have never heard of. Hmm. Perhaps it's time for the manual again. I grab it off the coffee table, where I keep it in case of an emergency, leaf through it and come to the correct chapter.

Leisure Time

In theory, the Robosapiens should provide some income to sustain himself and help you with all the household expenses. Unfortunately, some robots appear rather lazy in that area and will not perform labor functions to its fullest potential.

We can complete re-program him, but if you need a good short-term solution, you could try inserting a firecracker in his ass.

While he is somewhat prone to apathy regarding labor functions, he seems to have no shortcomings in the area of leisure. When left to his own devices, Tin Man will perform such activities for considerable periods.

He is currently programed to perform in several different areas, many of which are similar. Some involve moving small black and white pieces over a checkered board in a game known as chess.

He is capable of staring at this board for several hours a day. Sometimes a soft crackling noise can be heard, and one careless move may have disastrous consequences. He prefers this activity with humanoids that are just as single-minded and share the same aspiration: to win the Game. They use a mechanical implement that faintly resembles a time-controller but to the untrained eye appears to have limited use as it is set at strict 5-minute intervals. This is called a chess clock.

Of course, his opponents have no idea they are playing a glorified computer game. The Unit tries to make the Game a little more challenging by giving his opponents a vital piece like a queen or castle. He displays much pleasure playing at least 20 or 30 rounds of chess a day.

One other activity the Unit likes and performs with some accuracy is bowling. To observe his pleasure in propelling large, heavy bowling balls at several standing pins at a fixed distance is enchanting; his smile is never wider than when he wins.

He goes to a gym that contains many different mechanical iron implements three or four times a week. The true nature of these somewhat spherical objects is unclear to the casual observer, but the Unit seems perfectly capable of understanding the contraptions. He can be seen happily tossing these rather heavy objects in the air all the time flexing his impressive muscles and looking in the mirror admiring himself.

When he isn't playing chess, he will work behind the computer, as he is programed to look for **intelligent life on the web**.

His specialty is the use of languages, and Cross-Cultural Communication comes in handy.

The Unit uses the law of disciplined creative chaos to communicate and interact extensively with female humanoids.

(Note: our researchers are still trying to fathom out the reason for this peculiar practice)

PLEASE NOTE: Some quantum physics theories suggest that when the OCL is not directly admiring the Robosapiens, it may cease to exist or will exist only in a vague and undetermined state.

Due to an error in the programming at an early stage of development (which, unfortunately, our engineers have not yet been able to fix), the Unit developed an almost obsessive partiality to a small black boxlike object that sends images into dwellings of humanoids.

The Robosapiens has developed a peculiar infatuation for the SCF channel and spends many hours watching repeat episodes. Some loss of mobility can occur but hiding the remote control makes him eventually get up. If he is unable to locate the desired object, he complains bitterly.

(Note: the OCL is advised when that happens to pay no need.)

Another thing he can't resist is watching 22 people running around on a green grassy field, kicking a ball into two nested boxes on both sides of the area. This game is called soccer.

Watching is often accompanied by a yellow fizzy drink, called a beer and a large bag of potato chips.

If intending to take the Unit on shopping trips, he must be given some warning as he needs time for his relaxation exercises, meditation and breathing techniques. Not to mention adjusting his food habits.

As shopping is really against the Law of Nature, applying this technique enables him to be the perfect shopping companion.

The pleasure of dragging him for hours through the most crowded department stores and boutiques will have its own reward when you see the envious looks of other women. It doesn't take a rocket scientist to know they are green with envy and make you feel like Miss Universe.

Other activities haven't been mentioned yet, but the Robosapiens finds one of his greatest pleasures in receiving massages, preferably by the OCL of his choice.

(Warning: he can undergo these types of labor-intensive manipulations for hours on end until he is in danger of wearing the OCL entirely out.)

There is still much potential within the Unit for further enhancing its skillset in terms of leisure and other pursuits.

Therefore, the OCL would be encouraged to experiment and interact with the FQGC-01-747 and examine future possibilities.

The Unit enjoys being your chauffeur; this enables him to show his superior driving skills. It's noted in some Units the need to comment on other drivers' mental states will drive the OCL crazy. So far, all our attempts to prevent the Unit from making verbal comments have been in vain.

The Unit is an expert in various card games. Once put in the presence of other players, he will quickly find the different correct combinations using creative, critical thinking. The games encourage him to discuss strategies with his competitors, who fail to fool him as he is a savvy player.

Final note: The Unit has been implanted with a Game chip that one of our engineers installed in a none-supervised moment. So far, we have been unable to locate or remove the object. However, this unfortunate event has some severe consequences as the Unit is under the impression that he can't win if he is playing a game. Please ask Mr. Google for more information.

Damn! More uncertainties. Angrily, I walk to my computer, open Google, type in *The Game*, and wait for the result. It didn't take long, and a Wikipedia page popped up, and with growing dismay, I read:

The Game is a mental game. The object is to avoid thinking about the Game. Because when you do, you lose.

What? a Game? And we all play? Mind you. It is a highly entertaining one, but even so? I, as much as the next gal, like the challenge but this one sounds insane! Does he actually believe this?

But wait, what am I saying? He is a programed robot! He doesn't have any beliefs. Confused, I close the laptop with a tad too much force and stare blankly at the wall.

I need to find out how his brain works. Didn't I see a chapter before dedicated to it? I grab the manual and read.

Footnote: The Game Wikipedia source unknown.

Cerebral Cortex

Now we come to a complex subject concerning the cerebral areas of the FQGC-01-747 Unit. Just as in humans, its retina is directly connected to the cortex, resulting in perfect motor control and enabling him to distinguish color, depth, shape, and motion.

We must, however, state immediately that the operations of the Unit in this area are not always prone to scientific analysis. We found some results may be unpredictable.

So, the OCL would be well-advised not to subject the Unit to over-rigorous analysis and/or questions, but rather allow operations to take place and let the Unit perform in ways it finds acceptable (assuming, of course, that these occur with the OCL's own preferences!)

However, by and large, the FQGC-01-747 is programed to display the usual sorts of dynamic humanoid-like responses. So, for example, the Unit will display great pleasure during SSI functioning and fuel renewal processing, not to mention playing a good 30 games of chess once a day.

The Unit may display some sorrow if absent from the normal OCL for long periods. Because we installed a loyalty chip. Its activated, so prolonged absence from the OCL automatically causes feelings of loneliness in the FQGC-01-747.

Direct interrogation of the Unit will not always produce the response desired by the owner. The reasons for this are various, but we refer the reader to the previous section – the FQGC-01-747 unit is complex and cannot always correlate information in a manner that is capable of being interpreted by the OLC. The OLC would, in turn, be advised as to not interpret this as evasion, elusiveness or avoidance on the part of the Unit.

NOTE: Due to this particular behavior of the FQGC-01-747, the OCL may be absolutely clueless of why she started any verbal interchange in the first place, as it is clearly a lost cause from the start.

WARNING: This behavior should not be interpreted as HE IS SO NOT INTO YOU!! Which incidentally is the title of a highly acclaimed book written as a warning to females who wondered why their prospective friends/lovers didn't propose to them).

Higher cerebral programming

We aimed to exclude the psychological dangers of mind manipulation by the Robosapiens due to their artificial intelligence (this occurs frequently and exploitation is not uncommon).

Our earlier models tended to control female humanoids, so a non-manipulative GX chip is standard now.

The OCL can confidentially rely on the cognitive abilities and trust the Unit's judgment on life and death matters.

CONSUMER NOTICE: *Because of the "uncertainty principle," it is impossible for the consumer to ever fully grasp the complexities of the workings of a Robosapiens cerebral cortex.*

Right. That's it? I try to translate all this information into something I can comprehend, but it isn't easy. If I understand it correctly, he has problems distinguishing shape, color and whatever else? Also, I can't ask him any questions. Hmm - why ever not?

Perhaps I should ask Mark from sales for the address of his previous owner, that might shed some light on various things. She might have had a very valid reason to return him to the factory. In the meantime, I muse, what went wrong last night? Wasn't that the night he was supposed to have sex with me? If everything had gone according to plan, of course. I certainly hadn't counted on him getting angry. I sigh and feel depressed; nothing seems to work out as I intended.

I get up and redial Mark's number. Unlike yesterday this time, it rings, and he picks up on the second ring.

"Hi Mark, it's Silvia, who bought the second-hand Unit," I added for good measure. I tried calling you yesterday, but nobody picked up the phone. You weren't by any chance avoiding me, were you?"

"Ah no, so sorry we had a telephone problem yesterday. How are things going with," he paused for a second, "Peter?"

"Paul! Not good. I am afraid. It's turning into a bloody nightmare. Last night he accused me of misplacing his new pin-code. He was totally out of control, accusing me of all sorts of things. Is this normal?!"

"Well," he starts cautiously, "this particular Unit has some problems in various sections of his brain. I think that's why the previous owner returned him."

"I see. Can you give me her address so I can find out if there is anything else I need to know?"

"Due to our privacy policies, unfortunately, I can't do that." He informed me.

"You must have known something was wrong with him," I wailed, willing him to deny his earlier statement.

"All of our Units are having some problems, that's why we give our customers extensive manuals.

You must understand the complexity of duplicating a human male brain with hardware, and writing the software isn't easy.

Over the years, the Units tended to take on the characteristics of their human counterparts. Unfortunately, we have failed to correct these problems. We suspect it has something to do with the life-logic systems the Units are using."

"And are you telling me he is just behaving like a normal guy?"

"Not exactly. We take great care calling back all the Units yearly and take approximately 90% of his male counterpart's intricacies out of them, which have accumulated. However, the remaining ten per cent can cause their OCL's problems."

"You are dam right! I guess they don't live up to the claims you make?"

"Ma'am, all I can say is that if you push his buttons right, he does exactly what you want him to do."

I gulp, "Hmm, it used to be very easy to please a man. Just dress sexy, let him drink beer and go down on him".

On the other end of the line, he chuckles and says, "I guess the Unit still hasn't had sex with you?'

"To the bloody right he hasn't," I hissed seriously under stress. "I am almost looking forward to menopause, so my hormone level will drop."

He chuckles again, and helpfully offers, "have you fueled him?"

"Fueled him?" I echoed. "You mean I have to take him to the petrol station and stick a hose in an unmentionable part of his anatomy?"

His laughter boomed out. "No, why don't you send him back to the factory, and we'll see what we can do. On second thought, I don't live too far from your town. Why don't I drive up in ta few days and pick him up? I will send you a text when I plan to arrive is that ok with you?"

I feel a wave of relief as that sounds like a reasonable offer, and I agree. But as I hang up the phone, something is nagging at me. Do I imagine it, or does his voice sound familiar?

Santa

Over the next two days, I try not to let Paul know he will get a part lobotomy or a system reboot because I somehow have the idea. He isn't going to go along with that idea meekly. I feel tense, and I am sure it shows I have never been able to hide my feelings well. And sure, when I curl up on the sofa after work, Paul comes in carrying a mug full of hot chocolate, sits next to me and asks, "You have been very quiet the last few days. What's wrong?"

I stare at the candles, not looking at him. "I am wondering," I finally replied, full of trepidation. "Why your previous owner returned you." By the look of astonishment on his face, he would have won hands down if a prize were given for total lack of understanding. A slight frown appears on his face, and he checks his watch; his expression is stern when he looks at me.

"I told you last time I don't want to discuss it. Please let me be."

Ignoring his demands and holding the remote control so tightly in my hands that I am sure the indentations will never come out, I splutter, "did you have sex with your previous owner?" The anger on his face when he realized, I wouldn't let go was almost comical.

"Yes," he said guardedly.

I could not think of anything else to say and instead started drumming my fingers on the wooden side of the sofa. And he said softly. "Please, calm down."

How can I calm down as his words do nothing to soothe my brushed ego? I play in a weird drama except I don't know the words. If he had sex with his previous owner, why not with me?

"When you arrived, I thought you were Mr. Right but now, I realize your name should be Mr. Wrong! As far as I am concerned, you can sod off." I reply sharply. "You were supposed to solve my problems, but more than half the time, you are adding to them."

"You sound cross," he said.

"Why is the what-a-woman-needs chip not working? Let me tell you -something! They melt when treated properly but turn bitter if not used well," I spitted out the words full of venom.

He raises his eyebrows and snarls. "You are starting to sound like Glenn Close in 'Fatal Attraction.' You should have read my **TERMS OF EXCLUSIVITY!** Then all of this", he waved his hands. "Could have been avoided, and out of nowhere he produces a piece of paper and reads loudly!

For the first thirty (30) days, both parties agree not to ask questions about each other's past. After forty-five (45) days, if one party continues to be *unsatisfied, * the *wounded party* agrees to "give up."

My stomach flips, and a considerable shock vibrates through my body. Robo-boy came with a contract?

"TERMS OF EXCLUSIVITY? Nobody told me anything about that!" I wailed. It's like telling me all of a sudden, I sprouted horns.

Out of nowhere, he produces something that looks like a contract and hands it over. My eyes run carefully over the next bit of text he just read:

TERMS OF EXCLUSIVITY, GROUNDS FOR TERMINATION:

Any following will be grounds for immediate termination and final dissolution of said relationship.

1. **Infidelity**, running off anytime to console an ex-girl/boyfriend.

2. **Ending** any argument with the sentence, "My ex used to do that same thing.

3. **Undue** Interrogation of the third party. There it is!

And what is that? My signature at the bottom of the page is visible. Hell! I can't even remember signing it. How was that possible? Am I getting an early onset of Alzheimer's now? But then it hit me.

Didn't that good-looking delivery boy shove a form in my hand to sign, which I couldn't bother to read? Hell! I get up and stagger drunkenly to the fridge, where I aimlessly start munching on something I shouldn't. My mind goes in circles as I feel conned by the Robo-boys, conveniently forgetting I was the one who ordered the damn machine in the first place.

The threat of a tear is just around the corner, and I force myself to take deep breaths. How did I get into this self-inflicted misery? In all fairness, I must point out that my need for sex brought all this on. I massage my temples and sigh. Wallowing in self-pity isn't going to help me now. I have somewhere missed a turn. Only one thing left - I stagger to the fridge, pour myself a generous amount of wine and take a deep swig. The drink hits me like an avalanche, and I take another swig. Ah! As the warmth fills my belly, by magic the bleak thoughts evaporate as but just as I am about to take another satisfying sip, his hand shoots out, grabbing the bottle.

"Don't you think you've had enough? Are you trying to kill yourself now?"

"Hey, I just want a quick drink," I yelled. "Sod off, "and eye the almost empty bottle. However, he makes sure I can't get past him, and his stern look is about to crush any hope of a more permanent good mood.

My mind whirls. I get up, grab my car keys and head to the car. I need to de-robot. Not noticing the biting cold, I start the car and quickly look in the mirror. I see the havoc my emotional roller coaster ride has brought on. Red-rimmed eyes, unattractive gray skin, bags under my eyes and the absence of makeup makes me look like something out of a horror movie. A terrifying one at that! I am gripped by a sudden thought. Is that why he doesn't want to have sex with me? He must think I am way too ugly! Well, judging by my reflection, I can't blame him. I look horrendous. One part of me hopes Paul comes after me and apologizes, but that thought is instantly dashed when I see him through the window turning off the lights and heading upstairs. I feel completely shattered and lonely. With tears streaming down my face, I start the car and drive away at breakneck speed.

The window gets fogged up. I am not entirely sure if I am shivering now, from angst or cold, but I turn up the heat. The weather has turned noticeably colder, and the wind has picked up even more. I feel the car shake at the sudden onslaught, and to add to the misery, it starts to snow. Not a fairy tale, gentle falling of soft snow. No! Twirling huge flakes quickly obliterated the view, blanketing the road and making driving conditions treacherous. I slowed down. No use getting myself killed.

I take hold of myself, squaring my shoulders. Then, unexpectedly the darkness of an oncoming depression leaves me as the landscape transforms into a thick blanket of pure virgin snow. It's beautiful, like a sugary doughnut. Lucky there is little traffic on the road, and I finally reach the center of a moderately large town. Where the hell am I? Sanity takes over. I need to go home before the roads become impassable, but just as I am about to spin the car around and drive back, I spot a somewhat forlorn-looking Santa in front of a large department store sitting on what seems like a throne of plush red velvet next to a giant Christmas tree surrounded by heaps of kids waiting patiently in line to sit on his lap. I stop the car as Santa seems to be waving at me. Stunned, I look again. It is not my imagination as his hand beckons, and he shouts. "Come, it's warmer here!" Although the thick snow dampens his words, I recognize the welcoming invitation and his hand that unmistakably pats his lap. And I almost laughed aloud. What? Santa is inviting me to sit on his lap? I giggle. This is crazy. But when I look again, I see a determined look on his face as he shouts. "Come!"

For a second, I considered crawling onto his lap and asking for a boyfriend. Although I am not entirely sure Santa would grant such wishes, especially not for horny older women. I take a better look at him and see a weathered, crinkled face with a white beard, mustache and white hair. On his head, he wears a red fur-lined Christmas hat. It's hard to guess his age. For a moment, I envy him as he doesn't seem to give a damn about his pot belly; au contraire, he is displaying it proudly. Could I envisage myself as Mrs. Claus? My fantasy runs away with me. If I don't have to worry about makeup or holding in my tummy, I can just wear baggy pants, and everybody would be friendly, in case I rat them out to Santa! I giggle. I am being foolish. I need to drive away from temptation. Don't I have enough problems already?

But almost against my will, I spot an empty parking place and get out. Large silvery snowflakes descend around me. Crisp fresh snow crackles under my heels. I shiver. I am nowhere near dressed warm enough for this weather, and I question the wisdom of my overzealous act. Then I hear the sound of Christmas songs filling the air and smell freshly cut pines. Bright strands of twinkling lights are strung in the trees, enhancing the festive mood. I could surely do with a Christmas miracle to brighten the holiday season. I walk slowly as to avoid breaking my neck in the thick snow as I am wearing shoes that are far more suitable for a Saint Tropez beach, I approach Santa. Almost immediately, I notice his deceptively bulging biceps under his red coat and his deep tan that's more fitting for an Olympic athlete than Santa Claus. I may be wrong, but to my knowledge, the North Pole isn't exactly sunny. His face is quite handsome, and his cobalt blue eyes sparkle. The beard and costume make it impossible to guess his age. But I figure he is at least 15 years older than me. I feel a flash of envy as it should be illegal for guys to age better than we do. Our eyes lock, and absentmindedly he hands a girl a small, brightly colored gift. "Ho-Ho-Ho!"

"Hello, "I whispered when I came within earshot. "Any chance I can find you in my stocking on Christmas morning?" Shocked at my boldness, I laugh. It's as if my insanity has jumped to a whole new level. His hearty warm laughter doesn't disappoint me. "I was actually thinking that a warm scarf, mittens and a knitted hat would be much more appropriate, not to mention sensible boots," he smiled as he looked at my now visibly frozen toes.

His voice is deep and husky, very masculine, and I melt. His beaming, slightly smug smile tells me he knows exactly what effect he has on me.

"I am almost off duty; can I offer you a ride on my sledge?" He purred. "I have a battery of elves and reindeer standing by to assist me."

Witty and good-looking? What are the odds? Although the idea of sitting next to him on a sledge covered by a thick blanket is somewhat appealing, I am cautious.

"Tempting though that offer sounds, I am allergic to reindeers pulling sledges," I said as calmly as I could. "Anyway, I am so hungry I could probably eat one of them for dinner."

He chuckles." OK, so much for that idea. A ride in my car to a warmer place, perhaps? And then dinner? Seeing you are hungry?" For a moment, I didn't answer, and I looked at him in alarm, I thought he was serious.

"Won't Mrs. Claus object?" I probed. His reaction is unfathomable, other than perhaps for a small twitching muscle appearing on his cheek. "Mrs. Claus ran off with Mr. Jimmy Choo," he finally answered. "We were living on a shoestring budget at the time, but instead of downsizing, she expanded her spending, helped by a friend. I waited for the other shoe to drop, but it never did, so I filed for a divorce."

I looked at him aghast. "What a fiendish thing to do!"

He shrugged. "It was a long time ago, and I am doing much better now, so the joke is really on her! Don't let the costume fool you," he pointed to his coat. "I own a penthouse, and you can look at my priceless etchings any time." Did I imagine it, or did he wink?

"Your etchings?" I heard myself babble, stalling for a time.

'Yes," he answered, looking somewhat pleased with himself, "I have been collecting them for a while now. I even own one that is by Rembrandt van Rijn." I am not an art connoisseur, but even I recognized the name of the 17th-century Dutch painter and am suitably impressed. Santa masquerading as an entrepreneur or vice versa? Somehow, he seems a bit dangerous, and I wonder if there's some sort of safety drill I should adhere to before becoming involved with him.

Beware of Santa bearing gifts, I heard a small voice in my head. It was hard to imagine this Santa would make a fine boyfriend. He probably winked at everything in a skirt, I told myself. And what about mom? How can I bring him home and introduce Father Christmas as my new boyfriend?" Mum would look him up and down with disdain and then would tell me how grossly unsuitable he was and what bad choices I made in boyfriends, and she would probably be right. But I'm getting ahead of myself. For now, despite some reservations, I am strongly tempted to take him up on his offer for dinner. I nodded.

"I have to change" and he pointed to the entrance of the mall." Wait for me!" Sure, enough, he disappears through a door meant for staff only.

When he comes out, he takes my elbow and propels me rather brusquely towards an old red Range Rover. It was like being guided by Speedy Gonzales. In fact, it was so fast that I didn't have time to take a good look at him. I only saw an old sweater, jeans and a scarf covering half his face.

"Sorry for the vehicle. My other car has a service. Let's hope the heating works." It didn't, and shivering, I sat silently next to him. Fortunately, the drive to the restaurant is short. We got out of the car and I noticed that he looks guarded before he walks toward me. Yes, you are probably thinking what a nut bag that Silvia is, and you are right of course. I still cringe remembering it. This just shows my stupidity he either has a woman somewhere or the cops are after him. But as usually I wasn't thinking as I felt his hand resting lightly on my lower spine. The feeling is nice, and I almost purr as he steers me toward the small restaurant. Inside it's warm and cozy. I look around the plush interior. Candles adorn the table, and white starched tablecloths and napkins give the room a luxurious feel. A beautiful centerpiece of cascading white roses sits in the middle of the table and is absolutely gorgeous. Each waiter wears a crisp white shirt and an immaculate black jacket, with a folded napkin over one arm. They bow so deeply they almost fall over. This is a world unknown to me, a world of luxury and servitude. I feel a spasm of alarm, something tells me to be careful. My companion is effusively greeted by the manager, who is positively oozing servitude.

"How are you, Mr. David? Some champagne on the house, for you and your partner?" He raised his eyebrows inquisitively, looking at me.

"Silvia," I said, "Silvia Smith." He smiled with the truly false smile clearly used to kissing ass and solely reserved for the super-rich.

"Follow me, please," he walks us to our table, ensuring we can't escape and pulls up a chair for me. "Enjoy your evening, sir, madam," with a curt nod, he signals a waiter to attend to us, and he melts away. I must say I am slightly overwhelmed by the luxury of the place. Our table overlooks a well-tended garden, which is transformed into a fairy tale scene as sparkling Christmas lights are strung between the trees. Combined with the virgin snow, it gives the place a romantic look. A sommelier approaches silently, holding an extensive wine list.

"May I suggest a Chateau Latour, sir," he said, beaming.

"Excellent idea John!" John? Suddenly I realize I have no idea what Santa's name is, and I start giggling uncontrollably.

"What's so funny?"

"Well, we haven't even formally introduced ourselves. I keep thinking of you as Santa, but what is your real name?" His eyes glisten when he appraises me. His voice is husk. "I already know your name. Nice to meet you, Silvia. Mine is Luis. My mother was Spanish." His smile shows perfect white teeth that no doubt cost a fortune. I can't help thinking, hey, this one is high maintenance. I gaze into his eyes and am mesmerized by the blatant sensuous expression. He smiles, and his eyes crinkle. I still can't determine his age, but I guess somewhere between 70 and 80, yet he looks fit. And despite his age, I find him incredibly sexy. Without asking me anything, he orders a bottle for both of us. And says to another silently approaching waiter. "You know what to bring, right?"

"Very well, sir!" The waiter bowed and moved away. I feel the muscles in my face tighten and I roll my eyes, but he doesn't notice. What an autocrat! I am getting second thoughts about accepting his invitation.

I took a better look at him. Now that he has lost the costume, I see that his hair is gray at the temples, but I think it's still thick, and when he runs his hands through it, it bounces back straight.

Despite his age, he has exuded masculinity, and I am clearly attracted to him. A few minutes later, a waiter silently puts a salad in front of us. The green salad comes with cherry tomatoes, feta cheese, toasted almonds, bell peppers, goat cheese, red onions and high-quality olive oil.

Topped with fresh figs, which at first, I didn't recognize as I had never come across them before. To my untrained and sensual eye, they look like vaginas, but I wonder what they really are. But before I could inquire, the waiter, who must have noticed my puzzled look, asked. "A drizzle of dressing on your fresh figs, madam?" I throw him a thankful look, and he gives me a barely noticeable smile. "It's a mixture of honey and mustard." He volunteered further. I nodded. He drizzled not nearly enough, and I felt like grabbing his sleeve before he moved away. But I realized that would make me seem like the country bumpkin I am, and I restrained myself. For a minute, I admire the summery exotic salad before I pick up my fork and start nibbling.

Although I am still upset about my lack of say in the food choice, I can't help enjoying the greens. For a few minutes, we are both silent, and then he leans forward and places a warm hand on mine.

"I am enjoying your company, Silvia." His voice is smooth and sensuous. And sucker that I am, I totally melt. He smiles warmly at me, and I feel like a princess. Hell, he is talking to Silvia, right? Me? But before I can fully savor the feeling, the food arrives so quickly it makes me wonder if he had pre-ordered it when he changed out of his Santa costume.

"I hope you like some?" He inquired, pointing at the golden baked fish on our plates. "It's nowhere better than in this restaurant!"

I surveyed the grilled whole sole served with lemon, caper and butter. It looks delicious, and I can't wait to try it. I sprinkle some fresh lemon juice on my fish and take a bite. It is soft and luscious and melts in the mouth.

"Wow! It's like a mouth orgasm."

When he heard me, he spluttered and seemed profoundly shocked.

"What? Not in the restaurant," he hissed. I calmly observe his features as his eyes widen. Even when he is fighting an apoplectic episode, he is still handsome. But I realize he is indeed from another generation flummoxed I can't immediately reply. Clearing my throat, I responded calmly.

"It's an expression,"

"I know what it means," he said tightly, "but it is inappropriate to say that in public." I eye him silently, realizing this, whatever this is, isn't going in the right direction. I feel like a scolded child, and my cheeks burn.

"A slip of the tongue, it won't happen again." Silently we eat. The food is delicious, small roasted baby potatoes accompanied by freshly cut cucumber, avocado, lettuce, cilantro, and sweet Thai chili sauce. When I finished the last morsel, I contemplated licking the plate, but after looking at Santa's face, I decided against it. I don't want another generation- gap mishap. The delicious meal and the profuse amount of red wine have clearly mellowed him as he reaches out his hand to cover mine and gives me a heart-stopping mesmerizing gaze.

"Let's go," he said huskily, beckoning the waiter for the bill. When it arrives, he signs and says. "Put it on my account, please." The waiter gives a discrete bow after pocketing the hundred-pound bill Santa obtrusively places in his hand.

We exit the restaurant, and I can't help noticing he again looks around before heading to the car that now looks misplaced. I can only hope he isn't afraid of bumping into Mrs. Claus. Or a hitman. I think vindictively.

"A little kiss?"

I suppress a giggle, give him a little kiss, and then push him away before he can stick his tongue into my mouth. The little kiss is everything a little kiss should be, and I can't help thinking that perhaps the answer to my dreams is an older gentleman, one who is sophisticated and full of savoir-faire. Living in his mansion, attended by servants. We could travel to faraway exotic beaches and drink Mai Tai cocktails.

"Another one?" Before I could even react, I felt his lips pressing against mine again as his tongue tried performing an endoscopy. I almost choked. It takes all my willpower not to push him away. This is what he calls a little kiss? I can't help wondering what a big kiss would be—perhaps inserting his penis down my throat? With all my might, I want to push him away. Still, it feels rude, especially after he paid for such a delicious dinner, so I sit through the ordeal, calculating how long I need to endure his invading tongue and can end the kiss without offending him. The irony is not thinking about me being offended escapes me for the moment. But before I can decide how long I must endure this, his hand slides inside my blouse and starts fondling my breast. As his fingers squeeze my nipple, the instant treacherous reaction of my body betrays me and makes it hard to remember the tongue attack. After a few minutes of snogging and enjoying the feeling of sexual arousal, I almost forget the tongue until his warm hand leaves my breast and travels downwards, rudely altering my equilibrium. I grab his hand and yank it away, meanwhile pushing his tongue from the back of my throat.

"What's wrong?" he murmured in a low sexy voice. "Don't you like this?" Don't I like this? Of course, I like it. That's not the point. My brain tells me it's way too fast, and in a car? Hell, I have not had sex in a car since I was seventeen. At best, it was distinctly uncomfortable, and as I am old enough to be a granny, I don't have any desire to repeat that experience.

"I want to go back to my car. Can we go, please?" He sighed, clearly deeply exasperated but obediently did what I asked and started driving, each of us deep in thought. He stops the car when we reach my car, which is covered in thick snow. He pauses for dramatic effect and kisses me again. However, this time it's less aggressive, unlike before. I enjoyed it until he ended it all too soon.

"Shall we have lunch in a few days? I know a lovely intimate restaurant!"

I nodded.

"Great, it's a date. I will make the reservations. Is Wednesday good for you?" Without waiting for my answer, he says. "I will call you. Bye, princess."

"Sure, call me." Princess again? He noted my address and phone number and before I had time to blink, he was gone. Since

I was eight years old, I haven't been called a princess. Unsure what to think, I open the car door, let myself out, and walk to my car. I get in, start the engine and decide to wait a few minutes till the snow melts off my windscreen before I drive off. Once inside my house, I lean against the front door and stare blankly at my shoes. What the hell just happened? Perplexed, I go over the events of the night. Does the fact that he is much older than me explain his haste? Did he not want to waste a good erection? I grinned, speculating and eventually headed upstairs. Paul is nowhere to be seen; frankly, I don't care. I take a shower, and I can't wait to snuggle deep under the covers. But barely after my shower finishes, my phone alerts me with a text from Luis:

"I enjoyed our evening. You are such an interesting sexy lady. I didn't want the evening to end. Your kisses were delicious, and the feeling of your warm breast made me hard." I looked skeptically at the message and let a mean thought creep in, and I typed back.

"I bet you say that to all the girls!" Immediately his reply follows.

"NO."

As I am still processing this unexpected texting presence in my life, another Ping pops up.

"*I am already in bed. I have something for you,*" an unsolicited picture of an erect willie springs up wearing a tiny Santa hat. Surprised, I look at the picture. My first reaction is to laugh until I realize it's probably his penis. Is this a case of oversharing? Or a sense of humor? What the fuck! But before I can dwell on it...

Ping: "*Bells are optional!*" I shut my eyes and think, how many times has he done this before? Should I be embarrassed or revolted by this display? The fact that I am neither tells you something about me, I guess, and I laugh.

Ping. "Don't *you see I miss you already*?!" Hmm, in the restaurant, he seemed like an old dinosaur. But all of a sudden, he is a full-fledged techie sending pictures over the net. (And God knows what else I can't help thinking about). But although I am amused, I wonder why he sent a picture of his dick? Really? Does he believe he offers me something unique? Something I have never seen?

"*Is that a picture of your Santa's advertisement?*" I quipped. Yes, I know it's lame, but I can't come up with anything else.

Ping, "*Batteries not included!*" That's funny, and I can't help it. I laugh. Of course, this is not the first dick-pic I have received, but I had always dealt with them by blocking the guys who sent them. But this came from somebody I hoped to get to know better.

Not sure how to respond. I go through my list of answers required in situations like this, except I can't find anything suitable to reply to a retired, slightly overweight businessman of an undetermined age who just sent me a dick pic. Too soon for him to send such a picture? Hell yes! I fruitlessly search Google for an appropriate emoticon that conveys my emotion, and not finding any, I give up. I decided not to reply and instead ran it past Jane.

Quickly I forward the dick-pic. (Googling tells me 80 per cent of women share those with friends.)

Ping. "*Lol, where did you pick that up?*"

"It's *Santa's dick!*" I reply.

Ping. "You've *got to be fucking kidding, right*?"

"Nope!"

Ping. "*What is its owner like? I notice he left his face off the photo; did you reply*?" With the speed of a machine gun, she fired quick questions.

"Yes, I asked him, "Is this what I have to work with?"

Ping, "*Lol, you didn't!*" True, I didn't. To be honest, I am not sure if I even want to answer. "Should I ignore it, Jane? I feel this isn't the first time he has done this; don't you agree? I mean, for instance, where do you get a tiny Santa's hat from in the middle of the night," I lamely typed.

Ping. *"Well,"* Jane chose her words carefully, not directly judging. *"He could have photoshopped a hat on his willie. I mean, look at it, it's nothing special. It's barely 5.2 inches. He has to pimp it up for you even to notice it. LOL. But to be fair, he may have some special tricks. Who knows, don't you want to find out?"*

Slowly I type: "I think I want to see him again."

"Why don't you ask Siri? It's said she has an answer for everything." Jane volunteered. That seems an excellent idea., I can always blame Siri if it doesn't work out.

"Siri? How do I react when somebody sends an unsolicited dick-pic?"

Ping *"Who did Silvia?"*

"Santa!"

Ping, I swear I hear Siri laugh in the background, but as usual, she doesn't have a concrete answer, useless twat.

"Santa? In that case, I'd rather not discuss it."

I decided to put the pressure up with a loaded question.

"Siri? Do you know where Santa lives, and does he have a wife?"

Ping: *"The North Pole. I can see his house from the cloud."*

"Is his wife there?" I pressed.

Ping, *"Yes, she is currently located at the North Pole."*

"What is she doing?"

Ping, *"baking cookies for Santa."*

Hmm, that conversation is taking the direction I want, and I gaze out of the window. The moon has come up, and without knowing exactly why, I start daydreaming, wishing for a boyfriend who, for once, isn't a self-centered jerk, an undiagnosed but obvious narcissist, or a self-proclaimed dick-pic promoter. Well, look at the bright side. At least, this time, a man likes me enough to kiss me. Twice! I remember his smell, a mixture of pine and Paco Rabanne. I close my eyes, feel lightheaded.

I am skinny dipping in the ocean with the sun glistening over the water. Soft waves lap against naked bodies. A little wind comes out of nowhere, spraying us with the frothy foam from the waves, and I laugh happily. My date crinkles his eyes against the fierce sun. I am so wrapped up in this fantasy I think I will start a new Facebook group, Daydreamers Anonymous. I feel myself floating on top of the water and close my eyes. But unlike the sultry caress of the water, as I expected, it's cold, and something drips on my tummy. I snap out of my happy fog and open my eyes just in time to see the ceiling opening up, releasing a stream of ice-cold water onto my warm body.

"Jesus Christ! Holy shit." I yelled, and jumped up, shivering in shock. My befuddled brain can hardly accept the reality of a flooded bedroom. I look up and see that the initial gush of water has slowed down a bit. Thank God for that. I come to the brilliant conclusion there is a faucet break somewhere. Nothing does more to ruin a good sleep than a plumbing disaster at night. Moaning faintly, I get up, and survey the havoc. My bedroom will never be the same again. I jump out of the bedroom, grab a toweling robe and put it on.

Ping: another text. In a daze, I grab my now dripping phone, open the message and read. "*Hello, are you still awake?*"

"Yes, my bedroom has just turned into a swimming pool, and I think I will go skinny dipping." Silence.

Ping: "*What? Are you joking?*"

"NO!! And I quickly fill him in."

Luis arrives at what seems like the speed of light, making me wonder if he somehow orchestrated the whole thing. He took immediate control of the situation by making a few quick phone calls. I am still in shock, and he looks at me and frowns. "Get dressed. You can't stay here. I am taking you to a hotel."

Breathing hard and trying to control my panic, I pack a few items, dress, and burst into tears, my mind all over the place. Luis drops his phone into his pocket and takes me in his arms.

"Don't cry. It will be alright. Tomorrow the plumbers and the repairmen will fix it, come!" And he steers me towards the door. Meekly I do as he says, trying to control my sobbing. The drive to the Hilton is short. Without further ado, he checks me in while I look around, and even in my distress, I notice the Hilton looks like any self-respecting Hilton should, with cascading fountains in the reception area and substantial white columns made of marble from floor to ceiling, holding a magnificent, curved ceiling.

"Wow," I breathed, forgetting my earlier upset. "This is nice. I should have plumbing catastrophes more often." Luis turned towards me.

"You are still in shock, my dear. I am sending a car for lunch tomorrow. Get a night of good sleep. Unfortunately, I can't keep you company. My presence is required elsewhere. Here is your key," and he pulled a regretful face. "Sleep well, my dear."

He kisses my cheek, turns around, heads towards the revolving doors and is out of sight even before I can thank him. I watch him go, and I do not even wonder what he meant when he said his presence was required elsewhere. The next day a message from Luis with the time and the restaurant where he wants to meet me for lunch wakes me up. I take a leisurely shower, dress and do my makeup. When I go down to the lobby, another receptionist than the one from last night greets me as I approach and says. "Mr. Luis David, sent a car for you, madam, the silver Mercedes, over there," he points out. It beats me up how he even knows I am part of Luis's entourage, but I suspect it's how the very rich do things. Staff around him seem to bend over backwards to please him. My suspicions are confirmed when I approach the car. The driver opens the door and says. "Good morning, madam. I will be your designated driver today. Please get in, and I will take you to the restaurant." The ride was tedious and took longer than I had anticipated. I can't help feeling a bit nervous. When I arrive. Luis immediately spots me, and his face lights up as he smoothly gets up from the table and strides purposefully towards me, taking my hands in his. He kisses my cheeks and squeezes my hands ever so slightly. He is obvious pleased to see me, and I never smiled so broadly. He steers me toward the plushest dining room chairs I have ever seen, and I sink thankfully into one. As soon as I sit, the Maître d' hands me a menu before I can even take in my surroundings. I study it for a few minutes. Everything promises to tantalize my taste buds, and it's hard to choose. In the end, I ordered something called a confit of salmon with petite potatoes, shrimp and a dill salad.

The wine Luis ordered is cold, white and delicious, and after taking a few quick sips, I feel happy despite last night's plumbing catastrophe. He asks me if I had a good sleep, and we drift into the same easy conversation as the evening before. It's reassuring, and I take another sip of my wine. His attraction is undeniable. He is well traveled and amuses me with funny anecdotes that have me in stitches. At that point, a skeptic could say that I felt this strong attraction thanks to the wine, but I had the feeling I had met my soulmate. His warm smile melts as he bows to me and whispers in my ear.

"It should be forbidden to look so attractive at your age. You must have some excellent face cream. Where I come from, all the women have fillers, Botox and plastic surgery. How do you manage to keep this youthful look?"

"Wouldn't you like to know," I replied mysteriously, omitting the fact I had a very successful plastic surgery operation done by an excellent surgeon on my face and neck ten years back thanks to daddy's inheritance. Still, none of my friends ever suspected I had one done and only declared how well I looked after my vacation! Fuck all the creams that promise you to look young for eternity. My money was on the knife any time! I glance at him and grin, wondering why men are so easily duped. I notice that he wears a costly shirt and jacket, and I can tell its tailor made by how it clings to his broad shoulders. For a brief moment, I wonder how he makes his money. Smiling, I start playing with the salt and pepper shaker, only to be interrupted by his question.

"What's so funny?" he asked curiously. Not sure what to say, I fibbed. "I was thinking about you being Santa yesterday. Is that a work career or a hobby?

"It's a family tradition. I took over the job when my father passed on and luckily already had the grey hair and beard to make it believable."

"So does Santa grant wishes for Grannies too?" I inquired.

"That depends. Are you a Grannie?"

"Well, technically not, but I have a whole army of nephews and nieces. Do they count?" For a moment, he gazed into my eyes.

"I can make all your wishes come true," he whispered huskily and reached over, taking my hands in his. He is so close I can smell his expensive cologne. "I feel fortunate to have met you; we shall celebrate with champagne? Yes?"

"Yes." I smiled. "That would be lovely." When the waiter uncorks the champagne with a soft explosive sound, he pours it into two glasses and Luis hands one to me. "Cheers, my dear. To a happy relationship." The bubbles tickle my nose. It's ice-cold and delicious, and I feel a warm rush of happiness at his care and attention directed towards me. And I feel pleased that I had made the right decision when I got out of the car last night to meet Santa. He looks at me with sparkling eyes as he holds the neck of the glass and takes a sip, and leans back in his chair.

"We should do this more often," he whispered.

"That sounds wonderful." My words tumble out, although I have no clear picture of what kind of future, if any, we might have. Could it be that I have found my soulmate at last? And more to the point, would he be the right one this time? I had been wrong on more than one occasion, I muse. I am so lost in thought that I blurt out. "I am starting to believe in Santa." He chuckles. "You should."

"What kind of work do you do when you are not being Santa," I inquired as casually as I could, although I am dying of curiosity. He is silent for a few moments; then, cautiously, he answers. "I am in some quite boring family business. Let's not talk about that now. Tell me about yourself." Our eyes lock, and I need to tell him about my family, lovers, desires, hopes and despairs But I am lost in memories and fall silent.

"Do you have a current man in your life?" He wanted to know. Since I hadn't anticipated this question, I am unsure how he would react if I told him about the Tin- Man -cock-up. I stall for a time.

"Is everything OK, or did I touch a nerve?" Luis asked, obviously observing my hesitation in answering. I take another sip and say. "My last relationship didn't work out. At first, he seemed perfect in every sense except one. He refused to have intercourse with me."

His shocked gasp is so loud that the other guests look up from their plates.

"It's OK," I said calmly. God, even I am surprised by my skillful lying. "We parted amicably. I wished him all the best." The answer seemed to satisfy him for now because he nodded. "Would you like some dessert? I know what I want for dessert," and he looked at me with unbridled lust. "Let's go to your hotel. I am hard for you." Although I had heard similar words before, I had never heard them uttered by a 74- year-old man in a restaurant, and I audibly gasped, not quite sure how to react. As I fight to recover my composure, I play the words over in my head. I can't believe I heard him correctly. I mean, he is seriously OLD, right? Do older men really say these things? And in public? But despite my qualms, I feel ripples of excitement surge through my body and say. "God, are you for real?" His laughter is infectious, and I join him in giggling without my will. "Well, you must admit I never expected you to say that." He looks at me, winks and says. "Shall I get the bill? I can't wait to see you naked!" adding more eroticism to the already heated atmosphere.

The Revelation

He pays, we head for the car, and we get in. And as we do, his hand accidentally brushes against my breast, and I feel a new wave of desire shooting through me. However, I am a bit tense like always when I am about to have sex with a new man. Taking off your clothes is a big deal when you are older right? We no longer have the flawless bodies of a 20-year-old girl. No guy wants to look at your pudgy stomach, your sagging tits and your cellulite. Even the thought is quite sobering. We want to have as little light on as possible. Candlelight is perfect for first-date sex when you are the age of a grandmother. Only then are we more relaxed. But this is obviously going to be after lunch sex, and the room will probably be as bright as the bloody sun. Crap! In my head, I came up with a plan. Close the curtains, find candles, probably in reverse order, light candles, find music, (if possible) turn up the volume, take off skirt. Leave underpants on for now. Grind to the music, rub against his body. Take off his pants. Yes, also underpants. Kiss. Stroke his penis. And hopefully, soon, I will get a reaction out of him. (If not, send him on his way.) Climb on top of him, take off your underpants (mine) and hope that he is too preoccupied to check out your old body. Yes, I know he might want to, but at least you know he doesn't have the time to take a peek at your sagging tits and bum. Not to mention your grey pubic hair. Crap why hadn't I shaved? A man could easily get lost down-under. However, it didn't turn out as I had anticipated, he obviously had his own plans. As soon as we were in the room, he closed the curtains, took out his phone, turned some romantic music on, took me in his arms, and started kissing me. Expecting a similar onslaught to the one from last night, I am pleasantly surprised when the kiss starts gently with soft nibbles and his tongue playing with mine. I start groaning when the kiss deepens. His skillful hands reached under my blouse, found my bra strap and expertly unhooked it. The skill with which he did this should have alerted me, but I felt drugged by then, and I ground my pelvis against his body. His hands found my breast, and he squeezed my nipples, and bolts of pure lust traveled to my groin. His mouth left mine, and instantly I felt the loss of his warm mouth. He bends down and nuzzles my neck, God that feels good. He his pelvis rubs against my tummy, and he is fully aroused. His hand, almost of its own accord, wanders under my skirt, and one finger is inside my panties before I can even object to him touching my pussy.

"You are so wet," he whispered. His finger slides smoothly inside my panties. He strokes and enters me. I jolt involuntary, and I start moving in the old rhythm. The feeling of his touch down-under is exquisite, and all thoughts about the plan leave me as he strokes, kneads and nuzzles till I am about to burst with desire.

"Do you want me inside you?" He whispered. I can't talk, so I nod. "But before I do that, I will taste you."

"Yes, yes," I panted, tearing off his shirt. His skin has a healthy bronze glow. Is that the result of a tanning studio or a house in the south of France? Hell, I didn't care either way; all I knew was that I wanted this man to ravage me. The time is finally here after that long, long drought. I didn't realize I said it out loud, but I must have because he laughs. My body is throbbing with need, and I shiver. I will perish without his touch on my body. I can no longer think coherently. As he peels off my blouse and bra and leaves me standing only clad in my knickers in front of him. He ogles at me like a connoisseur. "I like your body. It's very soft and feminine, come." He leads me to the bed and softly pushes me on my back and in one motion removes my knickers and literally dives in."

"Ahh!" I moaned softly, and then I couldn't even do that anymore. The feeling of his mouth on the most intimate part of my body is exquisite. He sure as hell knows what he is doing. He licks, sucks, uses his fingers, and before I know it, I reach for a mind-shattering orgasm that has me panting for a few minutes. When I open my eyes, he is hovering above me with his dick in his hands, about to put it inside me.

"I have some condoms in my handbag," I had nicked them from the cruise, and they were probably long expired. He gives me a horrified look and says. "I don't do condoms."

"What do you mean", I inquired with a puzzled smile "You don't do condoms? You can't be serious."

"Oh, but I am," he reassures me, "I check myself regularly, don't worry."

"You check yourself regularly?!?" I blared.

"How often is that? Don't worry? What about me getting me an STD? Have you considered that possibility?" I wailed.

He is silent. Then he asked me.

"Did you ever have one?"

"No!" It has been a while since I had sex, well to be exact three years 45 days and 16 minutes, but I obviously wasn't going to tell him that, so I mumble something that sounds like: "Hormones, the tablets weren't good for me," and I trail off with a pained expression on my face.

"Spread your legs, honey," he said ignoring what I said. In the same expert manner as he was with oral sex, he has inserted himself in me before I can object, and I forget all about condoms. My heart is thumping with excitement, and for a brief moment, I think this is the way to die for damn sure. We make love for a few minutes, and then he asks me to reverse position because his knees are hurting, probably due to a bout of arthritis, I think, so I straddle him and do my thing until we come together in a shuddering release. Afterwards, we fell asleep like an old married couple comfortable in each other's arms. It's heaven, and just before I fall asleep, I think he may be the one I have been waiting for. A glow of happiness fills me and then I sleep only to be woken up by the sound of his phone an hour later. He releases his hand from my breast and answers it. A frown appears on his face, and he replies curtly, "OK, I am on my way." He turns towards me, kisses me and says. "unfortunately, duty calls. I will text you later. We had a wonderful afternoon. You are a good woman, and that was great sex."

I nod. "yes, we must do that again real soon." He doesn't answer. He is far too busy looking for his clothes, and his mind is clearly somewhere else. When he is dressed, he turns around, walks to the door and blows me a kiss.

Expectations

Luis sends me a text three hours later, telling me my broken pipe is fixed, and my bedroom is presentable again, and yes, he has paid the bill. I shower, dress and head back to my apartment, which looks pristine as though nothing had ever happened to it. For a few moments I stared at the ceiling. Whoever repaired it must have worked diligently throughout the day.

"Hello." Without me hearing him, Paul came in. I take a deep breath, ready for a confrontation. Where have I been, what have I done and so on, but instead, he asked. "What do you want for dinner?"

As if nothing had happened. Let's face it, an ordinary guy would have at least asked me where I was last night but not Paul, and for the first time, reality sets in. After all he is a robot and robots don't have feelings. If this afternoon had taught me anything, it was relishing the feel of two humans enjoying each other's touch. And I realize Paul is sadly incapable of this. I make a resolution that I will return him to the factory tomorrow. This adventure has been nothing more than a bloody and costly mistake.

I pick up the phone to make an appointment for his return. After all, they could always sell him to a frigid woman for whom he would be perfect. But then for reasons I can't even explain to myself, I put the phone down. Instead, I turned around and faced him.

"I want to invite a friend over this evening. Kindly stay in your room!" I informed him casually implying it wasn't a big deal.

"What do you mean?" He inquired quizzically and raised his eyebrows. As I am still buoyed by the afternoon romp, I speak haughtily. "Santa is coming bearing gifts." The quip is intended to hide the fact that I am a touch nervous. I don't know from where I have the confidence that Luis even wants to see me again. I try to remember what he said. Did he even mention coming over tonight? Hmm, I can't remember. Is this the onset of early Alzheimer's? I rub my forehead. I can't just send him a text and ask, right? That would surely betray an aging brain. Hell, next I will be drooling in my pillow. No, I definitely can't text him. Drumming my fingers on the table, wondering what to do I ask Paul. "Can you make me some dinner?" He nods and I dart a quick glance at him. His face is inscrutable.

Silence. Then unexpectedly he inquires. "Will I like him?"

What an odd question. I had expected some drama, and I am not sure if I am disappointed or not. I sit utterly still, then it comes to me I need a drink. I get up and pour myself a glass of leftover red wine to cover up my anxiety. The wine tastes like shit which does nothing for my mood. I look at Paul again. He is still waiting expectantly for an answer.

"Probably not." My voice sounded jumpy even to my own ears and trailed off. I must be nuts discussing Luis with Paul. No brownie points for me. Tears spring up in my eyes, and I attempt to gain control but to no avail. Why do I always get myself in a fix? I like to handle problems as fast as they come up, knowing postponing has devilish consequences. Postpone! Prevaricate! Pretend it doesn't exist, and it might acutely go away. Yeah! Like it ever will. I mean, let's face it, people don't postpone stuff forever until one day all their hopes and dreams fall apart. I sink into a chair and rub my eyes. I really have to get my shit together soon.

Ping: "*That was a delightful afternoon. Let's do that again real soon. Are you free next Friday evening? Perhaps I can taste your French cooking at your place. Please let me know in time, I have a pretty busy schedule.*"

Flabbergasted, I stared at the text. Next Friday? I am having trouble getting my head around it. Quickly I calculate that's in six days. Doesn't he want to see me sooner? A creepy feeling tingles down my spine. Did I miscalculate again? Does this mean he has a wife and a couple of kids tucked away somewhere? I ruffle my hair with my hands. Oh, sweet Jesus, talk about an emotional overload. Why do I always misjudge guys? I can almost hear my mom with her moral guns blazing, repeatedly telling me. "They just want you for the sex Silvia". She would shake her head and raise her eyebrows disapprovingly, "Are you nuts? In future, keep your legs together if you want a good man!" Mothers have the uncanny knack of pounding you in the pounding of your self-esteem. Even memory had the power to hurt. But could she be right after all? It would be humiliating to admit it to her as I couldn't even admit to myself that I am way too accommodating sometimes. Do I do it again? I growl inwardly. Make a note of yourself. As far as I see it, I have two choices, I can Ctrl-Alt-Delete further relationships, or comprise a checklist that I should follow rigorously.

Should I consult mom again? I wondered and winced. Perhaps I could cheer her up with a checklist, of what one man should adhere to. Not sure what I to do, I start gnawing at my cuticles and quickly write a list.

1 Why did you leave your former wife/lover/girlfriend?

2 Show proof of name with a valid ID

3. Are you free of any nasty diseases? (Ask for confirmation)

4 Are you faithful?

5. Do you like to point out flaws in others?

6. Are you dominant and overbearing?

7 How do you feel about having children?

8 Please state your yearly income.

9 Are you an alcoholic, a criminal, or a drug addict?

10 Do you fight for dominance?

When I read the list, I sigh, suddenly feeling a touch guilty towards Paul. After all, look at my requirements. He so fits the bill. Perhaps I am placing the bar too high, way too high. For reasons I can't even explain to myself, I pick up my keys and jangle them. Is this the age-old reflex of fleeing or staying? I throw my keys in the air and impress myself by managing to catch them before they hit the floor. Then I catch sight of myself in the wall mirror, I bought years ago in a cute antique shop. I groaned inwardly. No wonder he doesn't want to see me again soon. I look like an old hag. I hastily avert my face and make a mental note to go for a facial. After all, I need all the help I can get. In despair, I flop on the sofa. After analyzing the situation, I conclude my ego is mortally wounded. What had I been thinking? Regret wells up, and I feel annoyed. Hell! No wonder Jane laughed so hard when I told her. I can't say I blame her; I probably would have done the same if it happened to her. I resolve that this is perhaps the time I need to reflect on what's important!

"Dinner, Silvia?" As I was still reeling from Luis's apparent rejection, I had forgotten about Paul, who had asked me earlier if I wanted dinner. I looked at him sadly. He was so handsome with his chiseled cheekbones and wavy hair, but I realized that perfection doesn't exist however compatible he might seem. Not in real guys and not in Robo guys either. I wryly think. "Welcome back to the real world of dating in the old-fashioned style." Then when I recall the endless hours, I waited by the phone in the past, hoping in vain that a guy would call, I take a deep breath and come to the inevitable conclusion that I am way too old for this shitty game.

"Make me a tuna salad, Paul with extra mayo," I ordered throwing dietary caution to the wind. After all, if this is not the time for comfort food, there never will be a time.

"Very well," he nodded and disappeared into the kitchen. He is back in ten minutes with the food, and no matter how upset I am, it hasn't affected my appetite one bit, and I start munching. Some women stop eating when they are upset, but unfortunately, I find solace in food, lots of food. It buoys my spirits to the extent I should really join Food-orgasm-Anonymous. Unfortunately, after searching for it on Google, I found that such a group doesn't exist. Perhaps there is a niche in the market? I muse. But before I could even pour myself another drink and make plans to devise a new organization Paul interrupts me. "Silvia?"

I look up. "Yes?" I swear his face was as taught as an archer's bow.

"Will I like him"? He was tenacious, like a dog with a bone, and I guess he deserved an answer. "Well, if you happened to be a woman and he has just serviced you with his tongue and hands, then the answer is definitely a YES!"

"I guess you're being sarcastic,"

"Hell yes, of course I am," I retort and have the pleasure of seeing his eyebrows shoot up. An uncomfortable silence engulfs us, and awkwardly he says. "If you have no further use of me tonight, I will retire." He turns on his heels and disappears before I can react. Which rather proves my point that I now have annihilated two men. I switch the TV on and become almost physically sick when I watch a romantic movie. What a load of bull.

The Pewter Pot

The week slowly passed, except for Luis's brief text messages to confirm our arrangement.

"Hi," he greeted me jovially when he picked me up on Friday night, briefly kissing my cheek. "Is everything all right?"

"Fine," I lied. "It's my greatest joy in life to sit by the telephone all week waiting for suitors to call." The sarcasm escapes him because he answers. "Great!" while steering me towards a silver Mercedes. I perk up considerably when I get in and sniff the leather seats. It is a powerful aphrodisiac, and it never fails to arouse me. I could so quickly get used to this. I have heard of but never visited Luis choice of the secluded restaurant. Mainly it is because it's out of my price range. It's called The Pewter Pot.

"May I invite you to a mediaeval feast served by handsome waiters and buxom maidens in this tavern? Be prepared for a treat. In the old days' Kings used to dine here. I have been told," Luis boomed before entering,

I giggle at the use of the old-fashioned phrase buxom maidens and unsuccessfully try peeping through the windows, but they are heavily stained, whether on purpose or by natural cause, I do not know. But if they had, it would add some extra flavor to the authenticity of the place, and I chuckle. When we step into the dimly lit interior of the tavern, we indeed step back in time. The haunting mystical sound of a medieval ballad playing over invisible loudspeakers, accompanied by a spiritual lute, welcomes us. The song sings of heartache, loss and bygone wars, and I listen spellbound to the strangely captivating music. Closing my eyes, I travel back to a time of anguish and misery.

"Silvia? Please come." Luis interrupted. "Our table is ready."

Coming out of my almost dreamlike state, I look around the room and see several stained scrolls near the entrance that detail the tavern's history, roles. Swords and daggers adorn the walls, which are tinted in a burgundy color and support various mounted deer heads with spectacular antlers and stuffed small animals. They look authentic, and when I walk closer, their sad eyes bore in me, and I feel sorry for them. I hastily turn around and follow Luis to our table.

We pass a grand fireplace made of stones that takes up a large portion of the wall. It is big enough to hold a small army. In it, above a flickering log pile, sits a rotisserie holding a pierced suckling pig with its skin bubbling and crackling in the heat. It's turned every few minutes to give the pig's skin an even golden-brown color. It is stuffed with roasted pine nuts and sugar and gives off a delightful aroma that makes my mouth water. And I vow I won't leave this place until I have tasted the pork. My eyes travel further. On the ceiling hung crystal chandeliers that somehow are a crossover in design between the medieval and the eighteenth century. Placed along the wall are pillars that have flowerpots containing white hydrangeas and green vines. The artistry with which the designers combined modern styles with the mediaeval was genuinely impressive. We walked toward the crackling fire. The mantelpiece was decked out by a cascading curtain of green ivy, dried flowers, and carved candlesticks held large candles. I put my hands forward to soak up the cheerful welcome warmth until Luis puts his hand on the small of my back and steers me away. Feeling slightly miffed, I follow him to the table and observe that the tablecloths match the color of the walls, and intricate hand-carved candle holders are lit with tall unusual black candles, ensuring an intimate experience. Exquisite silverware was placed next to the plates. Wine and water glasses had been replaced by tankards of ale filled by the aforementioned buxom maidens.

Crisp linen salmon-colored napkins are folded into the shape of an elegant swan, and small decorative dishes hold bread and butter. Ceramic pots hold a delightful mixture of yet another bunch of wildflowers atop a rustic burlap runner that matched the medieval decor.

As soon as we sit down, a posh waiter wearing a crisp starched shirt, a bow tie and white gloves presents us with a menu. Discretely, he hands one to each of us and murmurs. "At your convenience, madam, sir." With a nod of his head, he silently retreated.

I open the menu, and inside, I read that the food is traditionally medieval and based on seasonal offerings and the chef's creativity. Judging by what I have seen so far, I have no doubt the ambience of the tavern will stretch to the food. On the next page, there is an apologetic note that although forks weren't invented in medieval times and people ate with their hands, the In-keepers have made concessions to the modern world and provide cutlery. However, the managers held fast to the etiquette of the time; therefore, cell phones were forbidden. Guests are requested to follow all rules, lined out in a second paragraph.

Dear customers. No blowing in one's soup, in case you have foul breath. No nose picking, spitting or hair scratching either because dislodged lice may land in one's soup. Please don't wipe your hands on the tablecloth, as we provide napkins. No licking of plates, burping or farting. And, of course, it's strictly forbidden to draw arms at the table.

I laugh. That's funny.

"What's so funny, my dear?"

"Have you read the flap inside the menu? About medieval etiquette? It's hysterical, but I guess in that era, these things were normal."

He nods. "Yes, they have a sense of humor here. Now I understand you want the pig?" He successfully distracts me.

"Yes, it smells delicious!" I dared not use the word orgasmic again since the use of that word was so disagreeable to Luis last time, and I had no desire to be the cause of another tantrum. And wonder why I always bend backwards to please a man, given that I pride myself on being independent and modern. Sighing, I take out my phone to Google a suitable synonym, for doormat, but before I can, a waiter approaches me, apologizes, and informs me in a calm voice that cell phones weren't invented in the Middle Ages and have I read the note in the menu? Would I be so kind as to put mine away? My cheeks flush, and hastily I drop it back into my purse. Did I imagine it, or did Luis give me a disapproving look? But he doesn't pursue it and, drawing on his previous experience in the restaurant, suggests. "Let's start with the soup. It is fresh and delicious."

"That sounds wonderful," I answered and noticed that my residual ill feelings towards Luis had somehow evaporated; no doubt it had something to do with the opulent atmosphere and how he treated me like royalty.

Earlier, when I opened the menu, I noticed something different when leafing through, but I couldn't immediately put my finger on it. Then I finally figured out why it looked strange – it had no prices. I wonder if I should send a text message to Jane and ask her about it? Little chance of that, seeing as the no-phone rule was strictly enforced.

We had finished the soup, and the main course was yet to arrive, so I excused myself to Luis and snuck off to the ladies. I swear the waiter is watching me like a hawk, and as soon as I enter the bathroom, I take out my phone and look over my shoulder, half afraid he has followed me.

'Jane, I texted, 'There are no prices on my menu. Why not?'

The reply was almost instant, *'Jeez, you are so naive. It's because they are astronomical. And in posh restaurants, they are old-fashioned and expect the man to pay.'*

My feminist side felt slightly insulted, but I liked being treated like a princess, even though that would make me a hypocrite, and the thought inspired a chuckle. I put the phone away and walked back to the table with a hint of a smile still on my face. As soon as I sit down for the second time this evening, Luis inquires. "What's so funny, my dear?"

I had to think fast, as I didn't want to tell him the real reason I went to the ladies.

"I thought that my first car probably cost less than this dinner!"

"Don't worry about it, my dear," he said patronizingly. "Drink your wine. It is delicious."

I take a sip, and it is as he said. And I quip," Carpe Vinum, I love this wine. It's even good enough for cooking with."

He turned towards me, shocked at my frivolous response, and retorted. "I don't care for the tone of your voice." Later I will learn that's one of his standard replies when offended. Slightly taken aback, I say feebly, "Well, you know me, I always have to joke." Thankfully we are spared a further calamity because the main course arrives. The aroma of the sizzling pork wafts up from the cast-iron plate on a wooden slab as it is wheeled in and sliced at the table. Gingerly the waiter places the hot plate in front of me and whispers.

"Please be careful, ma'am, it is hot." I throw him a grateful look and eye the juicy pork, which is still bubbling. The skin is thin, translucent and crispy.

The aroma is incredible, and I can't wait to start. It is basted and served with a rich honey sauce, salty and sweet, and the meat is very tender. It was the pig-I never-had-and-never-knew-would-be-so good! And I feel like I am in a gourmet paradise.

I had requested the pork to be drenched in garlic and was pleased to see they had not been stingy with it. Luis had ordered butter-fried garlic prawns. Thank God our tastes in food were compatible because garlic can be a dealbreaker on any date. The sauce was flavored with pepper, salt, honey and vinegar, dried grapes and fresh parsley and was delicious. I tore off a piece of bread and mopped up the sauce, reveling in the taste. I closed my eyes, it was so fucking good, and I vowed from now on, I should eat only roasted pork for the rest of my life. It was a feast for a King.

I looked up when a small bowl of vegetables containing carrots, turnips and parsley was set before us. And I swear I think that's how vegetables were supposed to taste hundreds of years ago. We eat silently, favoring the food. When we finally stuffed it, I pushed the plate away and spoke.

"I will never eat again. I am so full now!" Luis laughed and beckoned the waiter. "Do you care for some dessert? It's a honey-flavored almond rice pudding. "Would you care for some? We added some extra cinnamon," the waiter asked.

It sounds delicious, and I nod. "Oh yes, please."

"I like my women to have a good appetite," Luis beamed, sending alarm signals, *my women*? Is he a perpetual serial dater, I wonder? A Player? Well, as it turned out to be, he indeed was. If you be so kind as to bear with me, you'll find out soon enough.

After the meal, Luis produces a platinum credit card and inserts a hefty tip. He turns to me and says, "let's go, dear. The evening is just starting." He drives us back to my house, turns on some romantic love songs on his phone, asks me where the candles are, and lights them, setting a delightful atmosphere. He takes me in his arms and starts kissing me. For an old man, he had an incredible sex drive, and let's face it, just like last time we had sex, every stroke, every touch was for my pleasure. And based on my earlier assumption, I suspected he had been practicing his moves for a long-time pity it was to end soon.

A Convicted Criminal

I woke up, stretched lazily and looked at the man beside me who was still sleeping. He must have felt me observing him because he opened his eyes, entwined his fingers into mine, and said. "Hi baby, that was a great evening. What's the time?" He turns around and grabs his phone from the nightstand. "Holy shit," it's already nine; I have to get going!" he boomed. He removes the covers in one sweep, jumps out of bed, grabs his clothes, and hastily puts them on before I can even admire his bronzed body.

"You have to go already?" I asked feeling out of sorts. "I thought

we would have breakfast together or a coffee." He shook his head.

"No, I am already late, and I have to feed the dog first."

"Late for what?" I inquired. He doesn't answer and instead pockets his phone puts on his wristwatch, gives me a big kiss goodbye and makes a sharp exit. Before I can object or ask more questions. I shake my head and wonder why the hurry? Then a sneaky thought took hold of me. Does he have to go back to a wife or another partner? But how would he explain his absence for a night? And without a shower, he couldn't very well get close to a wife when the smell of sex was probably still hanging around him. I grab my phone intending to text him when I notice the time is five minutes past eight, not nine. And I text, "hey, are you OK? I looked at the time, and it is only eight o'clock." He replies almost instantly. "Yes, sorry I made a mistake; I'll call you later."

"Fine, not to worry," I texted him back. "I just wondered why you left as fast as a convicted criminal."

Silence. Then an ice-cold reply. "I don't care for your tone of voice," followed by yet another icy silence, as he hangs up the phone. Baffled by his response, I ring him back, and after a while, he answers and says. "Do I have to repeat myself. I don't care for your tone of voice."

Perplexed as I am, I realize the phrase's meaning could be unfamiliar to him (after all, he is Spanish, and English isn't his mother tongue). I tried explaining that it was meant to be funny, to get him to understand that the expression was intended for somebody who leaves in a hurry. I spend a good fifteen minutes trying to justify my flippancy, but he does not listen to one word. It's useless. When I finally give up, deflated, I stare in baffled silence at my iPhone when he disconnects. His stubbornness in refusing to hear me out seems an almost deliberate attempt to torpedo this whole relationship I thought we had going on. I feel resentful. What a jerk. Good thing this happens now before I make the mistake of falling in love with him. Then the thought occurs to me that perhaps I was right, he might actually be a convicted criminal. That thought cheers me up considerably, and I pick up the phone and fill Jane in. If I had hoped for some sympathy, I had deluded myself.

"*OK, look at it as your version of 50 Shades of Granny,*" Jane answered and laughed so hard I could almost hear her from across town. "*I hope you enjoyed your bit of fun,*" she added. "*Have you sent a warning letter to the old folks' home yet? Or better, write a Facebook blog. Your followers might get off on kinky geriatric sex. Even younger internet users may enjoy your adventures in senior sex land.'* I can hear her laugh so hard I know she is pissing herself. And I think vindictively I hope she is in a public place and leaves a puddle.

"Thanks a lot!" I growled. "Who needs enemies with friends like you," I retorted, only to hear her laugh again.

"I will design a special sympathy card warning about dating convicted criminals!" She giggled. "Lighten up, Silvia. You know you have a lousy track record with guys and remember if it's too good to be true... well, you know..." she trailed off. Groping for a reply, and feeling seriously pissed off, out of argument I snarl. "That's a fascinating debate, and we must do it again real soon."

"It's not the first time, nor will it be the last. And remember, if it doesn't pan out, you can start a new adventure and finally market your Granny Lube. What's the marketing slogan again? Without this edible lubrication, neither you nor your boyfriends will ever be very creative in bed again?!"

Jane refers to a homemade lubricant I concocted a few years back but never had the chance to market. I vaguely remember using water, coconut oil, aloe vera, corn starch, and other ingredients, like avocado oil. What was I thinking, hoping my next lover would be an avocado connoisseur? And would find every possible opportunity to eat me?

More likely the reality would be that he would snatch the jar and skip eating pussy altogether! I winced painfully. Up until Jane mentioned it just now, I forgot that I had spent days perfecting this lubricant. Before I know it, I head for the bathroom, looking for the jar. I find it, unscrew the lid and gasp when I see the once creamy substance has been replaced by a vile green substance that I certainly don't remember. When the stench reaches my nostrils, I throw the offending jar in one gigantic swoop out of the window and into the garden. Although I tried very hard, I couldn't recall the passion that drove me to make my own lube. Up until that time, I always had bought store lubricants with essential oils that, to my recollection, had made me feel like a true sex goddess. When I think how close I came to applying this now vile concoction to my private parts, despite wearing HRT patches which are a bit ridiculous at my age, sweat pours off my back.

Mark

Unable to sleep, I get up and head for the kitchen. I open the fridge and locate a packet of hamburgers. Wasting no time, I ripped off the plastic, grabbed a frying pan and some oil and threw in three hamburgers. A food orgy is what I need. As always, it surprises me how much I enjoy eating. I toss a liberal amount of mayonnaise and tomato ketchup on the hamburgers and wolf them down when they are fried. I slurp down half a bottle of orange juice, and finally, when I am full, I return the remaining burger to the fridge, lean back in my chair, pick up a book and start to read.

The book is about the spine-chilling tale of the two explorers that lived for two years in the remnants of what was once their ship. As they wander around in the bitter cold, I shiver in sympathy. When a bear attacks them, I am scared to death, and when they fall through the ice, I freeze. Enraptured by the story, I lose track of time reading through the night and only stop when

I finish the book. I have grown cold, and I decided I need a shower to warm myself up.

Afterwards, toweling myself dry, I catch sight of my face in the mirror, without makeup. I look closely at the fine lines along my mouth and forehead and make a mental note to inquire about Botox or fillers or a possible face-lift. I walk into my closet, grab a pair of pink pants and squeeze myself in. They are so tight that in most people's eyes they are probably not age appropriate. I select a matching pink sweater, apply makeup and make myself a cup of hot black coffee.

My day has started, and I weigh up my options. A few months ago, I hired myself as a consultant working from home, advising clients on how to streamline and improve their business. It helped me organize my hours. The company started slowly, but now, thanks to word-of-mouth advertising from grateful customers, it's starting to pay off. I decided I could spend some time at the mall and visit the local beauty shop and try out various beauty options which hopefully will increase my self-esteem. I pick up my car keys when I hear the ping of my phone. It's a message from Mark. For a moment, I frowned.

Who the hell is Mark? Then I remember he is the salesman from Robotics & Co, inquiring if he can stop by to pick up Paul for a possible reboot/rewiring.

"OK," I texted back. "I was planning a shopping trip, but hey, what are the odds of not coming out with a loaf of bread when I went in for one?" I sent him a laughing Smiley.

Ping, 😊, is my reward.

Punctually at 11 o'clock, the doorbell rings. I open the door, and look at the man standing before me, gasping in shock. It's Mark, Robo – my gallant rescuer airport Mark, the guy I met on my way to Singapore. Why hadn't I made the connection between airport Robo-Mark and Mark, the salesman from Robotics & Co? Beats me.

He looked just as I remembered him, somewhat weathered, with a wisp of gray along with his temples and, for some strange reason, I wanted to throw my arms around him, which I don't.

"Hello," he said softly, clearly remembering me too. "This is a surprise." He ogles my pink pants and continues. "You look good. Why didn't you call me. What happened? Let me guess; you didn't like my body odor? Or was it something simpler like losing my number?"

I blink and swallow hard, remembering that's precisely what had happened, and blush. I am way too old for blushing, and I make a mental note that from now one on I will wear a full-face covering. Unable to speak, I nod. When I finally find my voice, I croak. "No, when I arrived in Singapore, I wiped my face with the napkin on which you wrote the number; it was so terribly hot I never thought..." I trailed off.

He laughs. It's a pleasant sound that all of a sudden, I remember vividly. Shaking his head, he said gaily.

"Ah, it was over before it began. And it was such a special moment. At least I am having a second chance with you," he paused. "If I am fortunate, I may even see the notorious Bridget Jones pants," and he winks. It's so unexpected I grin.

"That depends. Are you a pilot or an astronaut? Because my mother always told me not to drop my panties in front of either of them."

"My father wanted me to be a shoe salesman, but they gave me the boot, pun intended, and the rest is history," he quipped back, rolling his eyes, and I laughed.

"Well, I believe that you can rule the world if you wear the right footwear." I, in turn, quoted Bette Midler.

He eyes me with amusement and downright admiration. "Well, if the shoe fits, and all that...you know I really like you; now that I have seen that you have no problem waiting for the other shoe to drop. Would it be presumptuous of me to think that you could easily fill my girlfriend's shoes? Think about it; you arrive just when I came to terms with being single for the rest of my life? What are the odds?" He joked, but when we looked at each other for a bit longer than was called for, I saw a hint of seriousness.

His features are relaxed, and with difficulty, I tear my gaze away and notice that I couldn't stop smiling. I am amazed at how well we seemed to be getting on.

"Let's see if I can find Paul," I said and turned around. "Please follow me!" We find Paul in the living room dusting my knick-knacks. He looks up from his task when we enter, and as he sees Mark, he politely greets him.

Realizing they would both leave, and I may never see either of them again I say. "Can you get us some coffee, Paul?" I know I am putting off the inevitable. Mark must have picked up on what I was thinking because he said it somewhat tentatively. "I'd like to take you out for a coffee or a meal if that's OK with you I will call you." Beaming from ear to ear I reply. "Yes, I would like that very much! You have my number."

After the coffee, Mark stops at the door, winks, and says. "That was a lovely start to the day meeting you again. I'll let you know about lunch and send you some papers to sign. Oops, sorry, Paul."

Before I can reply, they both depart. I slowly close the door and step back into the living room. The clock strikes twelve. The pure sound is oddly soothing, and a bolt of optimism shoots through me. My doubts and fears about whether I am still attractive have somehow melted away. Although having a date with Mark makes me realize, I have to review my wardrobe with a critical eye. At least this time I have an excuse to buy something new. Shoes? A dress? Or a pair of pants? Hmm, perhaps I can pick up a few good bargains. I grab my bag and drive to town, and just when I am about to park the car, I hear my phone pinging. Despite my no-phone-in-the-car rule, I take it out and look at the message. It's from Mark.

'Lunch tomorrow. I will pick you up at one.' I sent a smiley face back, and almost lightheaded with joy at the unexpected turn of the day's events, I parked and stepped through the automatic sliding doors of the mall. It's full of sophisticated shoppers that have flocked to the store because there is a sale on.

Excited, I look around the bustling mall that is overflowing with shops. It's posh, modern and glitzy and is renowned for its grandeur and vast range of exclusive goods. My eyes are drawn to a marvelous cascading waterfall placed in the middle of the mall that, however often I have seen it, still takes my breath away. On both sides are classic stylish boutiques, exclusive restaurants that serve superb food and wines, and even an art gallery.

The top floor houses an entertainment center with several top-notch cinemas, a bowling alley and a gaming venue. The mall owners who are reportedly wealthy Arabs have recreated an Asian floating market in the basement, with authentic cuisine to die for. The wafting aroma of the Asian food in the air is tantalizing, and I vow to come back later for lunch.

Passing the makeup and perfume booths on the ground floor, I purposefully maintain a good pace as I don't want to be distracted, and perfume isn't on my list. I head for the escalator, and go straight to the clothes section, trying on clothes I probably won't buy. When I stepped off the escalator, I walked straight past the sign petite knowing however lovely the clothes were, there was no way they would ever fit. Not to be deterred I intend to take full advantage of the huge bargains I see left, right and center. Picking up several garments I head to the fitting rooms. After trying on clothes, that on second thought don't seem suitable for a date with Mark. I sigh, and hand the garments back to the bored dressing room attendant with an apologetic smile. And continue my search through the bargain section for the eye-catching, stunning garment I have in mind. Not finding any I head for the designer section, hoping I can find something on sale that's in my price range. After searching through row after row, I suddenly spotted a beautiful black skin-tight skirt. What girl could resist such an item, right? I glanced at the price tag and realized it was not on sale. I pull a face, and with difficulty, tear my eyes away and stroll past the enticing skirt. Then I spotted a middle-aged woman who had snapped up a few bargains and now seemed to be competing with another shopper for custody over a lovely purple cashmere sweater. A thin lady of similar age shouts bitingly. "Let go, you cow. You don't need this piece. Dress your age."

This was turning fast into a must-watch event and I, together with a few spectators, gathered around in amusement. Both ladies tugged and pulled, and I winced when I heard a ripping sound. The lovely piece is being torn to pieces right in front of my eyes. The aggrieved ladies drop the now ruined garment and flee the crime scene together as if they had planned it all along. I suppress a giggle and forget them immediately when I see a tight elegant black dress. With a rush of excitement, I grab the hanger. This one has my name on it. I look at the price tag and see the green discount dot in the corner. 50% off. I smile and head for the dressing room. The bored attendant had been replaced by a more cheerful lady who pointed me to a vacant dressing room.

Hastily I strip and pull the stretchy fabric over my head and shoulders and look in the mirror. I'm glad I had the foresight to wear Bridget Jones pants that are so good at hiding little bulges. It looks good from the waist down, but the top part of me has somehow changed me into a sausage, a rather unappealing one. My breasts are squeezed flat, held hostage by the dress. I pull and tug, but the dress doesn't budge.

Sighing again, I try wriggling out of the dress, but that's not as easy as it seems. I pull, squirm, jerk and pull some more, anxious to take the dress off, but it's impossible. I dare not pull too hard for fear of ripping the delicate fabric. In despair, my eyes dart up and down. What now? Shall I call the attendant? But I feel too embarrassed to do that. This is fast, resembling the hot tub hostage experience of the cruise I took.

Surely not!

After one last desperate pull I gave it one more try and finally slid the dress over my head. Breathing a sigh of relief, I put it back on the hanger and headed out of the fitting room, pulling a face at the attendant as I handed her the dress.

"To tight." And I know exactly what she thinks when her eyes slide down my pink pants.

Bitch!

I wander through the department still relentlessly pursuing my goal, although I am feeling a bit deflated. And just as I am about to give up, I see a gorgeous white dress which would be totally unsuitable for a winter date. Excited, I approach the mannequin that wears it. The cut is exquisite, and the closer I come, the more I like it. I touch the soft knitted material and decide it's perfect. Perhaps they have another one hanging in one of the rows. Not seeing any, I look for a store attendant as somebody has to take the dress off the mannequin. Of course there is nobody in sight, and I head for the cashier, explaining I want to try on a dress that is presently adorning a mannequin. Shaking her head, she informs me that the staff responsible for dressing the mannequins aren't available and no, she can't remove it herself.

My spirits plunged. I sigh and babble something about a hot date and that I simply have to try it on! Although however sympathetic she is, she explains once more why it can't be removed from the mannequin. In disbelief, I take a deep breath, and just as I am preparing myself for some severe groveling and pleading, she excuses herself and walks away.

"Damn you," I muttered under my breath as I was left standing. Suddenly, trying on this dress has become the most important thing in my life, and I weigh up my options. Then, it comes to me in a flash. I will remove the dress myself since the cashier is far away and no shop attendant is in sight; it should be a piece of cake. Glad that I have a plan, I walk towards the mannequin, and around, to find a zip. Unzipping takes only a moment. Then, I realize that in order to take off the dress I have to remove her arms first. I grab an arm and pull, but it refuses to budge. I pause for a moment as I obviously haven't thought this through. There must be a trick to dislodging it.

I take my phone out and type in: *remove mannequin's arms* and a YouTube video pops up explaining the procedure. Hell, it's easy when you know how, right? I thank Google for being such a helpful little bugger, thinking I bet I could find out how to make an atomic bomb, too, just by searching. Giggling, I grab the arm, tug and turn, and voila, I have it in my hand. Great. I do the same with arm number two, and just as I am about to slide the dress off, somebody taps on my shoulder. I turn around, expecting to see a sympathetic female shopper but, to my dismay, I see the stern look of a uniformed security guard, who opens his mouth and barks. "What do you think you are doing, ma'am? Customers aren't allowed to remove garments from mannequins. Please be so kind as to hand me the arm," and he holds out his hand.

What now? Again, I weigh up my options. Grovel? Beg? Burst out in tears? Tapping my foot on the floor, I opt for the latter. I put on my saddest face and let a tear trickle down. "Oh please, sir, you don't understand. I simply must have this dress. There is only this one you see, and I need it to win my husband back. He ran off with his secretary, who is half his age." And for good measure, I suppressed a sob.

Immediately, he sees through my theatrical performance and repeats. "The arm please, ma'am." I realize that the game is over and silently hand it over. The guard grabs a phone out of his pocket, dials a number and gives the receiving party at the other end a number. "Wait here, ma'am, somebody is coming right over." We wait in silence, and I wonder what kind of trouble I am in. The stealing-arm-trouble or the removing dress-trouble? And what the penalty is, such an affront.

After a few minutes, a young girl walks toward us, introduces herself and asks, "Why did you take the arms off the doll, ma'am?"

I realize this might be the last chance for a sympathetic ear, and I quickly repeat the unfaithful husband story.

"I am very sorry to hear this, ma'am. I had a similar experience recently. My boyfriend ran off with my best friend and..." Here she trails off and seems to come to a decision. She steps forwards and removes the dress from the mannequin. "Here, ma'am, please try it on. I want to know how it looks on you! You need some help to beat a twenty-five-year-old bitch."

I throw her a thankful look, take the dress from her, and for the third time walk to the dressing room. Where I slide effortlessly into the dress. It fits like a glove, and unlike the previous one doesn't transform me into a sausage. I step outside and show myself to the girl who has been waiting. "Are you going to buy it, ma'am?" She asked, agreeing wholeheartedly that it looks great on me. "If he doesn't... let him go to other woman, he is a fool, and you are better off without him!"

Agreeing with her, almost believing in an unfaithful husband, I thank her profusely, and together we walk to the cashier where I pay.

"I hope things work out for you, ma'am," she said. She is such a lovely, friendly young woman that I almost spill the real story but stop myself just in time. Instead, I thank her again and leave the store.

Downward Facing Dog

When I came home from my shopping trip and checked my phone, I saw a message from Mark, unfortunately canceling our lunch, but he will call me the next day or so for dinner.

The next few days, I was a nervous bundle waiting for him to call. If my previous experience with dating has taught me anything, it is that dinner eventually leads to the bedroom with high expectations of a sensuous night. And then the inevitable breakup. But this time, after remembering the last disastrous experience, I wondered if that had been another wrong life choice. Perhaps I should not put all my eggs in one basket this time and see where this would lead. Hmm, should I consult Jane, my ever-reliable confidante? I pick up the phone, take a deep breath, a long swig of wine, and explain the situation after she answers.

"Why don't you do something different for a first date?" she suggested. "Dinner is always the same. It's food and wine... lots of wine, and you know what happens when you drink wine, right?"

"Err, well yes, that can be a problem," I admitted, stalling for a time. "What do you have in mind?"

"*Yoga!*" Jane stated firmly.

"Yoga?"

"*Yes, there is a new Yoga retreat close by. Why don't you meet Mark there? You could get to know him before committing to a *real* date. You may not botch things up as you have in the past,*" she argued.

Although she had a good point, I growled. I would never allow her to think she was right. Should I give it a try? Yoga had always seemed a rather tiresome and useless exercise to me. But as I am in the habit of making unfounded judgments, I decided to find out more. After some extensive Googling, I learned that, among other things, Yoga would enable me to touch my toes, something I always wanted to do. Perhaps I should infuse Yoga into my daily routine. It will supposedly give me spiritual guidance and calmness while managing my mental and emotional health. They made it sound like a walk in the park, something I have to try.

The Yoga classes were held nearby in a Zen Buddhist temple, and I decided to call them for an appointment. I had always considered myself energetic, healthy and sportive, so I signed up for the more challenging classes, planning to emerge as a whole new physical and mental being. Pleased that I had taken matters into my own hands for once, I waited for Marks's call the next day. I outline the plan, and although he seems slightly taken aback, he agrees to meet me in front of the Yoga building. I quickly gave him the address and time to meet and sign off.

Despite the light drizzly rain, the next day, I walked briskly to the Yoga retreat with a spring in my step in my pristine new white dress. Happy I would soon meet Mark again. Halfway there, however, the wind starts howling, and trees begin to rustle. I glance up. The sky has turned an ominous gray-black color, and a bolt of lightning tears through the clouds. What should have been a leisurely walk has now turned into a desperate dash for the Yoga building, which happens to be a long distance.

There is nowhere to shelter from the upcoming heavy rain, and I start running. Urged on by another startling bolt of lightning right overhead, making me almost jump out of my skin. And I wonder whether it is even safe to go on. Then the drizzle of rain changes into a downright torrent, and the matter decides for itself as I am not wearing a raincoat. In a minute, I am drenched. Scared of the relentless lightning, I keep running towards the building and sigh in relief when I finally reach the entrance. Under the covering of the overhanging awning, as I zealously shake off the drops that cling to my face and hair, I hear the sound of a car and lookup. An old rattling Volkswagen pulls up, and Mark gets out, running towards me. His face is crinkled with amusement when he takes in my appearance.

"You look like a drowned cat; why didn't you hail a cab?"

In my wet and miserable state, with my hair all plastered over my face, I fail to see the funny side of his joke and growl. In dismay, I look at my new dress; it's ruined. Covered in brown mud stains that I fear will never come out. Grinning, he puts his hand in his pocket and produces a neatly folded handkerchief. His mouth twitches. "Here, dry your face. It is clean!"

I do as told, and he knocks on the door. A Buddhist monk opens, greeting us with his hands folded devoutly in front of his chest and a slight nod of the head.

"Namaste."

Which sounded mysterious and exciting. Unsure what our response should be, we both clumsily copied him. Did I imagine it, or did he give us a quizzical look? I didn't dwell on it for too long as he turned around, grabbed two packets from a nearby shelf, handed them over, whispering. "Please wear this. Leave your underwear on and come out when ready; I will show you to the classroom. You will also find your yoga mats inside." He points to the changing rooms.

In the cubicle, I open the packet. It contains white pajamas that are wonderfully soft to the touch, and I vow to nick them after the session thinking they would make a great sleeping garment. I changed into the pajamas, took a step forward and almost tripped

"Damn!" I shouted, steadying myself against the door, and looking down at the offending leg pants, which were way too long. I pull them up, but the length doesn't change as expected. I should ask for a smaller size -these are a danger to my health. Holding on to the waistband of the pajamas, I hop forward and see the same monk who had greeted us earlier, holding a finger to his mouth and pointing to a sign on the wall that reads *SILENCE*. He whispers. "Excuse me, madam, talking isn't allowed as it will distract us from achieving peace and tranquility of mind."

I looked at Mark, who had also surfaced, and mouthed. "Is he serious?"

Smiling, he whispered back. "I am afraid so!"

Bloody hell, this isn't turning out as I thought it would. Talk about a rocky start! Relentless rain, then the tripping, and now silence? What have I gotten myself into? Surely this can't get any worse. The place is quickly losing its appeal. I glance again at Mark, who seems to know what I am thinking. Because he shrugs and mouths something like "wasn't this your idea?"

I had no time to dwell on it as the monk gestured for us to follow him to the classroom, where we were greeted by the yoga master with a smile and a hand gesture as to where to put our mats. A video playing on the wall outlines the procedure. First, we start with ten minutes of meditation. Which doesn't sound too hard. Then followed by some warming-up yoga positions.

We take our places on the uncomfortable mats, and, feeling positive energy, I emulate the Lotus position, folding my legs as instructed and resting my hands with open palms on my legs. See? I thought jubilantly, that wasn't so hard! I closed my eyes firmly and immediately realized how deafening silence could be. The unnerving, almost deathly stillness disturbs me more than I admit. Although I knew that the philosophy of Yoga was to connect your mind, body and spirit through meditation, the silence overwhelmed me, achieving quite the opposite effect. My nerves were screaming.

And what was that? Were we supposed to be hearing a thumping sound? Just as I was about to go into a full-fledged panic attack, I realized it was the steady thump of my heart. Relieved, I could barely suppress a giggle. 'Silly cow,' I muttered under my breath.

Fortunately, the meditation stopped after about ten minutes, and the warm-up, consisting of simple poses, started. Although I was able to copy them with some difficulty, I couldn't work out why my legs wouldn't stop trembling after a few poses. The significance of the word poses slowly filtered through, and I knew I had taken on more than I had bargained for as the Yoga-master took us through the *Camel Pose, Child's Pose, Cobra Pose, Corpse Pose, the Extended Triangle Pose, and Half Moon Pose.* And I broke out in a sweat. I will spare you the rest, for I knew with crystal clarity I had to leave NOW. I raised my arm and croaked when I had the teacher's attention.

"Can I be excused? I am afraid I have forgotten an urgent appointment!" Alongside me, I heard Mark suppress a stifled laugh.

The Yogi's only response was to point to the *SILENCE* sign. Need I say the torture continued? He took us through every conceivable position until all my body parts seemed entangled, like a nightmarish game of bloody Twister. This was not what I had signed up for! Why? Oh, what had I been thinking? All my instincts screamed go!

After that, everything became a blur. My whole body was screaming in agony, and I looked sideways at Mark, rubbing his calf, looking shell-shocked. Weakly I smiled at him, a smile which he returned equally weakly. Then unexpectedly, he pointed to the door and mouthed what seemed like: 'Let's go!' confirming that he wasn't enjoying this as much as I had anticipated. Perhaps I should have taken him to a funeral for a first date. Why didn't I think of that before? At worst, we would have been sad, but at least more comfortable.

But before I could react, the yoga master lowered himself until he was flat on his back, spread-eagled. He stretched out his arms, grabbed his feet, and held the position, making it somehow look easy. I copied him, vowing that this would be my last pose for the day. But for some weird reason, I couldn't spread my legs far enough and hold my feet simultaneously. Seeing my predicament, the master got up from his yoga mat and pointed to a sign on the wall that said: *'Happy Baby position'*. Something I couldn't whole heartily agree with as it felt more like an unhappy torture position.

Trying to achieve the near-impossible, my thigh muscles protested loudly, and I groaned. Observing my discomfort, the Yogi, as I will call him from now on, grabbed my feet, spreading my legs even wider until I feared he would rip me in half. Even in my wildest sex they had never stretched this far. Then, taking my arms, he forced me to hold my feet with both hands. I yelled in sheer agony as I heard the plop of some ligament tearing in my groin.

"What the fuck!" Was this supposed to happen? My yell of pain, needless to say, made no impression on Yogi because all he did was look at me disapprovingly and put a finger to his lips. Feeling sick from the pain, I eyed the other students. None of them showed any signs of discomfort. I admitted defeat, realizing nobody would come to my rescue. I look around to see the next and last slide, the *Downward Facing Dog position.*

Up to this moment, I had had my share of embarrassing moments in life, but they paled in comparison to what was going to happen. It was -*the mother of all humiliating experiences*-. Aware that I had been building up gasses during the lesson, I had somehow successfully suppressed them until this new Yoga position. However, the gas that I held in for so long could no longer be contained, and I accidentally let out a loud…, long fart. All the tranquility of the bliss-free *deeper inner world* I had hoped to achieve disappeared, with a swoosh of air accompanied by giggling and sniggering from the other students.

Mortified, my cheeks flushed with embarrassment, I sank down on the mat, bracing myself to run out of the room. I tried to, but that was thwarted by my inability to stand up. Weighing my options, I thought should I crawl out of the classroom? Oh boy, bloody hell! Why do I get myself into such pickles? I should not have listened to Jane. I should have just gone to dinner with Mark, and we would have drunk wine and screwed, and I would have spared myself the humiliation of the fart and the now imminent crawl.

No matter how hard I tried to get up, my torn ligament was not sending signals to my muscles, and I realized I was looking at an imminent visit to the ER.

"Please help. I can't stand up. Something is wrong!" I croaked. The yoga master walked toward me and must have seen something on my face. With a concerned look forgetting the *SILENCE sign*, he asks. "Can you get up? Do you need an ambulance?"

"Obviously, yes, I think I have torn something." I tried to sound casual, but somehow it came out as a whimper. Judging by the speed, he produced a cell phone from his pajama pocket and dialed the emergency number. I concluded people must regularly injure themselves during yoga classes.

In the meantime, albeit with difficulty, Mark managed to stand up, walk over and knelt beside me.

"It's going to be OK. I'll stay with you. I will change, get your things, and come back. Don't let them take you anywhere before I am back."

Fully clothed, he returned in less than five minutes, his arms laden with my stuff. Silently the yoga master handed him a plastic bag to put my clothes in. As we waited for the paramedics Mark stroked my hair, uttering sympathetic noises. After the ambulance crew hastily administered an injection that, in all fairness, was probably prompted by my swearing at them, things thankfully became a bit hazy. Had I not been in so much pain, I would have enjoyed the drama of driving in the ambulance with sirens blaring and lights flashing. But now, all I could think of was how long it would take before they knocked me out completely.

Hospital Gate

There are several advantages to arriving by ambulance at a hospital. First, they don't let you loiter in the waiting room, and second, if you have to be drugged to the eyeballs, there is no better place for it. They unload me, and an orderly wheels the gurney into a private room. I heave a sigh of relief, not realizing the room is only for changing, as all the cubicles with curtains for privacy are full. The nurse looked at Mark and asked "Are you the boyfriend or husband? If you are not, I can't let you stay due to privacy concerns."

Mark looked at her. His face crinkles with amusement as he answers. "Well, technically neither, but I hope to remedy that situation soon." He turns around. "I wait outside."

The nurse transferred me to a bed with the help of the orderly, handed me a white gown, and helped me change. Although the yoga pants were loose and oversized, she apologetically told me she had to cut them off, as it would be too painful to remove them the usual way. As I distantly saw the tattered pajama pants flutter to the floor and my underwear. "Are you sure you are old enough to see this?" I asked her and pointed to my pubis, which shows a wild jungle. You young girls all wax, I have been told. I tried it once, but if you ask me will you do it again? I say I rather walk under a bus!

She laughs. "Don't worry, mam, I have seen far, far worse, once I had a patient whose pubic hair grew halfway to her thighs, and as she laughed again at the memory, helped me into the short white gown tied in the back. After I was decent (a moot point), she wheeled me into the emergency room, where from my position propped up on pillows, I viewed a sea of misery. The place was filled at capacity, but the nurse, obviously used to this, positioned my bed expertly between two others in the middle of the room. On my right lay an old lady with thick-rimmed spectacles and neatly curled gray hair thrashing about as though in a terrible rage, audibly swearing. It was hard to understand what she was saying, but I could make out a few words. 'Bitch. She deserved it!'

It wasn't immediately apparent who the bitch was and what she deserved, or even why, until the policeman, holding a vigil at her bedside and whom I took to be her son, explained that she stabbed her neighbor for stealing a book and, in turn, was shoved down the stairs.

Looking at her now relaxed angelic face, I had difficulty imagining she could do such a thing. However, I'm aware that old ladies who claim to be sole owners of a car they're selling aren't entirely trustworthy, but this one took the term to a whole new level.

"She stabbed a neighbor over a book? Seriously?" I gulped, wondering if all my other fellow patients were also criminals.

The nurse must have noticed my discomfort and, unperturbed, said. "Don't worry, people say and do stupid things. But we even have a sign to try to remedy that situation, there!" and she pointed to a large sign that said.

WE ARE HERE FOR YOU!

Judging by the foul language I heard from the people around me, I could only conclude that most of them couldn't read or just didn't appreciate the care they were being given. I closed my eyes, trying to block out the disturbing impressions of the emergency ward. But no matter how hard I tried to eradicate the scene resembling Dante's Inferno, I failed.

Because even in my drugged state, I was aware that a guy on my other side had started yelling and cursing in pain, which led the room to instantly erupt with voices from fellow sufferers who showed no empathy whatsoever, reacting with a loud, "*shut the fuck up, asshole, we are all in pain!"* Our suffering patients took no heed of their reaction. If anything, he increased his ranting. This appealing human behavior hammered home how stupid I was to have gotten myself in this situation ending up in the ER.

It was a dumb... dumb...dumb idea of me to try my hand at Yoga. I could strangle Jane for even suggesting it. What was I thinking? To be fair, I needed to take my own responsibility. Why hadn't I left at the first sign when I knew I had bitten off more than I could chew? No! Idiot that I was, I had purposefully chosen to stay throughout all the poses, and where had it taken me? It had landed me into this hellhole, from which there was no hope of escape. Mark who had been allowed in after I changed must have noticed my shocked look because he gingerly stroked my face, soothing. "Don't you have private insurance so I can take you somewhere more comfortable?"

"No, I don't, but please get me out of this wretched place," I begged. "I don't need a doctor. Just take me home." Before Mark could act on my plea, the nurse came back with another nurse, unlocked the bed brakes, told Mark to stay put and wheeled me to the X-ray and MRI section. After about an hour, I was taken back to the emergency room. Mark had somehow managed to fetch me a coffee, and while we drank the lukewarm beverage together, we waited several hours before the doctor arrived. We talked a bit about nothing in particular, and glad he was by my side.

Now and then, we gazed at each other, and I found it difficult to process the aura of masculinity and power he emanated. So strong I could barely breathe. His attraction to me was compelling---was he the man I should pursue? What if it was one-sided? Inwardly I steeled myself for the inevitable blow that would come.

I bit my lip, trying to hide my reaction to him, so occupied that I forgot to play with my iPhone. Time passed slowly, but as we were very comfortable with each other, it didn't matter. A doctor with boyish features walked in after several hours, seemingly no older than sixteen, and I couldn't help but feel alarmed.

To ease my apprehension, I told him looked just like my third boyfriend when I was 20 years old and ad: "are you sure you know what you are doing? You just look like you are out of nappies." (Yes, dear reader, this shows you how antiquated I am).

He laughed and introduced himself. Ah, I may be young, but the advantages are that I am up-to-par with modern medicine and can make your scar look fashionable.

"Scar?" I shrieked. "What scar?"

"Let me explain, you have something called a Grade 3 sprain and a complete cruciate ligament hip tear when you did a yoga pose, and yes, it does require surgery! You have to be admitted, and in the morning, I have scheduled an early surgery for you. Given your condition, for now, all we can do is give you painkillers and icing to reduce the swelling. After the operation, you most probably need to stay in hospital for a few days. Oh, and one more thing, you'll need crutches. It might take you six weeks to two months to recover. And you can go home, but only if somebody is there to look after you!" As the gravity of my predicament hit me for the first time, I lifted my head and tried to sit up as fleeing at this moment seemed to be my best option. The piercing pain ran through my hip and leg, causing me to grasp Mark's hands so tightly that the tendons were clearly defined, and I started crying.

The doctor whispered something to the nurse, and she left the room only to come back with an IV bag, hooked me up and stuck a needle in my arm. Later Mark would tell me shortly after I started babbling incoherently about cruel Yogi masters, fairies/demons, Jane and other devils, and he felt it was time to leave.

He kisses me and whispers. "Rest. I'll be back tomorrow." He smiled at the nurse. "Please, look after her well, will you?"

Smiling back, she responds. "Don't worry, sir. Everything is being done to make her as comfortable as possible."

It was a long night but thank God throughout, they kept up a steady supply of drugs to ensure I was comfortable. The following day I was given consent papers for the surgery to sign and was told, 'no, you can't eat breakfast.' Which seemed a bit harsh for punishment, as I was hungry! But before I could complain, someone came in with a needle, injected me. "This will set you on your way to happiness"! He said.

His word was as good as gold, I felt a warm fuzzy feeling come over me, and I seemed to float above my bed with no care in the world. And just before I lost consciousness, I thought, 'I could sure get used to this feeling.' Several hours later, I woke up in an ocean of pain and groaned.

"Great, you are awake," said the nurse a little too cheerfully, adjusting something on the IV pole.

'Great? Wats so great about it?" I croaked. "Please, put me under again!"

Instead of answering, somebody wheeled me back to my room, and I slept off and for the rest of the day. When I woke up early evening, I saw Mark's face with his chiseled features and sharp cheekbones, looking at me concerned. His long-fingered hands holding mine. His thumb softly stroked the back of my hand.

"How are you feeling?" he asked.

"Water," I croaked with a sore throat. "Please, water!"

Mark reached over, grabbed a glass with a straw from the nightstand and held it to my lips, and I drank thirstily. Over the rim of the glass, I looked at him. He looked totally at ease with his deep tan and broad shoulders, emanating the aura of masculinity and power of a man who knows exactly who or what he is. And I felt as if I had known him for years. Nobody would ever say this was only the third time we had met.

Blinking my lip, something I do when uncertain, I feel the need to break the spell. Mark somehow has over me, and I joke. "Do you believe frogs can turn into Princes?"

A little taken aback by my silly question, Mark fought a grin and responded with a severe face. "You do know that not all frogs become Princes, right? Some don't want the hassle and prefer chocolate instead." The expression on his face was unfathomable.

"What about you? Do you prefer chocolate?"

"Ah! I think frogs can't live by chocolate alone," he quipped.

After studying his features, was he sending me a signal? Not coming to a conclusion, I forced myself to let it go, as it was more important to focus on my recovery. And as it was timed, the nurse came in, took my pulse and blood pressure. " You are doing great. Are you hungry? I will get you your dinner." She said.

She leaves only to come back a moment later with a food tray. She adjusted the bed and helped me sit up so I could eat. "I let you eat your dinner in peace," Marks got up from the chair and kissed me. "I'll see you tomorrow."

When he is gone, the nurse smiles at me. "You have a nice boyfriend, madam." For a moment, I have no idea to whom she is referring, then it draws on me, Mark. She thinks he is my boyfriend. I glance down fleetingly before laughing. "Oh no, he isn't my boyfriend. I have only met him three times. But he is charming, and who knows, right?"

After breakfast the next day, a nurse forced me out of bed, much to my chagrin. My protests that she was a cruel barbarian didn't make any difference as she babbled something incoherent that sounded like: you 'aren't a spring chicken, thrombosis, etc.' and told me the physical therapist was on his way, teaching me how to use crutches as I was necessary to take the weight off the hip.

The doctor came in shortly after that, checked me out, and told me I could go home the next day if I had someone to help me. They would book me into a rehab facility for a few weeks if not. "I'll see you shortly before you are discharged." On his way out, the door opened and revealed Mark.

"Oh, excuse me didn't know anybody was with you, Silvia. I'll wait outside."

"Are you Silvia's boyfriend, sir? If so, you may like to hear what I told her, that she can leave the hospital tomorrow, but she needs some home care. If not, we will book her into a rehab facility for a few weeks."

Mark turns his attention to the doctor and holds out his hand. "Hi, Mark Scott I am not Silvia's husband nor her boyfriend, but I will be soon, and I will look after her as long as she needs to. I'll pick her up in the morning."

He straightened up and took a step backwards. "Nice to meet you, sir," the doctor said.

"My name is Dr Nick Dale." He laughed. "She is a feisty one!" and laughed again.

My jaw dropped. How dare they talk about me or make decisions disgusting! It takes a moment to digest. "Hello," I said, trying to get their attention, don't ignore the granny! Both paid no attention to me. I try again. "Hello? Over here!! Hello??? Do you see this face? These lines? These are my what-the-fuck lines! You guys are mapping them out by complicating something simple, like asking what I want!" That got their attention. Both men turned as one, steeling themselves, and walked towards her. "Sorry sweety, you are right, but the doctor said you need help, why don't you come with me, it sure as hell beats staying in a recovering center."

"Let me think about it. I prefer to go home, but since that's not an option, perhaps Jane ..." and I trailed off. No bad idea. Jane is always out, going to clubs or looking after her grandkids. Besides, I am still angry with her for suggesting Yoga. No, Jane is definitely out! I decide.

"But how can I stay with you, Mark? We barely know each other."

"My sister and her baby live with me. She will be happy to take care of a friend of mine," Mark insisted. "I have a spare comfortable room on the ground floor overlooking the lake. You will love it, I promise. Please think about it, will you?" His pleading look was my downfall, and I caved. "Ok, it's settled, but I will move out the moment I feel better."

Mark turns to the doctor with a triumphant look. "I will look after her and pick her up in the morning."

Recovering

Unseeing, I stare outside. Several windows that run almost the length of the house facing the lake offer a great view. With its quiet water and gentle waves lapping along the shore, it is impossible not to be captivated by its serene beauty. Tall trees along the shore rustle in the wind, and the glass-like smoothness of the water gives an impression of stillness that is fast broken by an approaching boat. Squinting my eyes, I try to determine who is steering, but the sun's glare reflecting on the water is blinding, and I fail to do so. The boat passes and silence returns. One cannot be other than impressed by the beautiful view that should have had a calming influence on my mind but instead, the profound stillness evokes a deep sense of melancholy.

I had not seen much of Mark. The three of us had shared only a few dinners as Mark left punctually at 7 am each morning, and after dinner, knackered after using crutches the whole day, I couldn't wait to retire for the night. I recalled the day I had arrived at his home. When he picked me up from the hospital, it was a sunny yet cold day, and Mark wrapped me in several shawls. His thigh brushed against mine when he lifted me out of the wheelchair. His proximity made my senses whirl. He was close enough, so I could smell a hint of an expensive aftershave which combined with his masculine smell made it difficult for me to pull myself together. Without any apparent effort, his muscular frame ushered me into the car.

When we arrived, he walked to the passenger side of the car and helped me out. The ride had been short and uneventful but had still tired me out following my surgery. After I was shown the room that had been prepared for me, Mark noticed my exhaustion and asked Mathilde to bring me a tray of food. Thanking him with a weak smile, I could only nibble when it arrived, as I was too exhausted to eat. I undressed and got into bed where I fell into a deep sleep.

Over the last five weeks, I have grown accustomed to the view of the lake and the boats that come and go on the water. The boatmen and their families always wave to me as I watch them.

The crying of Mark's sister Mathilde's baby takes me out of my reverie. I get up from the settee which is placed in front of the window and walk to the cot. The baby stops crying as soon as she sees me and smiles. I had promised to babysit for an hour until Mathilde returned from shopping. Putting my crutches to the side, I pick the baby up, take a few unaided steps and sit down on a nearby chair. Earlier, Mathilde had prepared the baby's bottle. My hand reaches for it, and I place the teat into the baby's mouth, where she starts sucking hungrily. She is a lovely sweet-tempered little girl with a shocking mop of brown curly hair, and I love babysitting her. Mathilde had taken such good care of me during my rehabilitation that I took up every opportunity to repay her by babysitting.

Now five weeks later, I feel my healing is complete, and when she returns, I tell Mathilde that I am now ready to go back to my own house. She protests that I am not strong enough and can stay as long as I like, but I am determined to leave before Mark gets back. I had already packed the few things Jane had fetched from my house. When I had told her about my accident, aghast at my injury, she hadn't stopped apologizing for suggesting I join a yoga class. But after I assured her that it had been my fault, we settled into the same friendship routine as before the accident and had spent hours texting. I had arranged for her to pick me up at two in the afternoon, and she arrived promptly. I bid my farewell to Mathilde and the baby and asked her to convey my thanks to Mark. He was currently in Japan and had texted me a few times to enquire how I was doing. I sent him pictures and a video of the baby trying to crawl, along with some stories of what I had been doing.

In the meantime, I no longer needed the crutches as my doctor had given me a clean bill of health, after warning, chuckling. "Don't try yoga classes for a while."

"Don't worry, I think that yoga is more suitable for a concentration camp; from now I will dedicate my time to finding a cure for AIDS," I replied. Sharing a smile, he nodded. "Make an appointment with the nurse in about four weeks' time. I want to see you again. Goodbye, please be careful.

QT

Back home two weeks later, I once again looked outside at the bleak winter's day. Rain is slashing against the window, and I feel a burning need to see Mark for reasons I can't explain. After I left his home, I had only received a single message and the words. "I'll see you in a month. I have to go to Hong Kong!" That was seven weeks ago, and I wondered why I hadn't heard from him since. Had he airbrushed me out of his life? And why? I found it hard to contemplate. Wearily I shook my head and picked up a trashy magazine, aimlessly leafing through it only to put it down when the phone rang. I take the phone off the table and look at the caller's name. It's Mark!

"Hi," I answered, a bit breathless. "Glad to see you. Are you still alive?"

He laughs. "Did you miss me?"

"Sure, like a sore thumb." I replied, slightly peeved.

"I am sorry, I should have called you sooner, but I have been swamped with work. I'm glad to say I am back now. Are you free for dinner?"

I am inclined to say no, but the prospect of seeing him again makes me throw all caution to the wind, and I say. "Yes!"

"Great, I'll pick you up at seven; wear something pretty!"

Happy and excited, I walk into the kitchen and make a cup of tea. Looking dreamily out of the window, I see a little, wet puppy in my garden. The fence is broken, and it's easy for anybody or anything to walk in. I scan the street for his owner, but the dog is alone and soaking wet, and my heart melts. Not realizing my life would change forever, I walked out the door and called the dog. Not knowing his name, I try. "Come, doggy! Come!." He stops exploring and looks around, then with a wagging of his tail, he runs towards me. I pick him up and see that it's a boy.

"Here now, where is your mommy?" I inquired. It's silly, I know, he isn't going to answer me. I judge him to be about six weeks old, too young to leave its mother. Having never owned a puppy, I am at a loss as to what to do with him, but since he is scruffy and covered in mud, I decided to start him off with a bath.

I take him to the kitchen, put the plug in the sink, run him a warm soapy bath, and discover he is white. His soulful big brown eyes never waver when he looks at me, and he doesn't mind me washing him. I towel him dry and put him on the kitchen floor, where he promptly pees. Do I imagine it, or does he look guilty? I place a few newspapers in front of the door, pick him up and tell him.

"This is where you pee, OK?" His light bark makes me think he understands me but, as I discovered later, he didn't. House training him will be a work in progress for quite some time and stressful too. I Google what one needs to do to care for a new puppy and read that I need to train him properly. That will be a lengthy process so it will have to wait for now. Not the most brilliant move, as I will later regret putting it off.

I rummaged through my fridge, trying to find something edible for him to eat and found half a hamburger. I mash the diced meat, put it in a bowl and offer it to the doggy. He paddles closer, sniffs, and wolfs it down. I water down a bit of milk, and after licking the saucer dry, he waggles into the living room and starts chewing on an old slipper. I pick him up and put him on my lap, where he snuggles up and falls asleep, knowing I am a goner. After I left Mathilde's house, I had not realized until now how much I missed the baby, and I felt a void filled just by holding the puppy.

I pick up the telephone and make an appointment with a vet. I am lucky, he can see me right away, and I put QT, yes, I decided to name him QT, as he is the quietest, most lovely, sweet dog one can imagine, in a bag and take him there.

When I arrive, the vet tells me he is a Bichon Frise and will not grow significantly. He checks if he has a chip to locate the owner, but he hasn't.

"What do you want to do, ma'am?" He asked. "If you want to keep him, he needs to be vaccinated, chipped, and..." he looks at the bag in which I transported him. "A proper bag, a leash and a doggy bed, not to mention puppy food. Are you ready to take on such a responsibility?"

I look at QT, who looks back at me with his lovely brown eyes, enthusiastically wagging his tail as if to say something. "Yes, yes, please, mommy, adopt me..."

I nod. "Yes, if nobody claims him in the next few days, I will keep him!"

"Very well," answered the vet and continues his examination. "He is a healthy little fellow, and these breeds are the easiest to take care of. You are lucky. I will chip him and gives him his vaccinations."

QT takes it all in his stride, not even barking or growling.

On my way home I stop briefly at a pet store to buy him food, a bed, a leash, and some toys. Once back home, I installed his bed beside the sofa and sacrificed my old slippers. For the rest of the day, I played with him and walked him several times, and he kept me so busy that I almost forgot my date with Mark. If he hadn't sent me a text with an: 'I am on my way,' I would not have been ready. Hastily I put QT in his bed and ran upstairs to change, I had no time to shower or wax and out of breath, I answered the door when Mark rang the bell a few minutes later.

"Hi" I greeted him, eagerly grabbing his hand. "Look what I got!" And drag him into the living room. As Mark enters, QT sleepily opens his eyes, wags his tail, jumps out of his bed and licks Mark's outstretched hand.

"Hello, little fellow. Where do you come from?" I quickly explained the situation, and Mark looked at me. "You will make a great mommy. He is adorable." He picks him up and kisses his little face. "I made a reservation for seven o'clock. If we want them to hold the table, we should leave now." He looks at me. "Will he be OK till we come back?"

"Let me put his bed in the kitchen for now." I answered. "He may need to pee; I will put some fresh newspapers on the floor."

The restaurant Marks takes me to is on the top floor of a 66-story building and can only be reached by a sleek glass-encased elevator. I hold my breath as I watch the river Thames flow gently through the city from the vantage point of this high-tech ride, which also provides me with a dramatic view of the Tower of London.

When we enter the rotating restaurant, with its scarlet curtains, I see it is ornate with trendy zebra-covered furniture. We are greeted by a hostess, and after Mark gives his name, she walks us to our table. It is decorated with white linen tablecloths with burgundy under cloths that give the room a dramatic appearance. The candles have the same striking red color and contrast starkly with the white starched tablecloth on which the plates stand.

After Mark orders a bottle of red wine for us, we are handed a menu, and I choose a pasta dish with a Parmesan dressing and oven-roasted beets. Mark orders the Devon crab that comes on razor-thin cucumber slices with a hint of truffle oil.

Both dishes look delicious. At ease, we both taste from each other's plates. At the same time, our conversation is sprinkled with banter and laughter, and the evening flies by. We have the hot apple crumble with freshly whipped cream for dessert, which is to die for. Then the evening ends only too fast as Mark signals for the bill, and he drives me home.

Mark gets out, opens the car door, walks around, holds out his hand, and helps me out of the car. We walk to the front door, which I clumsily open.

Suddenly uncertain, I look at Mark. "Do you want to come in for a coffee or something...?" I trailed off. He doesn't immediately answer, but then instead of agreeing, he says. "Don't you need to check on QT? He is, after all, a puppy and has probably used your kitchen floor as a toilet."

"Shit." I had forgotten I had a new addition to the household! How could I have been so stupid? I turn around and walk to the kitchen. Standing on the threshold, we are greeted by an adorable ball of fluff wagging his tail to celebrate the fact that he has destroyed my once pristine kitchen.

I survey the scene of torn-up newspapers, puddles of pee, and, if that was not enough, a ripped garbage bag with its contents strewn out over the floor. In his defense, I must point out, his bed was pristine. I pick him up and gently scold him for what it is worth.

"Let me walk him, and you can tidy the kitchen". Marks said calmly. I nod. He picks up the leash and walks outside. "Give me a few minutes."

I grab a new garbage bag, toss all the rubbish in, mop the floor, put new newspapers in front of the door, and wait for Mark to return. When he does, he puts QT in his bed and tells him to stay put. We look at each other for a moment. "Do you want a coffee?" For some reason, my voice sounds husky.

He doesn't immediately answer. Uneasily he runs a hand through his hair. Edging closer, he bends his head and presses his lips against mine. For a few moments, the world stands still, then starts spinning. The kiss deepens, and I forget all my previous heartbreaks. Lips playing, tongues exploring. His arms are strong around my body, and a delicious giddy heat surges through my loins. In answer to his unspoken question, I press against him. I need to feel he is aroused, and I am not disappointed. The firm bulge assures me he wants me as much as I want him. Strong impulses surge through my body, and I moan. We don't move for a moment -all of our senses spinning out of control.

What sweet heaven was this? His hands stroked my back slowly, sensually. Then, both hands slid from my back to my waist, feeling touching. His hands slide up, cupping both my breasts. The bolt of pleasure shooting through me almost makes me swoon, losing the ability to stand. Searching, probing, penetrating each other's souls we breathe as one. The sensations are too intense, and I close my eyes again. His hands caress my breasts. Squeezing and fondling, a soft sound emanates from his lips when he finds my nipples hard as a rock. He circles and gently presses. A raw, primitive urge drives me deeper and deeper into the rising abyss of passion. My breathing goes slower. My heart is racing and almost stops altogether. I opened my eyes again, looking at him. Will this be my love that never dies? Deeply I inhaled his scent. Wanting nothing more than to be in his arms forever. The sensations are too intense, and I close my eyes again.

Almost mutually, we withdrew our lips ending the kiss. Shakily we look at each other. Words are no longer needed. Our smoldering eyes tell their own story. Mark removes his hands from my breast and steps back. Feeling the warmth of his hands disappearing, I feel robbed, denied and even rejected for a brief moment. I whisper uncertainly. " Where do we go from here? "Don't tell me I need to kiss another frog?" I waited, hardly breathing.

Mark must have seen something in my eyes because he took my hand. "That depends entirely on how handy you are at catching flies," he replied huskily.

I open my mouth and close it. "Time flies by fast enough. I don't see myself catching your dinner." My wit must have amused him because he roared with laughter.

"A well-balanced diet of flies is important. We have been around for 200 million years, that must tell you something,"

Marks responded. Cupping my face he continues. "Don't worry, we frogs are survivors."

My mouth twitches. "I wouldn't know the difference between flies and other bugs."

"It's easy if you don't let the flies take advantage of you."

"Are you telling me nothing bugs you when I feed you correctly?"

"Hm," that depends entirely on how well you cook! he grinned.

I look at him. "I guess condiments are overrated?"

He nods and laughs again. His eyes sparkle, the air is electric, and I want to ravish him.

"Well, I wouldn't go that far, but I tell you one thing, once you have tried frogs, there is no going back," he winked.

Trying to sound nonchalant I say. "I am confused about something. Does this mean when I say jump, you ask how high?"

His face drops and half-jokingly he responds. "No, that would be a mistake. But let me ask you something, do you have control issues?"

My smile disappears. Is he implying I could be dominating? God, I remember in the past, I was accused several times of just that. But let's not go there. Is he letting me know his boundaries?

Or jesting?! I dare not looking into his face. Does this convey something more serious? While I am still trying to work it out, he grabs my hand. "There is a proper way to catch and handle frogs. Perhaps you aren't aware of how fragile we are?"

I look down. What is he telling me? Before I can work it out, I am distracted by my phone. As my hand reaches my pocket, I pull the phone out and peer at it.

It's a message from Jane. No doubt she wants to know how the date went. What can I say when I don't even know? How can I explain it went from heavenly to nightmarish, or did it? Perhaps the change in tone was only in my imagination. After all, I have been known to overthink events. On the other hand, he may have genuine issues in his previous relationships. Brilliant. Just what I needed. Suspiciously, I ask. "Am I wrong, or do I detect some problems with former spouses and/or ex-girlfriends?"

Do I imagine it, or does his voice sound strained when he answers? "I don't want to discuss it right now."

God, he sounds just like Robo man. I stared at him for a moment, at a loss for words. My question has certainly raised some serious issues, and I say defiantly. "Are you dealing with personal stuff?"

He looked at me steadily. "Although dating frogs has many advantages, you can't control them. And not all women are that pliable." His eyes darken. "I find my way is often the best, although it can cause conflicts."

Pliable? He wants his woman to be pliable? He thinks he knows best? I gulp. Something has shifted, and not in a good way. I give him a fake smile and reply with a hint of sarcasm. "Hmm, I can see a few problems arising with that line of reasoning."

Mark raises his eyebrows. "Women have a way of controlling relationships. My ex was a perfect example of that. Frankly, I don't think I can deal with that again."

It's out in the open; I force myself not to overreact. I can't face the fact that we seem to have encountered our first problem. After an eternity, I say. "Just my luck encountering a frog with ownership issues."

My face must have given something away because he attempts to diffuse the brewing strife. "Sometimes a frog is just a frog."

"I thought I kissed one." I muttered. "But I don't think he turned into a prince. Perhaps it was a toad."

"Being a frog has its advantages," he said quietly. I can't think of an appropriate reply off the top of my head, so I grab my phone and Google 'magic frog.' To my dismay, I read a whole bunch of superstitious drivel, ranging from the toxic nature of frogs, to witchcraft to their supposed healing properties.

"What are you Googling?" Mark asked.

"Magic frogs," I mumbled. "I need to know if they bring luck."

"If you carry a frog in a pouch around your neck, it will prevent seizures." He said with a straight face. "Always handy at our age. So, you see, we do have our uses." "Plus," he pauses for a moment. "We don't need to rent costumes for a masquerade ball. Think how much money we save!"

God, I hope he isn't a cheapskate, I ruminate. I honestly can't deal with another one. But wait, he already bought me dinner, didn't he? Am I being too judgmental, assuming he is tight with money? I look at him. His gaze is steady, and his finger strokes my cheek and the outline of my lips, and I have trouble remembering my name. Then I come to my senses and snap. "I hope you aren't turning out to be a cheapskate or a smart-ass; I detest both."

He frowns, taking his time. "I never argue; I simply will explain why I am right." He answered in an unexpectedly forceful manner.

Stricken, I stare at him. Somehow, our earlier communication had decreased considerably in tone. Just when I thought it was going well. Can he see the anguish on my face? Oh God, I hope not. Do I have to start kissing more frigging frogs? I don't think I have the stamina for it. I drag my attention back and bristle. "Please don't tell me frogs come with manuals!"

He removes his hand from my face and folds his arms. "If you master frog handling, you will find we are mostly harmless but can sometimes irritate."

I glared at him. What is he telling me? We were about to fuck our brains out just a few moments ago, and now he's lecturing me on how to handle frogs? Confused, I chew my lip. This felt so right earlier! Fighting tears, I turn my head away. He mustn't see me like this. My jaw is trembling, and I randomly pick up a porcelain frog from the side table nearby, remembering it was given to me by my grandmother, a sagacious woman who told me: "It hurls and jumps, but is also slimy and slippery. And most of the time, when you kiss them, it's still a frog." Needless to say, I never took heed of the veiled warning. I fight an instinct to smash it on the floor but stop just in time. I would kill myself before I let him see how upset I am. I have to sort out my thoughts. Is this what I want? Being reduced to tears every time a guy makes a condescending, arrogant remark? I should have my head examined. I am way, way too old for this sort of shit I think grudgingly.

We look at each other silently. How did we go from allies to adversaries? The blossoming relationship I thought we were building has just unraveled with the speed of light. I stare at him. His face is stern, and because I don't want to give in to my sudden miserable feelings, I inquire in the sweetest voice I can muster. "Did I kiss a frog that is toxic?"

"When treated right, we are mostly harmless!" He countered.

"You mean I can't cook and serve your legs with cream sauce?"

My attempt at humor must have hit a sore spot because suddenly, he blazes. "What's wrong with you?"

I leave the question dangling. I know what's wrong. I have, as I usually read way too much into Mark's advances. Will I ever learn? I gave him a withering look intended to reduce him to ashes.

"You know, back in the old days, they used frogs for condoms."

"Money can buy you a frog but can't make him jump!"

It's clearly a stalemate. Brilliant. What happened to the amazing feelings that began this evening? Or our sparkly banter? The mood is clearly ruined. The knives are on the table. I am trying to pinpoint when or how the conversation changed. But I draw a blank. Perhaps I can defuse the tension by coming up with something silly.

"Listen," I say, clearing my throat. "Let's play a game. I start, and when I stop, you finish my sentence." Without waiting for him to agree, I continue. "Once upon a time, there was a bitchy Princess. Her favorite place was a pond near her father's castle. Every afternoon she sat down and washed her hands that were full of ashes from cleaning the hearth. She was always grumpy as she didn't sleep well. Every night, there was a darn pea under her mattress, and no matter how many times she took it away, it always found its way back." I stopped.

Mark picked up the story seamlessly. "Once when the princess was very tired, she fell asleep leaning against Jack's beanstalk, which grew close to the pond. Earlier she had tried climbing it, but with her glass slippers, she found it impossible and gave up. She didn't know how long she slept but was woken by voices."

"Sleepily she opened her eyes and saw Dopey and Bashful looking concerned at her. She explained there was no need for concern - it was just her lousy footwear which made her tired." Eventually I faced Mark, who looked somewhat uncertain. Nevertheless, he took a deep breath.

"Because she was getting older, she found her glass slippers didn't fit as well as they used to. Her feet had started to sag, A corn had reared its ugly head, and the callous on her feet was cracked making every step excruciating."

He stops, clearly running out of steam. My subterfuge to diffuse the tense atmosphere had worked, judging by the amused expected look on his face.

I take a deep breath and continue the story. "It is clear this was exacerbated by her ill-fitting glass slippers. It's a good thing the prince didn't come along. He would undoubtedly think twice if he saw her calloused old feet."

I started to enjoy this and mischievously against the rules I continued. "The princess took out her iPhone and looked at Little Red Riding Hood's message. You probably remember her; she is the one with that annoying, overbearing grandmother who was eaten. Sorry, I see you thinking, what is this about, shoes, Cinderella, wolves and Grannies? Actually, it's about nothing, but I like fairy tales, not shoes. Only Cinderella and the booted cat love footwear!" I paused. Mark gave me an approving look.

"The Princess kicked off her slippers carelessly, and one landed in the water. This didn't unduly worry her. She knew Kermit would retrieve it. After all, he was the one that gave her the slippers a few weeks ago and told her to attend the ball the prince threw last week." He stopped. Without missing a beat, I continued.

"Glass slippers? What are you thinking? Have you ever walked on them? There is nothing more excruciating than walking in glass slippers. And on top of it, dancing all night long? No wonder she left early. Her feet were killing her." Triumphantly I looked at Mark, who scrunched up his forehead, clearly thinking.

"The phone in her hand rang. It was her friend Belle from Beauty and the Beast. Inquiring how the ball went. Quickly the princess told her she left early due to a glass-slipper catastrophe. Belle, in her turn, told her she was silly for leaving early. A princess meets prince charming and then leaves at midnight! Do you really think she deserves a prince?" Mark left the question dangling. Damn, I have to think fast. Then it comes to me, and I cry out. "As it turns out, the princess was roaring drunk. Clearly, any self-destructive princess didn't deserve a prince.

"Unmistakably a brainless twat." Mark agreed, laughing. "Who can resist a horny Prince?" Did I imagine it, or had the air turned electric again? I grinned. My plot worked. We were back at our old easy footing of careless banter.

"Anyway, I digress." I smiled. "Most fairy tales aren't fairy tales at all, and the advertising boys have finally found out that

Sleeping Beauty prefers not to be woken by horny princes with leery grins on their faces."

Mark squeezed my hand. "Don't they? Have those ad boys fooled us all along?" I laughed at ease again, and he moved closer. Exhilarated because our careless banter is back. I look at his mouth and can't pull my eyes away. There was no denying the chemistry between us. I know he is my oasis in the dessert and parched. I run to him metaphorically as he is standing close to me. He, reaches over and takes me once more into his arms. His voice is low. Cupping my face in both hands, he draws me closer and whispers. "I want to kiss you again."

A shiver of delight runs through me as he ravishes my mouth, plunders, and explores, robbing me of my will. I press closer to him. My need is strong, my body throbs. His hand tugs at the zip of my dress, but not finding it easy to slide it down, he ends the kiss and murmurs. "There must be something remarkable under your clothes because the dress guards you better than Fort Knox."

I giggle. Obligingly, I turn my back towards Mark.

He brushes the blond hair away from the nape of my neck and unzips me, this time without any effort. I wriggle out of my dress, forgetting I wear the horrendous Bridget Jones control pants. "Shit, fuck." Mortified, I stutter something like, "I knew wearing these tummy-sucking-fucking pants was a mistake." I try pulling up the dress that is now in a bundle around my ankles. He stops me with his hands and protests.

"No, no, lucky I was a jailer in a previous life, and I can help you out of this uncomfortable contraption easily." It was so unexpected I giggled. The ease with which he defused my embarrassment is sweet and reassuring. And I quipped. "This is what you get for dating grannies. We come with huge knickers, saggy boobs, and wrinkles every geologist would be proud to call fissures. And live in the hope that one day we will date the collagen detective that finds it for us."

He looks at me in admiration. "Do you think this," and he points at his bulging biceps. "Is the result of hard work? Nope, they're rentals that have to be returned."

How funny and sweet did he handle my garment mishap.

"I like your wit. It's refreshing and unusual. Don't worry, I think you are a wonderful, witty, great woman. I love spending time with you and finding out more about you daily. I am so glad I found you again. After we said our farewells at the airport, I never realized it would be such a long time before we met again."

I wince. "I can be a real bimbo. When I tossed the napkin, I forgot it had your phone number."

He nods and jokes. "Well, the connection was there, but you grounded it." God, he is fast I think, and laughs.

"Step out of the dress," he ordered. I stepped aside and shivered, only clad in my ugly supporting granny compression-pants and lacy bra."

"Bedroom"? he inquired.

Silently I wave him in the general direction. He pulls me in his arms, plants a featherlight kiss in my mouth and scoops me up. In the bedroom, he gently drops me on the bed.

His hands are on my skin, which is hungry for his touch. He bends over me and kisses me deeply. I open my eyes and see his eyes are closed. A soft moan escapes his lips, and he pulls me closer if that is even humanly possible.

"I find you incredibly sexy with or without grannie pants," he murmured. "Can't you feel how much I want you." His bulge is firm, and I wriggle my hips. For a moment, Mark grinds into me, then rolls off me. His hands are on my granny pants, pulling them down and revealing my messy bush. Oh God, I cringe; I knew not shaving was a mistake! Brilliant!

"Wow, aren't I the lucky one?" he purred. "I like treading through mysterious jungles." And his hands slide up, as he is close to the honey pot, it hits me like a freight train. 'Dam I need lube'! The essential (extra strength) no grannie can do without is in the drawer of the nightstand. Fuck. Horror. How can I grab it and apply it without him noticing? Why or why did I not keep it in the bathroom. At least, I could have excused myself. Shit. I growl inwards. For a moment, I considered putting my fingers in my mouth and bringing them to my pussy. It had worked well in the past, though. I am older now; and I probably need something more substantial. Something developed from space technology with super-power strength. I sigh. What a way to kill the mood. He trails his fingers up my thigh and comes alarmingly close to the no doubt dry-tight-pussy problem.

Shit, I have to think fast, but before I can devise a sensible plan, he has reached my vaginal lips and slides effortlessly his finger in. I sigh in relief and moan, incapable of solving problems, dry or wet, as he searches, strokes, and when he finally puts his mouth on me, I dissolve in a puddle. Ahh that feels so good! Even if he did stop short of my orgasm. Hastily Mark removes his clothes and straddles me. I moan again. My body is in overdrive. I want to feel him inside me and when he finally enters me his breath caresses my cheek and blows gently on my lips, taking a little nibble. The feeling of him moving inside and how he teases my lips sends my body into a frenzy of need. Unlike most fairy stories, we don't climax together. He sends me first in a full-fledged orgasm. I could have happily died at that moment. He moves a few minutes longer then, with a groan, he reaches his climax. The feeling we are as one is exquisite, and I marvel at how close I feel to Mark. As he collapses on top of me, I plant sweet kisses on his head and smile wider than ever before. After a few minutes, he starts snoring, and I need all my strength to push him away. I grab my phone and try Googling 'magic frog' again. I need to know if somebody else shares the same joy and happiness, but to my dismay, I find the same bunch of superstitious drivel that was there the previous time, and I am none the wiser. Is Mark really the frog that has metamorphosed into a prince and brought my search for the right man to an end?

I am sorry dear reader, from now you will have to use your own imagination.

The End

Ingram Content Group UK Ltd.
Milton Keynes UK
UKHW020652240723
425668UK00013B/567